the 13 MOONS

~

for Al,
Thony.

ANTHONY HANDY

Anthony Handy.

'Our mistake is to confuse our limitations with the bounds of possibility.'

William Golding

*

*'This is my grief. That land,
My home, I have never seen;
No traveller tells of it,
However far he has been.'*

Edward Thomas

*

*'Be grateful for whoever comes, because
each guest has been sent as a guide from beyond.'*

Rumi

ISBN-10: 978-1493769766
ISBN-13: 1493769766

TO MY CHILDREN

WITH LOVE AND GRATITUDE

Copyright © 2013 Anthony Handy

All rights reserved.

CONTENTS

PROLOGUE	7
THE TREE-MOON CALENDAR	9
THE FIRST YEAR	
Birchmoon (1)	11
Rowanmoon (2)	44
Ashmoon (3)	71
Aldermoon (4)	89
Willowmoon (5)	98
Hawthornmoon (6)	107
Oakmoon (7)	115
Hollymoon (8)	134
Hazelmoon (9)	137
Vinemoon (10)	145
Ivymoon (11)	154
Reedmoon (12)	166
Eldermoon (13)	182
Mistletoe Day	188
THE SECOND YEAR	
Birchmoon to Hawthornmoon	191
The Inward-Looking Houses	223
SAHADA, the House of Stars	230
MILFA, the House of Masks	237
USBA, the House of Healing	247
SAFIN, the House of Mercy	254

PROLOGUE

Last year I went abroad to stay with a friend of mine, an archaeologist like me, but of much higher standing and accomplishment. We went for a trip into the desert, to a remote valley where he had been engrossed in some 'individual' fieldwork. Some of his more tolerant colleagues called it 'eccentric', whilst others just considered that he had gone crazy from too much desert sun!

This desert is not all endless dunes and quivering distances. There is undulating scrubland with thorny bushes, and great outcrops of rock just the same colour as the sand from which they emerge, as if camouflaging themselves.

As we wove our hired camels (for there's no access to motor vehicles, even so-called 'all-terrain' types) between the sharp thorn-bushes and chameleon-outcrops, quick, bright lizards flicked the edge of my sight and disappeared, like stars that dissolve in our full gaze, having beckoned from the corner of our eyes.

The valley, as I said, is remote, and we travelled for many days, much of it silent and tedious, because it was too hot even to talk, or to do anything but sit on the backs of our uncomplaining beasts, carried through the oven-trembling air, silently observing the startlingly vivid colours of sunbathing snakes, and the dull, slow passage of minutes and hours. Occasionally, our camels skirted the gaping skull or wreckage of ribs of some unfortunate creature, and then our eyes would switch with an involuntary flick from the dusty grey-gold floor to the white-blue, cloudless intensity of the pitiless sky, scanning for the still-winged birds of prey that were never absent, ever patient. We passed several great fluxes of rock, as if the desert had erupted at some long distant time, and instantly petrified to form intricate channels, through which my friend seemed to know the only possible route. It was via this path we finally came to the valley in question.

Here, the valley floor was dotted with smaller outcrops of the same sand-coloured and wind-sculpted rock. We set up camp in the shade of the overhanging ledge of one of these rocks.

The following day, we began our archaeological work, sifting sites he'd already begun, and searching the area for new sites of interest. It was on the eleventh or twelfth day that we discovered, in caves close to our camp, a dozen or so sealed jars in which were collections of papers. To our amazement, we found that these papers comprised a set of diaries, maps, observation notes, recipes, logs, letters and so on, kept by one Kip Smith, a fellow countryman of ours. Some of the seals were damaged, and the contents of these jars were variously faded, or nibbled by age, worm, wasp or mouse, but scraps survived in a legible enough form to decipher valuable information.

Within a few months of returning to this country, my friend died of a condition that had plagued him for years. He asked me, during his final days, to complete his work, and I have spent a long and painstaking period sorting, translating, deciphering and collating Kip's papers (sometimes from just skimpy notes or shreds of reported dialogue) into something akin to a continuous narrative (along with what I consider to be apposite quotations from literature, and organised within a framework of his culture's lunar calendar), so that they could tell of the extraordinary experiences of the young man who wrote them, and of the great work in which he was, and we all are, involved.

THE LUNAR TREE-CALENDAR MATCHED TO OUR OWN

< V	J	F	M	A	M	J	J	A	S	O	N	D		**KEY TO**
	BIR													***13 MOON-TREES***
1/	09	12	12	15	17	20	22	25	28	02	05	07		BIR = BIRCH
									VIN					
2/	10	13	13	16	18	21	23	26	01	03	06	08		ROW = ROWAN
3/	11	14	14	17	19	22	24	27	02	04	07	09		ASH = ASH
4/	12	15	15	18	20	23	25	28	03	05	08	10		ALD = ALDER
								HAZ						
5/	13	16	16	19	21	24	26	01	04	06	09	11		WIL = WILLOW
6/	14	17	17	20	22	25	27	02	05	07	10	12		HAW = HAWTHORN
7/	15	18	18	21	23	26	28	03	06	08	11	13		OAK = OAK
							HOL							
8/	16	19	19	22	24	27	01	04	07	09	12	14		HOL = HOLLY
9/	17	20	20	23	25	28	02	05	08	10	13	15		HAZ = HAZEL
						OAK								
10/	18	21	21	24	26	01	03	06	09	11	14	16		VIN = VINE
11/	19	22	22	25	27	02	04	07	10	12	15	17		IVY = IVY
12/	20	23	23	26	28	03	05	08	11	13	16	18		REE = REED
					HAW									
13/	21	24	24	27	01	04	06	09	12	14	17	19		ELD = ELDER
14/	22	25	25	28	02	05	07	10	13	15	18	20		MD = MISTLETOE DAY
				WIL										
15/	23	26	26	01	03	06	08	11	14	16	19	21		
16/	24	27	27	02	04	07	09	12	15	17	20	22		
17/	25	28	28	03	05	08	10	13	16	18	21	23		
		ASH	**ALD**											
18/	26	01	01	04	06	09	11	14	17	19	22	24		
19/	27	02	02	05	07	10	12	15	18	20	23	25		
20/	28	03	03	06	08	11	13	16	19	21	24	26		
	ROW													
21/	01	04	04	07	09	12	14	17	20	22	25	27		
22/	02	05	05	08	10	13	15	18	21	23	26	28		
23/	03	06	06	09	11	14	16	19	22	24	27	**MD**		
												BIR		
24/	04	07	07	10	12	15	17	20	23	25	28	01		
											ELD			
25/	05	08	08	11	13	16	18	21	24	26	01	02		
26/	06	09	09	12	14	17	19	22	25	27	02	03		
27/	07	10	10	13	15	18	20	23	26	28	03	04		
										REE				
28/	08	11	11	14	16	19	21	24	27	01	04	05		
29/	09	//	12	15	17	20	22	25	28	02	05	06		
									IVY					
30/	10	//	13	16	18	21	23	26	01	03	06	07		
31/	11	//	14	//	19	//	24	27	//	04	//	08		

THE FIRST YEAR

BIRCHMOON
(December 24 - January 20)

'For who would bear the whips and scorns of time...'
William Shakespeare

'Ever since I was a child I have feared mummers.
It always seems to me that someone,
A kind of extra shade
Without face or name,
Has slipped in among them.'
Anna Akhmatova

Birch is the tree of inception; it represents beginnings, and was often the chosen wood for making cradles.

Birch-whips and sticks were used for flogging out evil spirits and, by association, flogging out the spirit of the old year in 'beating-the-bounds'.

This moon begins immediately after the Winter Solstice, and so is the month of the Lengthening of Days.

Chapter 1/ BIRCHMOON

I

1ˢᵗ Birchmoon *from Kip's journal*

My name is Kip Smith. I live at the forge in Straight, the village where father and I smith on Staple Street, the highway chiefly used by shepherds and wool-merchants in moving their flocks and fleeces between pastures and market-places.

This is my journal. Since mastering the art of writing, by my own application and with the inestimable guidance of a local man of learning, it is to be my delight to keep this journal.

I shall be enabled to have discourse with myself without being overheard by my father, who is suspicious of my book-learning, a suspicion which he articulates with spit and sneer. The old scholar who taught me to write, Samuel Sloethwaite by name, also taught me reading, mathematics, a couple of old languages, a modern tongue, some logic and some sciences. He said I had a gift for words 'and maybe more besides' –whatever that meant!

It is the first day of Birchmoon, the first moon of our New Year. The days are short and cold, the nights long and colder.

12ᵗʰ Birchmoon

It is even less easy than I had anticipated to find the time or the privacy to keep my journal. But I shall persist in my endeavour; I shall persevere if only in gratitude to Mr Sloethwaite, who has given me an education from the goodness of his kind heart, simply because we became friends when I was a little boy, and I showed an interest in his books.

14ᵗʰ Birchmoon

Enough! I cannot find any time and space to myself. Having my journal like a friend demanding my company and attention has brought this to a head. I must leave; a life of smithery in this place is not for me- (I quite like this word, which I suspect I might have made up, because it seems to blend the name of the trade with the word 'misery'). Indeed, the very thought of spending the rest of my life in Straight causes me to break into a claustrophobic sweat. I am breaking free; I have even told my parents! My father announced that he was glad that his son was going to show himself to be a man of the world and display some initiative- though he did add the words 'At last!'. Unnecessarily, I thought, but typically uncharitable: I've never known him give a kind or encouraging word to anyone. I thought I had finally shaken off the desire to please him until I noticed the flicker of pleasure when I thought he was giving me an encouraging and supportive send-off. Those words 'At last!' may have finally done the trick. Anyway, he then, contrarily, began to moan about the smithing business and to ask how he could cope alone; but I'm not to be deterred.

Now, strangely, there comes to my mind a day from my childhood.

The village of Straight, where my family home and its adjoining smithy are located is, as I mentioned, on Staple Street, the main drove-road of the island. Many people pass by: travellers, local farmers and merchants going about their business, shepherds with their flocks. The children of Straight use the dusty track of Staple Street as their playground.

Once, we children were playing a game of our own invention, using pebbles. I forget now what the game was, but it consumed our whole attention at the time. The weather was cold, but the company and the fascination of the new game meant that we were unaware of its bite, despite the fact that the time of year was around the winter solstice, with the days at their shortest. It was late afternoon and growing dim. One or two golden lamps were filling the cottage windows with their warm light, and an owl's hoot had just begun echoing in the twilight, when suddenly one of our number pointed north, up Staple Street.

"Who's that?!"

We all peered into the shadowy distance of the drove-road and could make out, against the last light of the evening sky, the silhouettes of a collection of dark figures and small, covered wagons heading towards the village. As they approached, we discerned that they were oddly dressed: it was the mummers, who travelled the fells every winter during 'the dark days', performing their play at each settlement in return for 'hospitality', which amounted to nothing more than being allowed to pitch their encampment within the village for the duration of their stay without any undue harassment. I was never aware of where they went to 'out of season'. Indeed, the thought never entered my head as a child: when it wasn't the mummers' season, the mummers didn't exist!

I say they were oddly dressed, which -although not in costume- they seemed to my young eye to be. Maybe it was an unfamiliar regional variant of dress, maybe a raggedness brought about by the constant travel. I don't now recall. It's even possible that the subsequent fantastic nature of their costume and performance simply now colours my memory of their arrival.

Anyway, like sheep we children stood in an instinctively protective huddle, half fascinated and half fearful, and watched them trudge past, the pots and pans clanking on the sides of the wagons, to a small patch of waste grass beyond the forge where they set up camp. There were no greetings, from them or us. We sidled to the edge of the 'green' and gazed at their activity until, soon after their campfire was lit, we were called by our parents. Even the adults, I think, were wary of the mummers.

******

The mummers kept themselves to themselves. They didn't drink at the inn or alehouse, they didn't mix or even pass the time of day with the locals. They were accepted by villagers as part of the annual round: they were 'the mummers'; they came, they performed, they moved on- that was that. So people went about their usual business the following day, behaving as if the encampment didn't exist, apart from the fact that, as they passed the encampment, they kept their heads more intently bowed than normal, though I'm sure they didn't resist glimpses from the corners of their eyes, if only out of native curiosity.

However, this acceptance meant that the evening revolved around the mummers: meals were eaten early, children were hurried along ('Come on, our Kip. Don't want to miss the mummers!') Suddenly, it was alright to mention them, acknowledge them. Their time had come.

So my family, along with the rest of the local population, headed for the yard of The Raddled Tup Inn, where the performance, according to long tradition, took place.

******

The evening, although early, was dark and cold; as we gathered round the edges of the yard with our backs to the stable-doors, our breath curled in wreaths about our faces, then rose and drifted to nothing like the dust of an invisible stampede. Or, if you blew hard, a trumpet of mist was momentarily formed reminding me of illustrations of personified zephyrs in the books of learning in Mr Sloethwaite's library, blowing their winds from the cardinal points of old maps.

Soon, we heard music from out on the highway: fiddle, drum, whistle and pipe heralding the entrance of the mummers. My young eyes drank the glitter of frost on the frozen yard reflected in the canopy of flashing constellations above. For a moment, which lingered for an age, I was aware of a shadow slipping into the yard. Something in my boy's perception became aware of something beyond the world I had so far known; beyond the village; beyond the fells and mountains; beyond unknown seas; beyond horizons, the moon, the stars. And yet a simultaneous conviction that it (whatever 'it' was) also lay in the core of my own being. I shivered with a sudden chill and pulled my collar closer, aware —as in a dream- of a creature stirring in its sleep in an intimate, distant cave.

Then the mummers burst in through the gates of the stable-yard, dressed gaudily and fluttering with ragged ribbons. In came the characters so familiar to the villagers since they could ever remember: to a burst of cheers, The Fallow Knight entered in his golden helmet, with suit of saffron, and a dazzling tawny robe of tattered ochre, orpiment, cream, gamboge, looking like a great mythic owl; all this fronted by a huge, circular, bronze shield with a 'protective' central eye of amber. He represented 'daytime', 'the light', and appeared to me to be a magical embodiment of everything heroic.

Then there followed, to a venomous tirade of booing, The Mazarine Champion in a suit of indigo, shawled by a mantle of cobalt blue, and bearing a great foursquare shield of ebony. From its centre shone a defiant, brilliant eye of lapis lazuli. He represented 'night-time', 'the dark', and I believed him, in my childishness, to be wickedness incarnate, an errant raven of doom and ill omen with a heart as dark as sloes.

After the two main combatants of this imminent drama of dark-and-light, we saw The Old Dame- a stout, masculine man with a grisly beard and squeaky voice, wearing flounces, lace and bonnet; a respectable, bespectacled Doctor Of Physic, with potions and powders and a bag of tricks and instruments; several heroes and villains of our island lore to be the chief adversaries'

armies; and, finally, a buffoon, dressed lu(
outsized shoes, and constantly tripping and
poking so that the initial awe caused by
characters was burst with laughter.

The play ran its course. The army of The Mazarine Champion was routed and left dead on the battlefield, their chief warrior was defeated in single combat by The Fallow Knight and fell amongst his late supporters; the magical doctor was hailed and duly performed his trick of resurrection, after which all were reconciled: the turning of the year had been honoured and acknowledged, we all now knew that days of warmth and light would return in due course.

The landlord and his staff circulated with hot punch and pies, everyone chattered, and children immediately began to re-enact their favourite parts of the performance. I found myself standing slightly apart, watching the scene of bustle and conviviality. Inwardly, I was disturbed by conflicting tides of emotion. My hero had, to my delight, been victorious; yet I alone- or so it seemed to me- had felt a pang of remorse and pity for The Mazarine Champion when he had fallen. Also, when all the characters were revived and reconciled, something deep within me wanted to shout to the tawny hero, 'No! It's not alright! Don't relax! Don't turn your back!' Something in me did not trust the happy ending.

The mummers kept in their own huddle and were, for this one time only, given food and drink (one could barely call it 'hospitality') as due reward for their performance. Suddenly, I was aware that one of them, The Old Dame, had left his conclave and, unprecedentedly, was acting just like a local resident, walking about and pushing his way through the crowd. She/he seemed inexorably to come towards me, closer and closer. Finally, he/she stood by me: I could hear the breathing caused by the effort of pushing across the yard to reach me, I could smell the strange, foreign smell of her/his sweat. I was frozen with alarm, almost terror, yet outwardly calm. The strange thing was that, although we were part of a bustling crowd, no-one took any notice of us, not even my parents, even though fraternising with the mummers was unheard of.

"Well," said The Old Dame, not in the squeaky, mock-female voice of the play, but in a deep, gruff bass. I just stared back at him, transfixed. He scrutinised me quite openly, as a child might do an adult, only this was the other way round. There was an uncommon force in his eyes, and I was suddenly aware- from some inner well of intuition- that these eyes were, in fact, feminine. More than that, they were female. This wasn't simply a man dressed up. I waited in silence, returning her gaze, aware of a muted quality to the surrounding crowd which distanced it as if we were inside a bubble. Finally, she spoke.

"Yes, you are the one." It was hard to reconcile the gruff, male voice, physique and face with the woman's force from the powerful eyes. I stared back, unresponsive for some moments, till I replied, "Who are you?"

"Who am I, Kip?" I started in surprise at the use of my name in her mouth. "Who am I? Showman or shaman? What do you think? But never mind that."

He took a small bundle of rags from a pouch hanging at his waist.

"Take this," he commanded.

The voice was solemn, wary, imploring, urgent: "Keep it safe. Keep it secret. The mystery must be hidden from all idiots. Find him who is of the earth."

I stood agog, seized by repulsion and horror at this being whose interior and exterior seemed not to fit together. Suddenly, her eyes became gentle, and, in a voice that was somehow utterly reassuring, she said: "Do not look at my bodily form, but take the gift that I offer."

Later, when I was alone in my room, I uncovered the scruffy parcel. Inside was a curious object, the like of which I have never seen in my life. It comprises a series of carved wooden spheres, one inside another, each successive sphere slightly smaller than its containing sphere, and each one (there are, I think, thirteen in all) made of a different type of wood, as far as I can make out. How the whole was crafted I cannot tell. There are no apparent seams to show how it was all joined into one. The patterns are complex, and beautifully and skilfully carved.

******

Now that this memory returns, I know that whatever he/she gave me back then is the cause of my going on my…journey? adventure? task? At the time, as a child, I didn't question that 'Yes, you are the one.' But now I am baffled: what does it mean? Still I am bemused to think how the old woman-man knew that I would have to go. I don't even know how I know! In other words, I don't know where I'm going, or why I'm going , only that I *am* going.

II

'Along all roads and
Towards all thresholds, slowly
A shadow advances.' Anna Akhmatova

Forest of Yate. An eyeblink. An eye that was shuttered flicks open, and the resulting vibrations of the eyelid echo into the deep mysteries of space. The eye listens, this way and that. It has a predator's vigilance, meticulous and sure. Yes! It has detected something. Something miles away, yet strangely close at hand; it hears the stirring of something. A great, dark beast blinks both eyes heavily, as if stirring from a long sleep, and then heaves itself up. There is a journey to be made, a prey to be stalked. The eyes sting as it hauls itself into the cracked light of the pine forest. Glistening nostrils dilate, shrink, dilate, playing the air. The forest creatures seem to pause, suddenly aware of a presence hitherto unnoticed. A golden eagle on a natural tower of Dolgirth granite high over the beast's cave sees with its god-like eye, and barks its warning; a colony of rooks in some high, wind-wild pines rise and fall like surf in a sudden tumult of concern; a red stag freezes motionless beneath its canopy of horn; a sleepy wolf raises its head like a dog at the hearth and, feeling a disturbance from its dreams, lets out a howl which moves like an omen amongst the pine and rowan branches; red squirrels crouch deeper in the dry leaves of their dreys. The beast slouches off towards the west, the first saliva of appetite in its mouth.

III

19th Birchmoon

My plans for leaving have been thrown into some confusion. There's a girl. No, no! Nothing at all like that! No, she's simple, you see. She just turned up one day. No-one could find out where she came from. For months enquiries were made up and down the trade roads, with merchants, innkeepers, drovers and shepherds; but not a sign or a whisper could be discovered. It was as if she had just appeared from nowhere.

They call her Maddy, which is cruelly appropriate, 'cos that's what they say she is: "...as mad as..." Well, that's what the people in our hamlet think, anyway. But the folks hereabouts don't appreciate ways other than 'the way we've always done it', as I know well enough from the times I've tried to speak my mind on village affairs, or from people's reactions to my helping myself as a child to read and write from printed ballads, bills and scraps of paper that I begged from amused passing travellers, and from my association with Mr Sloethwaite, whom my father distrusts, mainly because he's different to him: "You want to be careful, lad, getting above your station."

Now my father is an impatient man, and does not 'suffer fools gladly', so it was ironic in the first place that his name should have been the one drawn from the hat at the village council meeting held to settle Maddy's situation and assuage the conscience of the community. Anyway, this Maddy is given shelter and employment by my father, to whom, by the way, I was apprenticed when I was 12 years old, before eventually becoming the latter part of Smith and Son; she fetches and carries for us around the forge, and helps my mother with domestic duties.

Yes, someone had to keep her, and it fell to the blacksmith, my father: but with what bad grace. He never was kind to her: humiliated her with his tongue; snapped at her when encouragement was all that was required; remained sullenly silent when just a kind word would have made her day; struck her sometimes. His behaviour towards her stirred up memories and feelings from my childhood and apprenticeship that I would rather had remained dormant, and I had to look on and just try to ease Maddy's misery with secret smiles, sympathetic eyes, a quiet word or just a friendly wink.

But this morning the old tyrant lost control of himself. It was just an accident when Maddy knocked over the water-pot and drenched his feet and legs, but something in his mind just seemed to snap, and the old bully grabbed her and began to beat her. He was shouting at her, awful profanities and swear words; thumping her with those great blacksmith's fists like giant mallet-heads, and slapping her back and forth with the front then the back of his huge, crab-like hands. I stared with increasing horror as her mouth split and blood began to pour down her chin and from her nostrils. Then I got scared for her and yelled at him to stop, the first time I'd ever raised my voice to him. He paused just long enough to oath at me "Shut your mouth!" and that he'd deal with me later, before returning with renewed violence to beat the nearly unconscious girl. My own mind suddenly went as red as the fire I was bellowing.

Now my father is strong, but his best years are past (he was in his forties when I was born), and I've worked with him for some years now, hard work (no choice with him as taskmaster!), so I'm almost a match for him in strength, but I also have my youth with its vigour and agility.

So the next thing I knew was that I'd got hold of him and pushed him to the ground before he was even aware that I had left my post. He would never have expected such a thing; always enjoyed taunting me with the label 'Gentle Giant' because I didn't go along with his crude and vicious ways. But when he stumbled up at me growling like a great silver-grey bear, I was too quick and kept dodging him, being reluctant to hurt him. This only infuriated him still further.

"Stand still and fight like a man!" he yelled. I attempted to pacify him.

"Father, calm down!"

"I'll calm down as soon as I've taught you a lesson you won't forget, you bloody young upstart. How dare you tell me what to do, you... you ~~~~ changeling!" he added with a disowning sneer, the taunting name voicing his years of unease at having a son who did not share his narrow outlook on life, and, worse, actually read books!

He charged at me and I sidestepped him. This time, in his fury, he picked a large poker from by the fire-pit. I could see that I would have to act or something irreparable might occur. So, as he lunged with his makeshift weapon, I feinted a leftways dodge and winded him with a punch in the pit of his stomach.

Then, whilst he gasped on all fours like a hunt-weary beast, I picked up Maddy and carried her to our cottage adjoining the forge where mother tended her. Whilst I helped my mother tend to Maddy, I was inwardly bracing myself for my father's return. I assisted in getting Maddy to a straw mattress and returned to the cottage just as my father entered, silent and sullen. However, the storm of violent curses I was expecting didn't come, which was a revelation to me. Even as it was occurring, I sensed a sea-change was happening to our relationship. As the moments went by and he didn't turn on me, I felt somewhere in my perceptions as if a door was slowly opening onto a new world, in which my father was, if not scared, then at least wary of me, and in which new possibilities had become available to me.

After a while, he turned from sulking to wheedling, saying that we shouldn't let 'a little difference of opinion' come between us in our partnership, but I replied to him, with an assertiveness that astonished me even as I spoke, that I'd already settled on leaving anyway.

"Leave! You can't leave!" he spluttered, and I detected some desperation, almost fear or panic.

"You're a blacksmith, a simple, working man. Not a scholar or a…a…an adventurer!" Again the sneer, as if it were the most contemptible description he could possibly muster.

"You're getting above yourself, my lad. Stick to what you know, boy!" All the time he spoke, his tone veered between cajoling, admonishing, threatening, warning. He was in new territory, and didn't know how to cope with it.

"No good will come of tramping off into the world. It's not seemly for a blacksmith."

"I'm not a blacksmith, father. You are."

This he took to be a stinging insult, and gave up the argument for the time being, turning his attention to Maddy.

"So what about this moon-child?" he remonstrated, suddenly angry. "She can't live here."

I reminded him about the village council, though the words seemed separate from me, as if it wasn't really me involved in this man-to-man exchange with my father.

"Damn the village council. I've had enough of her. I've done my share."

"O, don't burden yourself," I shouted back with some sarcasm. Then I added, "She can come with me." The last five words were spoken and hanging in the air between us before I'd even realised they were in my head! Another voice, inside me, was protesting, "Wait a minute! This isn't part of the plan!!"

IV

Fragments written by Kip based on a packer's log

<u>PACKERS</u>: *merchants and dealers transporting wares in packs on strings of mules. These men dealt, when travelling north to south, in salt from the northern brine-springs at Minford Bregan (locally 'Bren', cf. brine) which are believed to be fed by natural underground channels from the sea. On the return journey from south to north, they brought spices and tobacco from the southern isles. Some packers dealt locally, buying salt at the salterns, and selling in the market towns of the island. Others took salt to the southern ports of the island and exchanged them there for the incoming spices and tobacco, which they then sold en route north to the salt-springs.*

17th Birchmoon

He was always glad to leave Minford Bregan. Despite the fact that it gave him his living; gave him, indeed, his name, Brag Drufus: Brag from Bregan, the salt town, and Drufus from the mountain ridge due north, Drufus Brow. He still found it inhospitable, this place of scree scoured by the pitiless easterlies that cut across the bitter fells. Its buildings of dark grey stone and slate were like formal concentrations of the natural stone. Salt had seeped into the town's water, so to speak: all its rheum was salt- not only when it cried or sneezed, but even when it spat. The evaporating pools at the salterns epitomised it. If the town itself were to evaporate, salt was all there'd be left, glistening like quartz on the dark grey bone of its skeleton.

22nd Birchmoon

His mules were loaded and standing patiently in the street by one of the salterns. One of them licked at a salt-cat. Then Brag joined the lead mule and led his string towards the road south. The early morning sun through mist was saline, white and fuzzy, like sediment in a crucible. 'I'm always glad to leave my hometown,' was his feeling, even if he didn't actually think it to himself, let alone voice it. He might even have been offended if you'd suggested this disloyalty to him.

23rd Birchmoon
Evening. Drakenfold, land-harbour in the fells, a haven from the winds and wolves. Some shepherds at The Stopping-House Inn. Snow due, they said, and who would argue with their hard-earned weather lore. They knew the fells. As well as the shepherds Jim Scalla, a packer like Drufus, heading north with near empty packs, having sold all but a fraction of his Dark Braxil tobacco and his spices, this remaining fraction the portion for his dealings in Minford Bregan, and some baccy for himself, of course. Somehow, the smoke of those strange, dark leaves from over the southern sea evoked such feelings, as if hinting of things past, like a reminiscence or a homesickness.

24th Birchmoon
The east wind- honed by the heights of Dolgirth and Gabb Knap as it funnelled between them, then shepherded south by Ransgall and Drufus- had risen all day, cutting ever more cleanly through the packer's long-coat. But now the mules were safely stabled. It had begun to snow while he was still four miles short of the town. About an inch was lying by the time he arrived at Pegford. This is the capital for northern shepherds: all the Scallafell sheep were gathered, bought and sold at the sheep fair every August, a few weeks after shearing. By the time of the fair, the wool-packers had all gone with their loads of wool, heading for the great wool-market at Cromber on the southern downs, way off along Staple Street.

25th Birchmoon
The ale-house parlour at the village of Straight.
'Made it, spite of t'snow!'

'Ha! Tha need worry. Tha's heading south. Tha'll be off t'fells in a day or two.'

26th **Birchmoon** *Late Afternoon*

Every mule had its head low, ears pinned, eyes in slits. The packer, Brag Drufus, at the head of the string, walks with his shoulders slightly forward, as if to cleave his way through the cold, to force the door of the snow-gale. His long-coat clings to his shape, by turns his hat is slapping or exposing his forehead as the broad brim buckles or stands perpendicular in the gale. The spare length of his hat-string lashes his cheek constantly. The wind is made visible, white wind's contours. And the snow is driven with such venom that it stings even the merchant's weathered skin. As he pushes mechanically, instinctively onward, his mind toys with the word 'snowflake'. 'Flake. Snow. Flake. Down. Soft. Down. Goosedown. Bed. Soft. Sleep. Soft. Flake. Dreams.

Soft snow. Soft flakes….' on and on. These and other variations accompany, fever-like, his steps which leave a trail across the fells alongside the wake of hoofprints, all too soon covered by the surge of the blizzard. The howl of the wind makes him think of the fell wolves, but also of cosy times when, as a child, he had listened from a warm bed to a gale outside thrashing the window with ropes of rain, and it had heightened his childish sense of warmth and security to hear it and know that he was out of it. And so, playing with words and memories to try to shut out the elements, he plods on towards the bluff of Duns Tow, the edge of the fells, at the foot of which is the fellside town of Hawkby. There: company, warmth, ease, talk, food, drink, sleep…!

A sudden shriek of storm scoops the comforting thoughts from his skull and whips them away into the desolate reaches of the blizzard; the wind-shriek becomes a mule-shriek mixed with a wolf-snarl, and Drufus' attention is hauled back from his mind-play to the pressing moment.

The rear mule has a wolf on its back, and the packer runs back drawing a dagger as other mules begin to bray and scream and buck. Nearby wolves run off as Drufus approaches, but the assailing beast, after dropping from the mule's back and taking a few strategic paces away, stops and turns its head. An unearthly leer reveals its fangs, and the fixity and intent of its stare seems more than animal. But then it turns away and disappears into the swirls of snow.

V

Birchmoon *otherwise undated*   *from Kip's journal*

Today I visited my old friend, Samuel Sloethwaite, who lives humbly in part of a rambling old dwelling long in his family called Sloethwaite Hall, but known locally as The Court House on account of the large entrance hall being used as a venue for parish business*, including the adjudication of local disputes.

(* On the island there was no organised 'church' such as we know it. People held beliefs and practised their common rituals, but these would be considered pagan nowadays. Their word 'parish' therefore had no religious connotations: it simply defined the socio-geographical divisions within the island, over which communities carried out self-jurisdiction under the aegis of the Island Council.)

The single door leading from it into Samuel's living quarters is kept permanently locked. Indeed, he has a dresser against it on his side, and I would readily believe that he has even forgotten that the door exists.

The house, as I mentioned, rambles. It is built of the local dark-grey stone, rather bleak-looking. It has a crenellated tower, hinting at former times, almost beyond recollection, when raiders came across the seas and through mountain passes to impose themselves on resident inhabitants.

Samuel is an old bachelor and a learned man, different from the other villagers. It is said that he used to be a professor at the island's seat of learning in Aphambold, a place way to the south, and only heard about by 'us Northeners' in travellers' tales.

However, some deep sadness came to him- I think the death of someone loved, but he does not refer to it- and he retired to The Court House here in Straight long before I was even born. One day, when I was a young boy, I was drawn into the mysterious driveway that led to the big house which could not be seen from the road. I was suddenly struck with awe and fear as I saw the old man approaching me, but, although a private man, it was with kindly words that he addressed me, and, for some reason, we immediately took to each other. To cut a long story short, he soon began to take me under his wing, and began my education, which I loved and lapped up like a cat takes cream. Perhaps he regarded me as a son he never had; I don't know. Anyway, apart from his housekeeper, Mrs Bowerbank, I was the only person that entered his home, as far as I was aware.

Although The Court House is so extensive, Samuel Sloethwaite inhabits just three rooms: the kitchen as his 'everyday' room; his study for business, comfort or relaxation; a bedroom for sleeping. Other than that, all the rooms are kept locked and undisturbed.

The interior of the house is dark-panelled and restful, as if occupying a sidestep from passing time; goodness knows how still and quiet the unused part of the house must be! But as a child, and then a young man, I always found the sombre, tick-tocking, book-musty, bachelorish chambers fascinating and tranquil, and I became a frequent (and always welcomed) visitor from the very start.

Today, after my lessons, he made tea, and while we sat sipping, I talked about my decision to leave, and the row with my father, though I didn't mention Maddy. You will understand that this man, who has befriended and educated me, is like a second father to me: the one in whom I can confide about personal difficulties, and from whom I can confidently seek advice. In my naivety, I imagined that he might feel a degree of betrayal in my leaving, but his response was warm and encouraging, almost as if it was something he had waited for, even expected.

"You mean you don't mind?" I asked innocently.

"Mind? I have been educating you for the time when you went into the world. I would expect nothing less of you!"

"So you think it's a good idea?"

"You must go, Kip."

"But what about my father? The business? He expects me to take it over."

"You must respect your father, but that doesn't mean you have to do everything he expects. There are plenty of strong and reliable young men who would jump at the chance to be apprenticed to a master smith."

"I've no idea what I'm going to do," I said, as if trying to talk my way out of my decision.

"I don't suppose you have. But you are- if I may be so immodest- well educated, and you have a sound head on your shoulders. You will fare decently well, I dare say."

So that was fine! Except that I was nagged by the fact that I hadn't mentioned the complication of taking Maddy with me.

VI

Kip looked at his loaded cart, considering what to do with his secret gift: the one presented to him by the 'widow' from the mummers. Should he take it with him, or hide it in his room where it would be safe from whatever scrapes awaited him in the great world beyond Duns Tow and the edge of the Scalla Fells.

He unwrapped the secret and gazed at it. Its concentric carved and hollowed globes had long been a mystery to him, but their beauty held an inexplicable fascination for him, as if in that beauty lay some undeclared significance. Somehow, and for no reason he could put into words, he suddenly resolved that the spheres were integral to whatever journey he was about to take, so that he sighed resignedly, folded the rags back round the object, and pushed the parcel into the large 'poachers' pocket inside his coat, buttoning the flap over it.

He looked at Maddy who stood still, quiet and patient as a draught animal, looking at the ground in front of her.

"Well, Maddy. Let's make a start."

VII

Looking down from a great height, an eye can see the rugged backbone of northeast-southwest running rock that is the ridge called The Lament (from the way the easterly winds moan through the gap between it and Long Brow), and, parallel to it, a silver bootlace meandering south which is the River Apham. Wheeling west over Scalla Fells, The Eye rushes through acres of light and air, spies a small village on a long, straight stretch of highway, marks out a pair of young people heading towards the fell-town of Hawkby. Just a young man and woman with a horse and cart carrying a few possessions, and yet the eye scrutinises them more closely than all the landscape features or inhabitants so far. Then, with a sudden scream, the creature banks and heads back in the direction of the river. The air-stream slips over its golden tawny feathers and sloping forehead, its curved beak. The eye sees the land rushing up towards it as its creature stoops on folded wings. The eagle lands on the mossy bank of the Apham, somewhere among the pine-trees of Knapshott Forest. Then the eye feels the cold, liquid caress of river-water on its unblinking surface as its creature, now scaled and finned, shimmers away through Apham's depths, heading south.

VIII

It was dusk, and only a few Hawkby folk were about when Brag Drufus finally entered the main square of the fellside town. After a slight pause, during which he had taken a lungful of the icy air as if to dilute the memory of the hostile, snow-smothered, wolf-haunted fells, he stepped out across the open space towards The Buzzard Inn, his habitual resting place in this town.

Those natives north of the oakwoods were a taciturn and undemonstrative people, so the old ostler took the leading rein from the packer with a cursory, though not unfriendly, 'Sir!', even though he'd known Brag 'man and boy', and his father and grandfather before him. The Drufus family had been packers for as long as anyone could recall, and Brag had known The Saltway ever since he'd begun to travel it in the company of his elders as a small child. Brag climbed the steps to the inn: an interior of lamplight, polished wooden screens, table-tops and settle backs. A grove of squared timber trunks held up the high ceiling. The landlord, John Redna, nodded almost imperceptibly and went to get a supper for the merchant. Mrs Redna, of a more open nature than her husband, enquired, "Well, Brag, how goes it?"

"Much as ever, Mrs Redna," came the packer's stock reply, as he took off his greatcoat and gauntlets. The landlady poured him a mug of hot, dark ale. The scent of liquorice, cloves and nutmeg warmed him even before he tasted the brew, melted the recent memory of blizzard and sinister wolf.

"I suppose we'll start to see the traders and entertainers passing through to Lolsdun Candle Fair any day now," ventured Mrs Redna, whose mother hailed from Mountbury, far away in the south of the island, so passing to her daughter a more conversational leaning than was common this far north.

Before the packer could reply, if indeed he intended to with anything more than a slight facial gesture, they heard the sound of cartwheels and hooves in the stableyard. "Now who could that be?" mused the landlady.

IX

25th Birchmoon *Noon* *from Kip's journal*

I fear that I have acted with great foolishness in bringing young Maddy along with me. She needs looking after in safe surroundings, such as the village afforded. Bringing her on this... this... well, 'adventure' is a kind word; bringing a simple, innocent girl is, I fear, irresponsible. I know it... I knew it when I instinctively hid it from Mr Sloethwaite.

Already she is showing signs of nervousness and being unable to cope with the instabilities of a travelling life. Earlier today she began to look edgy and said that there were eyes looking at us, even though it was plain to see that the bleak fells stretched emptily away on all sides. I tried to reassure her, but she insisted we were being followed. No amount of soothing talk or indicating the unpeopled spaces surrounding us could put her at her ease. But I must be patient with her- she is young, she is simple, and doesn't understand. I must even say that her concern amuses me by its utter contrariness with reality, for we passed not a soul all the day apart from a pedlar and a couple of shepherds. Indeed, the only living creature I saw apart from Scalla sheep was an eagle which wheeled high above us for a while before diving away in a sudden hurry, presumably having seen some likely prey. Now that I come to think of it, perhaps it was this innocent occurrence which upset her fragile sensibilities, for it was only after that that she began to display her unease.

25th Birchmoon *Early Evening*

We are camped at the foot of Duns Tow, a great upheaval of land that forms a bluff which marks the southern extremity of the fells.

Since I wrote my earlier entry, Maddy's behaviour has begun to unsettle me. My humour and tolerance were perturbed by an afternoon filled not only with sudden movements of hers to look behind or simply to freeze on the spot and listen intently, but also with disconcerting warnings like: "The hills are watching us, Kip"; "We are being followed"; "What was that sound?"; "Can you hear breathing?" In the end I'm afraid that I became annoyed, and rather too curtly told her to desist, to calm herself and keep her comments and questions to herself, though I was immediately full of remorse at her look of hurt. Maybe I can find a kind old dame tomorrow in Hawkby who will take her in. I have enough in my savings to pay for her keep until I return from… whatever it is that awaits me. I'll see what can be arranged.

25th **Birchmoon** *Late Evening*

A stroke of good luck! A traveller came to our camp just as we had finished our supper. As he approached, Maddy became agitated, giving nervous little sideways twitches to her head and mumbling something like 'Doubletongue, doubletongue' over and over again.

However, all was well. We chatted amiably for a while, exchanging pleasantries, during which we discovered that the traveller, who introduced himself as 'Bob', was also heading for Hawkby where he has a couple of days business. When I agreed to his travelling with us 'for company', he gave me a spontaneous hug, and I felt a surge of fraternal warmth for his openness and natural affection.

We sat down by our little wayside hearth, and Bob entertained me with a couple of funny stories, after which he leaned into the shadows out of the firelight and picked something from the ground close by.

"Is this yours, Kip?"

I felt the lifeblood drain from my face when I saw him holding up my precious bundle: the rag-swaddled ornament, the strange gift of the man-woman. My hand went instinctively to my poacher's pocket, which Bob watched without comment. I could not think (still can't) how the bundle could have worked its way from this deep pocket and through the closed flap. It was lucky, to say the least, that Bob's sharp eyes detected it.

"Tha-thank you, Bob" I stammered, feeling discomposed.

"Not at all, Kip. No trouble. Glad to be of service to a new friend."

"Ubble-ung, ubble-ung," I heard Maddy mumbling across the fireglow.

" Maddy's my sort of ward. Don't mind her…," I said, "…she's just a bit simple," I added in a whisper.

X

27th Birchmoon

As the maid fills his ewer with hot water, Kip questions her about a man to whom he had spoken briefly on arriving at the inn late the previous evening. It had been a simple exchange of comments about the weather, but something about the man had impressed him.

"O, Mr Drufus," said the maid after Kip began a vague description of him. "He's a packer, a salt merchant. Everyone knows him!"

"Drufus… I've heard the name, other than the mountain in the far north of course."

"They're a packing family," added the maid as she hung a couple of towels on the wooden rail. "Mr Drufus comes from a long line of merchants."

"Yes, but not dealing in wool, they've always used The Saltway, so I've never met them. I lived on Staple Street." The use of the past tense relating to his home echoed in his head and shocked him as he spoke. "What's he like, this Mr Drufus?"

The maid took up a pile of towels that she was delivering to the other four rooms along the passageway and stood with her hand on the doorknob, about to leave, but looking at Kip.

"Keeps himself to himself. Straight as a die. Few words, even for these parts. Salt of the earth, if you take my meaning." She raised an eyebrow at him in a slightly quizzical manner, and left.

Kip sighed and considered the task of preparing for the day ahead. Then his jaw slowly fell open, and his eyes seemed to him to dance in his head. He took a quick breath to stop the maid, but immediately realised it was too late.

"Salt of the earth," he said to himself. "I wonder…" He recalled the words of the bearded woman in the mummers when she handed him the rag bundle: 'Keep it safe and keep it secret. The mystery must be hidden from all idiots. One day you must find its place. Find him who is of the earth."

"…of the earth… Then this is it," he said to himself, suddenly certain. "It has begun already."

He washed quickly, knocked on Maddy's door, and they went down to breakfast, Maddy gabbling excitedly about the snow which, overnight, had come from the fells and whitened the town. Kip noticed that the sight of the packer, who was eating his breakfast at the communal table, made his heart miss a beat. He wasn't sure why this should be so.

"May we join you?" asked Kip, following communal table etiquette.

Drufus seemed to weigh the simple, polite, rhetorical question as if his answer were a judgement of life or death. After what seemed a period when they were held in suspension , he nodded: "Aye."

They sat in silence whilst breakfast was brought, and ate without words for a few minutes. However, there was no feeling of unease, Kip noted.

A butterfly that had come indoors to hibernate during the progress of Autumn lay dead on the windowsill. Maddy finished eating and, turning her head to look into the street, saw the insect lying flat on its side.

"Poor butterfly. Pollen and dust."

Brag stopped chewing and glanced at the girl

ruminatively.

"Oh, don't mind Maddy," Kip said apologetically.

"I don't," replied the merchant.

"She had to come with me...." And the young smith found himself telling the story of his dispute with his father and of his departure with Maddy in tow. He felt as if he couldn't stop talking, as if this man would see right through him if he let fall his screen of words.

"He's kind," announced Maddy with childlike directness.

The packer nodded to her with a half-smile.

She picked up the dead butterfly and left the breakfast room to put it somewhere that she felt to be more appropriate.

"She's just a simple girl," Kip explained self-consciously. "I'm going to try and find a place to put her up, here in Hawkby. She'll find a long journey too alarming."

Brag let out a bark of a laugh. "And what's your mother's maiden name?"

Kip was flummoxed. "What do you mean?"

"Well, lad, I've not met you before, or you me, I've not even finished my breakfast, and yet I've heard half your life story. You don't play your cards close to your chest, do you?! So... a long journey."

Kip suddenly felt a sense of exposure. The packer spoke sparingly yet searchingly, and the young man experienced an irresistible need to talk to him, along with an accompanying confusion as to how he could keep his secrets in such circumstances.

"Mr Drufus," he continued, and now his temples thumped in apprehension; he felt as if he was about to jump out from a very high place into the unknown, but, to balance this fear he felt that an inner prompting which he trusted was being obeyed. "Mr Drufus, this may seem odd after so short an acquaintance, but I need to tell you the story of something that happened to me when I was a little boy."

Brag poured some more of the steaming brew into his mug and looked at Kip silently and intently over the rim as he sipped.

"It started when the mummers came to my village. One of them, the old dame, gave me a parcel. She told me to 'keep it safe and keep it secret'." Kip paused because the packer put his mug on the table with a sudden thud, but as he didn't speak, the young smith continued.

"So I did. I kept it safe and secret. I told no-one. Not my mother or father. Not my friends. Not even Mr Sloethwaite. No-one at all… until now."

Kip related the whole story in detail, and then drew a bundle of rags from his pocket, laying it on the table between them and resting his hand softly over it, his eyes fixed on Brag appealingly. All through the telling, the packer had done nothing to encourage or discourage him. He just chewed his breakfast, and sipped, and watched. Kip felt that he had never been given such attention before.

When he had finished his tale, he felt somehow light, as if he weighed almost nothing, like thistledown. It was like the lightness that comes on mornings when one wakes to discover that it has snowed overnight, and a curious cold brightness fills the windows and reflects from the ceiling, filling the room. But it was also more than this.

There was a sudden scuffle in the entrance passage outside the breakfast room.

"No, leave me alone!" cried Maddy's voice.

Kip leapt to his feet, sending his chair crashing back onto the floor, and rushed out.

Looking down the passage from the doorway he called out: "Hey! Leave her alone!"

A pair of journeymen— or so they appeared to be from their worn workclothes— seemed to be trying to persuade or force Maddy out into the stableyard.

"Oh, and who's going to make us?" one of them

retorted.

Kip advanced down the passage but suddenly stopped in amazement. The man he was about to confront was the traveller who had joined them on the first leg of their journey and so kindly directed them to the inn.

"Bob?" Kip felt as if he were in a dream, because the young man displayed not one hint of recognition, but just caught hold of Maddy's arm roughly.

"If you don't leave her, I'll deal with you soon enough!" Kip heard himself saying.

"Kip, take care!" Maddy said softly, using his proper given name for the first time he could remember.

"You and whose army?" jeered the aggressive assailant.

"Forget it," urged his companion, obviously not relishing a fight.

"Shut up!" The two spat syllables stung viciously at his weak accomplice who shrank back. "So," continued the bully, "I repeat: who's going to make us?" He looked threatening with his face full of derision and aggressiveness, his fingers already touching the handle of a dagger beneath his jacket.

"I think it'd be best if tha left now." The voice was quiet, but somehow undeniable. It came from the doorway of the breakfast room.

"Oh, sorry, Mr Drufus. We didn't realise she was with you," stammered the bully's friend, eager to be out of the situation.

"What difference does it make who she's with?" demanded the packer.

The bully stared at Brag with a surly belligerence. His voice was almost a whisper, but full of venom. "Mr High-and-Mighty Drufus, aren't yer? And what are you? A packer!" He filled the word 'packer' with all the contempt he could muster. "Nowt but a packer." He spat on the hall floor.

Brag raised himself ever so slightly, and his eyes flashed. The bully's bravado seemed suddenly to drain away, and he turned on his heel with a curt command to his pathetic companion to follow.

Kip sighed with relief and led Maddy back into the breakfast room, assuring himself by questioning that she alright. Returning to the table, where two or three other patrons were now being regaled with bacon and beer, Kip's knees went weak and his head began to spin. His bundle had gone!

"It's gone!" was all he could say, and that weakly.

"Keep yer package safe you were told," scolded Brag. "Which includes not leaving it lying around at inns filled with the likes of Bob Nixon− not to mention packers like me who you hardly know from a bar of soap!" Maddy giggled at the metaphor, and Kip looked abashed, then crushed.

Mr Drufus sighed and gently ordered his young new acquaintance to sit down at a small table in the corner. He pulled the bundle from his own pocket and pushed it across the table. "Now… keep it safe! What's in it anyway?"

"Open it and see." Kip already felt that he could trust this man, even before this recent proof of his honesty and reliability.

Brag peeled back the rags and his eyes widened. Maddy smiled. She reached out her hand across the table and touched the object tenderly with fingertips. "Lovely moons," she whispered, almost to herself.

The object was a sphere, not solid, but carved into a fretwork frame, and containing thirteen other spheres, one within another, getting smaller and smaller, like Russian dolls, except that these were also fretworked, so you could see them all, or parts of them all, in one glance. Each was made of a different wood, which represented the trees of the months of the calendar in use on the island. This was an ancient lunar calendar, comprising thirteen 28-day months, and a spare day which formed the hub of the year, Mistletoe Day or Yew Day, depending which part of the island you came from.

Brag took all this in during a moment's glance. No sooner had Maddy touched it than he quickly wrapped it and glanced round the room. Pushing the bundle towards Kip, he hissed, "You're going to have to be a mite more secretive than this! Keep that out o' sight, for pity's sake. Especially with the likes of Bob Nixon about."

"Why? What do you know about him?"

"He's just a no-gooder," Brag replied evasively.

"I'm sure he's the person who travelled into Hawkby with us, but he didn't show a flicker of recognition."

"What worries me," said Brag, "is that if he's about, then happen so are others far worse. Far, far worse."

Kip dropped the subject of Bob Nixon and studied the bundle of rags in his hands.

"Mr Drufus, what is this object that I've had to look after so carefully; that I somehow knew was important to bring with me; that…you seem to know something about, judging by the way you reacted when you unwrapped it?"

But the merchant seemed distracted by his own thoughts and didn't reply.

XI

In a dark side-street of Hawkby, the last day of Birchmoon, an eye blinks. The only sound is a steady, hoarse breathing with an occasional soft, bovine cough. Has a bull broken free from a market pen? The breath moves towards the main street, swirling silver in the freezing night air, but itself warm and sweet as silage. However, the figure that steps out into the main street is not a bull, it is human, and leaves boot-prints in the crisp snow. But the figure's head seems of monstrous size, and maybe in the moonless night there is an impression of two great, curved horns, or is it simply the silhouette of the upturned collar of a greatcoat?

An eye flicks up and down the empty street, and then settles on the upper end, where the thoroughfare merges into the town square. The eye looks at the silver-dirt floor of the square where many feet have trampled snow and mud into a mess, then focuses on a building across the open space: The Buzzard Inn.

When it reaches the door of this building it glances to left and right before entering. Imagine the sudden, violent scraping of chair-legs, the tables overturned in panic, the terrified shouts and screams and disbelieving stares as this beast with a bull's head and human body bursts into the front bar.

Inside, Kip and Maddy are sitting at a table sipping hot cider, Brag is leaning at the bar counter talking business with a storekeeper who wishes to buy some barrels of salt. The door from the square pushes open and some of the occupants of the bar look up to see who the new arrival is, then… they return to their conversations or private thoughts as the newcomer is a stranger. The beast enters and no-one recognises it. The beast enters and they do nothing. But Maddy shivers and suddenly feels uneasy.

"Are you cold, Maddy? We could move closer to the fire," offers Kip.

"No, I'm alright. It must have been the icy draught when that gentleman came in." But a coldness settles in her bones.

The newly arrived gentleman buys a drink and sits in a corner by the fire, and whenever Maddy glances his way, he always seems to be watching them.

Kip broaches the subject of leaving Maddy at Hawkby. Maddy is displeased. Kip persists. Maddy remonstrates. Kip insists that it is for her own good. He admits that he hasn't found a suitable place yet, but he is convinced that he will, and that she will be safer and happier there. Maddy folds her arms and sinks into a stubborn silence.

The gentleman rises from his place by the fire and approaches them. He begs indulgence for the discourtesy of invading their privacy; he is so apologetic, so well-mannered. He is so sorry, but he could not help overhearing their conversation. If he might make so bold, he happens to know of just the residence where Kip might leave his charge with an easy mind. The young blacksmith stands courteously and offers the gentleman a place on his settle. The two men discuss the details. The lady in question is the gentleman's sister. She is out of town but returns tomorrow evening.

Kip explains that he must leave in the morning. If Kip would be so kind as to honour the gentleman with his trust (he is so gracious, so kind), he would be only too pleased to look after Maddy for the day and introduce her to his sister personally. He is sure that Maddy would make just the young companion she is looking for. Kip is about to shake the gentleman's hand when something akin to that scene of panic and uproar we erroneously imagined at the gentleman's entrance startles him. Maddy erupts into a fit of screaming and yelling. She pushes over her small settle which crashes back onto the flagstone floor. She dashes her cup to smithereens next to it, then flings herself onto the cold stone, moaning and screaming by turns, and chanting words that seem to be a repetition of 'cold bones, cold bones!'

Brag rushes over and, leaning over her, takes her in his arms and by sheer physical strength subdues her flailing arms. Kip is shocked, spellbound. Maddy pulls the packer's head down to her own. She is moaning and feverishly whispering, then suddenly appears to pass out.

Mrs Redna appears. Before marrying John Redna and coming to The Buzzard, she had been a midwife and has some knowledge of medical matters. She takes charge of the young woman.

When Kip turns round to apologise to the gentleman, he finds that his new acquaintance has disappeared.

28th **Birchmoon** *from Kip's Journal*
Already, so early in my journey, I begin to have misgivings. I seem to have stirred up a hornets' nest. Mr

Drufus spoke to me earnestly this evening, after Maddy's fit. He made it unequivocally clear to me that we must take her with us. He would not say why he was so insistent, except to hint that there were dangers abroad, which meant that it was best that she were not left alone, i.e. out of our company.

"Not," he added worryingly, "that even that will mean we're in the clear."

"Excuse me, Mr Drufus. You keep saying 'we'."

"Aye."

"Well," I stammered. "Er…" I found his monosyllabic directness disconcerting. "Well, does that mean that you are coming with me… us?"

"Nay, lad. It means that you are coming with me! I was already heading for Fiskemouth, which is where you are now going!"

XII

In a dimly lit room, a man reaches out a gnarled countryman's hand and draws a brass globe round on its axis with his horny fingertips. The firelight and candle-glow just disclose that the surface of the sphere is inscribed with maps of the night sky, with the main stars, planets and constellations picked out in strikingly coloured enamelling.

In the hushed tones of someone used to living alone, he muses to the black cat on his lap, "Well, Snowy, the stars tell of visitors."

The cat mouths a short, silent miaow in reply, a sort of feline assent, and the man continues, as much to himself as to his companion, "Brag Drufus is due, which is lucky as I'm almost out of my baccy. Perhaps it's him who's indicated."

A feline and rather uninterested 'Yes, probably' from the cat.

"But somehow it is and it isn't. I don't know. Both seem to be indicated. Oh well, we shall see soon enough."

ROWANMOON
(January 21–February 17)

'To have gathered from the air a live tradition
or from a fine old eye the unconquered flame.
This is not vanity.
Here error is all in the not done,
all in the diffidence that faltered.'
                              Ezra Pound

'It is the spirit that quickeneth.'
                              The Gospel of St John

Known also as the quickbeam, the rowan is the tree of life, and this is the time of the Quickening of Days.

Rowan wood was used as a prophylactic against lightning and witch-spells, and a rowan-stake driven through a corpse was said to cause the death of the ghost.

The moon of the rowan contains the first of the year's four fire-feasts, Imbolc or Candlemas, and the rowan's poetic name is 'Delight of the Eye', that is LUISIU, or 'flame'. The festival celebrates the reawakening of the land after the long Winter sleep.

Chapter 2/ ROWANMOON

Rowanmoon 5 *from Kip's journal*
Left Hawkby early yesterday morning, entering oak-woods after a while. They were dark and shadowy, but afforded some protection from the cold north-east wind.
Reached a woodland settlement cleared from the forest, and named after its inn, The White Hart, where we lodged for the night. Spied the new moon through the window-pane.

Rowanmoon 6
Today we left The White Hart and its small clearing, entering again the seemingly endless oak-woods, where the snow had only penetrated in delicate, powder-like patches where the forest canopy allowed. Occasionally, when there was a gap, for example where a tree had died, the snow might fill a hollow with light folds like a sheet on an unmade bed. The track winds on over the damp carpet of brown oak-leaves, which the cutting hooves of the pack-mules reveal to be a sort of soggy crust over a black humus comprising centuries of old Autumns. The air is pungent with leaf-mould scent, and motionless, almost as if it is listening.

The oaks themselves are an individual race: some are slender and graceful, reaching towards the light which pierces the leafless canopy here and there; others are squat and warty, sprouting thin branches from low on their boles; more than a few are strong, spreading, royal-looking specimens; yet others are broken-limbed and of sorry appearance, like old soldiers.
The day was mild for the time of year, and dripping with thaw-water. Twice I saw red squirrels drawn from their snow-nap after the recent white cold.
In the late afternoon, the track we were following was joined by several others, and deepened, sinking between

root-strengthened banks. Mr Drufus explained that this was where many of the paths, tracks and drove-roads came together, like tributaries of the great Saltway. The deep road is also a remnant of an access to an ancient camp used by the tribal inhabitants of this land thousands of years since, a camp long re-inhabited by the tribes of forest trees. Eventually, this road emerged at the wood-edge, allowing us to look down a broad, rabbit-cropped ride, silvered with only a dusting of snow, and revealing further off the valley of the Fiske, enclosed by high hills cloaked in a continuation of the woodland. I felt a sudden surge of feeling for this homeland of mine, which surprised and unsettled, at the same time as affording me comfort. Was it motivated by an intuition that I should not look on this vista again; that, whatever adventure lay ahead of me, I would not return from it? Who can tell?

From our vantage point, we could see the roofs and smoking chimneys of the village of Openshaw, and we descended to discover a clean and comfortable inn where we put up for the night, and where I am now writing this entry in my journal.

There was a sense of unease about today's travel which I shall try to represent by relating an exchange which occurred at one point:

"For goodness' sake, what's the matter?!" asked Mr Drufus in an exasperated tone.

"What?!" I exclaimed, a little startled by his sudden outburst. "What do you mean," I added, perhaps obtusely, as part of me knew exactly what he meant.

"All day, you've been glancing over your shoulder every few minutes. What ails thee? If there's something amiss, you need to say."

"Oh," was all my reply, abashed by the revelation that my 'clandestine' watchfulness had, in fact, been all too obvious.

" 'Oh'. Is that all you've to say? 'Oh'. Come on, lad. Out

with it."

There was a sudden commotion in the mule-string as one of the animals nipped the creature in front. Mr Drufus went to check on matters and, during the delay, I cast a quick, furtive, sidelong glance at Maddy, who had caused my nervousness in the first place by whispering that we were being watched, and murmuring 'Cold bones' to herself over and over again. She, however, now appeared preoccupied with some wizened, red berries lying in the snow like drops of dried blood on white linen.

"Well?" asked Mr Drufus on his return. "Gee up!" he called, resuming the progress of the string of mules.

I sighed. "It's nothing. At least I've seen nothing." I was trying to protect Maddy, though why she should need protection from Mr Drufus I can't say. Protectiveness had become a habit in me where she was concerned. "It's just a feeling."

"A feeling?"

"That we're being followed."

"Who by?"

"Tantrum Bobus!" Maddy suddenly squawked, although she had apparently been absorbed in the passing scenery and not interested in our conversation.

Almost imperceptibly, Mr Drufus's step faltered before he continued walking, but he looked hard at Maddy, and a deep frown troubled his brow.

*****

Stopped at an inn tonight. As we entered, the landlord immediately recognised Mr Drufus, of course, due to his lifelong association with The Saltway, not to mention the previous generations of his family before him.

"Evening, Brag! O, before I forget- you know me and my memory- a stranger was here earlier. Asked me to tell you that he couldn't wait, but would catch you later."

Mr Drufus says that this message is very troubling. For

some reason, it shows him that I am carrying something of great value, and that my journey is of immense importance. If he is right, I seem- whether I like it or not- to be in the very centre of something that is far beyond my comprehension.

"Why me?" I pleaded.

He seemed unsympathetic. "Why not you?!"

Rowanmoon 8

Why do I feel uneasy? Nothing has happened really. So why do I sense someone following? There's never anyone there. Is it all just the power of suggestion, even from one as innocent as Maddy, or does this feeling grow from something real, an unseen but actual threat? Are there innocent explanations? My head cannot reason it out!

I spoke to Mr Drufus about it this morning. His response astonished me.

"We'll detour," he said.

"Detour? From The Saltway?"

"It's the logical thing to do. If someone is anticipating our journey and leaving messages to taunt us, then we'll find our own route to Fiskemouth."

So we took a sidetrack off The Saltway in the late afternoon and found a small, insignificant alehouse which had a spare room that the owner agreed to hire out to us for the night, though we had to put up the mules in the farmyard opposite as the alehouse had no stabling.

We sat in the attic-room after setting it up: travelling rolls on the floor for Mr Drufus and me, the tiny bed with a straw mattress for Maddy. Outside, the wind blew and caused the window-hook to scrape backwards and forwards on the dormer-wall below the window. This persistent sound seemed to emphasize the silence inside our small, dingy attic-room.

"Well, we're certainly off the beaten track!" I commented to Mr Drufus, more to relieve the silence than anything.

"No-one will find us here."

" Happen," he replied in blunt dialect. His tone did not have the ring of conviction. I sighed and glanced at Maddy who, as usual, was not taking any apparent notice of our conversation, but was involved in the childish game of breathing on the little square panes of the leaded window and scribbling on the resulting mist with her finger.

I looked back to Mr Drufus and tried again to engage him in conversation.

"What's the matter?" I asked him.

"Don't know," was his curt reply.

Aware of a certain oppression, and wishing to counter it, I suggested that we go down and get some supper. "Oh, yes!" shouted Maddy, jumping up with the enthusiasm of a six year-old and clapping her hands. She is delightful company sometimes...

The public room: a wall-clock talking to itself, persistently and patiently counting out its portion of eternity; two labourers drinking and talking about pigs; and a note left at the bar by a stranger that the landlord had just matched to his new arrivals and handed to Mr Drufus:

'Dear Travellers, Somewhat off-course, aren't you? Still, a snug little alehouse, isn't it? I hope that our paths cross before too long. Sleep tight. Your fellow traveller.'

How do you elude a pursuer who is ahead of you, and who seems to know your mind before you do yourself?

******

Rowanmoon 10   *The Kingfisher, Fordhope*
"The knock at the door announces a stranger: by definition, one to be feared."
    H. Halpert & G.M Story (Christmas Mumming In Newfoundland)

My hand is shaking as I write. We took rooms at the Kingfisher Inn, which stands by the River Fiske where it is forded by The Saltway, and earlier this evening, I strolled out to take the air and walk off some of the effects of the excellent food and ale that the landlord had regaled us with at supper.

It was dark, so as I wandered down the main street I could see the lantern-lit interiors of many dwellings, which was entertaining. A little beyond the end of the last terrace of cottages, a large house, set back and peeping through its bounding yews, caught my attention, particularly as a gibbous moon approaching the full was adjacent to its roof, apparently sitting on its shoulder. In the top of the house's three storeys was one lighted window, the only one illuminated in the whole house. From where I stood I could see a figure sitting with its back to the window. Then, for no reason that I could see, I suddenly had a strong feeling of foreboding, even fear. I was just telling myself how silly it was to let my imagination frighten me at my age, when the figure slowly turned and looked out of the window, staring as if to dissolve the darkness with the intensity of its gaze. I was dressed darkly, and the moon was casting little brightness where I stood: it was not possible that I could be seen from that high room. Yet I felt sure that the figure was looking straight at me, concealed by yew boughs and shadow though I was. Then, as if something had just caught its eye, it craned its head towards the window right in my direction, stood up and picking up a lantern which was the only light, left the room.

I felt a wave of panic as my scalp prickled. I thought 'Why? Why am I scared? What is there to be scared about?' My breathing began to come in short, quick exhalations. The light of the moving lantern appeared briefly at a window on the stairs on the first floor.

"I must leave. Come on, Kip Smith!" I told myself as I remained rooted to the spot, staring at the house.

The swinging lantern-light now appeared in the fanlight over the front door as the occupant arrived on the ground floor. Now I knew what a rabbit feels like at the approach of a weasel; I felt the ice of terror in my veins. My limbs were frozen- there was a gap between my brain and my body. Then the sound of a door-bolt snapping open roused my body to life. The silhouette of a large figure stood in the doorway, holding a lantern high and casting its great head slowly from side to side, as if sensing my presence out in the lane but not actually seeing me, almost as if it were sniffing the air. Then, uncannily, its head stopped its side to side searching motion and once more craned in my direction. With a sudden resolution it took a step or two towards me, and I turned with an involuntary whimper and fled down the street for the inn.

As I turned my head to ascertain how close my pursuer was, a trick of the light (or should I say 'a trick of the dark') made it appear that he had put down the lantern and dropped onto all fours. The next moment, as I hurtled down the dark street, I heard a menacing outbreak of snarls. I felt hopelessly doomed, awaiting the first agonising clutch on my leg of sharp fangs, but kept running in an automatic way, perhaps through some basic urge of survival. Suddenly, as if by magic or grace, I was at the inn and slammed the front door behind me. Without hesitating, I ran upstairs.

Maddy was asleep. Mr Drufus was asleep. Should I waken him? What do I tell him if I do? "Mr Drufus, I got frightened in the dark. A man quite reasonably thought he detected someone lurking in the lane outside his house, and came to investigate with his guard-dog, which chased me down the street."

How could I sleep? I was so jumpy! Every scratch of a mouse in the walls, or scrape of window-hook in the breeze, made me freeze with momentary fear. I had to sit with my back to the wall and watch the door.

Suddenly, there was a quiet knock at the door. I scarcely breathed. Maddy's shoulder rose and fell as she slept. Mr Drufus gently snored. Another three small knocks, as with a knuckle. I could almost hear the vibration of listening from the other side of the door. Then footsteps receded down the passage.

An hour or so later
Now I am *really* confused!
Maddy stirred in the bed as I sat on my bed-roll, and the conversation went like this:
"What's the matter, Kip?"
"It's nothing," I replied, not wishing to alarm her unnecessarily. Who knows what effect the horror I felt could have on her delicate sensibilities?
"But," she persisted, peering at me through the moonlit space of the room, "you look terrified."
"It's nothing, Maddy. Don't worry. You go to sleep. There's much more travelling to be done tomorrow."
A scratching noise at the window made me gasp, and we both saw some sort of claw or paw feeling for purchase on the sill. Maddy seemed astonishingly unconcerned, but I was frozen with disbelief and fear.
Then a startled cry, half human, half fox-yelp, screeched just outside the dormer, and the paw suddenly disappeared, as if something had jolted whatever it was away from the window. Maddy sprang up and opened the casement.
"Gone,' she observed with a calmness and detachment that must of been born of her uncomprehending simplicity.
"Shut the window!" I shouted, thawed back into responsible action by the sudden threat. "It might be dangerous," I added, attempting to find a middle way between maintaining safety and not alarming Maddy.
"Oh, we're quite safe, Kip," she said, in one of those occasional serious and assured manners she has. Then she continued, "I drew a protective symbol on our window in case the follower tried to get in."
I was confused into silence. I remembered her breathing

on the window and drawing on the resultant condensation with her finger.

Is she just playing childish games? Or does she know something? No, surely not. I must keep a sense of perspective.

Apparently, Mr Drufus slept soundly throughout the whole episode!

Rowanmoon 11

Mr Drufus listened to my fear-filled narration of the previous evening's occurrences with evident concern. I was prepared for the moment when he would begin telling me that I was letting my imagination run away with me. And I was ready to be reassured by his reassurances! But he promptly announced that we must leave without delay, and get to a friend of his who lives about twenty miles south of here, on the other side of Tyner Hill.

I think that this friend must be extremely learned- even more so than Mr Sloethwaite- if Mr Drufus needs to consult him! And not only learned, but imposing. I can't imagine what it will be like in his presence.

Rowanmoon 12

We have walked hard all day from Stoatland village, and endured the steep, winding climb up Tyner's northern side. However, I forgot my fatigue coming over the top of Tyner Hill as my amazement grew, for hoving into view at each step was a lonely, majestic ring of thirteen standing stones, measuring about sixty feet in diameter. For some reason that I presumed must be to do with the imminent quarter day, a small bonfire was laid outside each old monolith.

As we came closer, I noticed that a group of rustics was gathered just outside the circle, and the men and women in the group were chatting, though they stopped to scrutinize us as we approached. I paused to gaze in awe at the stones, whilst Maddy skipped round the as yet unlit bonfires. Mr Drufus proceeded towards the group of country folk.

"Tis Mr Drufus, the salt-packer," a slight old woman with white hair declared.

"Why, so 'tis, Miss Dapplethorne," agreed a short, rotund and rubicund man, who resembled an apple made human.

From where I stood, I could discern at the edge of my awareness that a conversation ensued, full of pleasantries, in which Mr Drufus was more animated than normal, but still left the bulk of talk to his interlocutors. There were frequent bouts of banter and laughter, especially from the 'human apple'. Much of the talk seemed to be around a celebration that was to take place at the ring of stones, including the lighting of the bonfires I had noticed. The ceremony was linked, as I had surmised, with the quarter day which was approaching (the 18th Rowanmoon) and each monolith in the stone-circle (known locally as 'The Old Uns') represented one of our lunar months, thirteen in the whole year. Most communities celebrate the four quarter days, but they don't all follow the same pattern.

Gradually, the group dispersed until there remained only 'Mr Pipkin' (as I had named him to myself, after the famous local varieties of apple: the Pipkin of Lete and the Curney Pipkin). Imagine my utter astonishment when Mr Drufus introduced us and announced that the gentleman was called 'Mr William Pipkin'! My look of disbelief seemed to give him no end of amusement.

"But you can't really be called that. I just made that name up for you in my head!"

"And what else would I be called, young man?" he replied, beaming at me with a twinkle in his eyes. Apparently, it was ancestors of his who developed the two famous apples, though whether the fruits were named after their creators, or the family gradually came to be known by the names of the apples, well... this knowledge is lost, as they say, in the mists of time.

The three of us continued in his company towards the village, which comprised thatched buildings of mellow, golden stone which stepped down the hillside. When we reached his cottage, the topmost in the steep village street, he invited us in for some refreshment. I was a little frustrated when Mr Drufus accepted the rustic's invitation because I was eager, as well as anxious- to get to the friend who Mr Drufus thought could help us.

We followed him up his garden path, with the old countryman proudly pointing to his bee skeps in his orchard, for which he'd invented some curious-looking extensions, so that they rose in tiers to resemble a Babel-like tower. This was so that he could collect what honey he needed without having to kill the colony, which he thought outrageous.

"Just take the amount of honey that you need, and leave enough to see the colony through the cold months," he said. "It's important to respect Nature and live with it on Earth without hurting it."

He regretted apologetically that there was not more for us to see in his garden, and as he rambled on, with quips and chortles, I began to relax and to forget my concern for reaching Mr Drufus' friend. Mr Pipkin seemed to have a gift for making people feel easy in his company, and the more he spoke, the more I felt drawn into conversation.

The room into which we were led was a homely chamber, and also dark, due to a combination of the small, deep-set windows and the overhanging thatch. Bill was obviously not a tidy man; the room was a jumble of domestic paraphernalia climbing out of the shadows which were still and grey now, but must, I could imagine, be a pool of restrained, dappled, and dancing green light in Summer: the promise of the climbing plants which now clung leaflessly to the thatch-eaves and window-frame. There were cluttered table-tops, cupboard tops, sideboards and shelves. In just one sweep I noticed writing quills, tins marked 'Seeds', a stuffed kingfisher, a bread-crock, tied bundles of dried herbs, strings of onions, coat-pegs with layers of heavy tweed coats, corduroy jackets and felt hats, a creased leather armchair with a lokum-coloured velvet cushion upon which slept a black cat, curled as neatly as a seashell.

We drank sweet parsnip wine and munched a rich, moist fruit-cake, homemade bread and home-reared honey. And I, oh dear!, I completely forgot Mr Drufus' friend whom we were supposed to be so urgently seeking. It was a haven, this simple countryman's home, with the uncluttered pleasures of the garden and its fruits: all my fears and anxieties fell away without me noticing, so that when Bill, in his hospitable country way, insisted that we stay to supper, I was delighted at the prospect and happy to assume that Mr Drufus knew what he was doing when he accepted, with a helpless, smiling glance and raised eyebrows at me.

So supper and pleasantries mingled for the next hour or so, until we settled before the open fire, Maddy and I on a long, upholstered stool, and Bill and Mr Drufus in battered leather armchairs. Now that the talk took a more serious turn. For the first time in my experience, Mr Drufus began speaking, and kept talking uninterrupted. He told our kindly host everything, to my mounting dismay: firstly because he had drilled into me the necessity for caution, and secondly because I wasn't sure that this simple man would be interested or would understand. I was agitated and perplexed. Maddy alternately wandered about the the room looking at objects or sat and gazed into the flames in the hearth. I watched the two men: as Mr Drufus spoke, Bill sat staring into the fire whilst he listened intently, his elbows on the arms of his chair, his thick fingertips touching and gently supporting his chin, nodding his head occasionally. The only hint of any concern was to raise his eyebrows suddenly when he heard about the messages left for us, and to knit them slightly when he heard the names of Bob Nixon and Tantrum

Bobus.

Mr Drufus eventually completed his slow and purposeful rendition, delivered in his deep, even voice with its blunt, northern accents, and drew his pipe from his pocket, offering his tobacco pouch to Bill. Soon the room was fragrant with a strange, sweet aroma of smoke that drifted and eddied gradually but inevitably towards the fireplace, to be drawn at last into the flue in the main current of air.

After some minutes, Bill finally spoke.

"Nice bit of leaf you've brought with you this time, Brag."

"Mixture of 'Butterleaf' and 'Sweet Lily'. A good year," replied Mr Drufus.

Another few minutes passed. Then Bill rose carefully and went to a tall cupboard built into the corner of the room. He lifted out a large, etched brass globe on a stand and placed it on a small table between the armchairs, then drew it round slowly on its axis with those worn, sensitive fingertips and scrutinized it closely. From my seat, I began to discern in the lamplight that the markings on the sphere were constellations, maps of the night sky. My perplexity deepened, but I was intrigued. Who was this simple countryman that Mr Drufus trusted with our story, and why did I feel safer in this cottage than I had for the entire journey so far? The beginnings of my speculation were interrupted as Bill turned to Mr Drufus.

"I must consult my books. Come through. My workshop might interest your young friend."

We followed him out of the cosy parlour, moving in the wake of lamplight that he and Mr Drufus bore through the scullery and rear lobby, where general household and gardening activities were evident in the boots, gardening coats, flowerpots, pottery sink, and two barrels - one for his ale and one for his cider - and demijohns where his country wines were busy quietly popping to themselves next to the copper. From the lobby, one door led into the back garden, but Bill unlocked and entered another doorway, through which very few guests - I discovered later - were ever ushered.

The place we entered was startling after the workaday domesticity of the parlour. This room was open to the apex of the roof and gave the impression that the cottage was much bigger on the inside than seemed possible from without. A flight of wooden open-tread stairs led to a narrow gallery on the opposite wall, where there were shelves of old books; workbenches ran along the opposite and right-hand walls of the ground floor, and a large work-table occupied the middle of the 'hall'; a huge fireplace sat back-to-back with where the parlour fire must be.

The benches and table were covered with a mass of extraordinary objects: pots, pans and crucibles containing various coloured sediments; tripods and gauzes; measuring instruments such as bottles, jugs, rulers, calipers, sextants; orreries, globes, astrolabes; jars of gold-leaf; old, smooth-handled woodworking tools; various sized knotless wooden panels of lime, birch and alder; piles of folded linen; sets of lenses; tightly corked jars (some holding messy, brownish liquids, others strange pigments of off-white, ochre, woad, madder, umber; larger jars containing resins like amber, oils such as linseed; phials of powders, chalks and alabaster; pots bristling with brushes; and an unpleasant, fishy-smelling substance in a large cooking-pot bubbling quietly over a low fire in the inglenook.

To say that I was amazed would be such an understatement as to be meaningless.

Bill lit a couple of lamps close by and, leaving Maddy and me, climbed the staircase to the gallery with Mr Drufus, whistling a country dance tune to himself. While Maddy showed her usual interest in her surroundings by playing with an orrery, I decided to follow on to the gallery. I could see by the newly-arrived lamplight that yet another leather easy-chair stood at the far end of the gallery from the stairs, and that a white cat was curled on its cushion.

"Ah! Hello, Jet!" exclaimed Bill. "Hard life for cats, eh?"

he added.

Totally ignored by Jet, but chuckling at his rhetorical question, Bill squinted at the volumes on the shelves. To assist his search, he ran his fingers along the spines of leather, fabric, velvet and other materials, before pulling out a large old volume, more like a folder of loose-leaf pages in various materials than a book, which displayed many columns, numbers and symbols. After studying it for some while he nodded and tapped the page with his gnarled, scarred countryman's forefinger.

"Well, well, Jet. Fancy that, eh! Well, well..." Jet blinked slowly and without interest.

Bill turned to Mr Drufus. For the first time in my short experience of him, the apple-bobbingness had gone from his voice.

"It's serious, Brag. This is it!"

Very well, readers, I have to confess that this was the moment (although you, I'm sure guessed ages ago) when my VERY slow wit suddenly realized that this was the friend that we had so urgently travelled to consult. I was embarrassed at the recollection of my condescension. As Mr Drufus and Mr Pipkin were murmuring earnestly to one another, I retreated downstairs, thankful to hide my discomfort.

I sat on a bench and considered my naivety, my unfounded arrogance, and resolved to purge them by confession and apology. At this point, Maddy walked up to me with a sympathetic smile.

"Cheer up, Kip!"

"I've been foolish, Maddy."

"Who hasn't?"

"I thought that Mr Pipkin was just a simple countryman; worse, a bumpkin."

" Close... apart from the 'just'... and the 'simple'... oh! and the-"

"Yes, alright!" I interrupted her with a self-deprecatory laugh. "No need to rub it in."

Again, in talking to Maddy, I had that feeling that she was not the person whom I thought she was. I was beginning to feel very unsure about my ability to assess people. My self-confidence, my whole picture of myself, was being undermined.

We sat in silence, Maddy and I, and a stillness deepened inside this strange room, and also inside me, so that I had the curious impression that my inner self was bigger than the body which contained it; that I was bigger than the room in which I sat; that the room was bigger than the cottage of which it was a part. Like peeling an onion to find each successive layer bigger than the one outside it. Impossible worlds within worlds...

I was summarily awakened from this reverie by a dull, snapping thud as Mr Pipkin abruptly shut the book he had been consulting and, replacing it on the shelves, descended from the gallery, after courteously bidding Mr Drufus to go first.

"Let us return to the parlour," he announced.

"Wait!" I cried, surprising myself with the unexpected volume of my voice. More quietly, I asked, "What is all this?" indicating the mysterious workshop with a sweep of my arm.

"I make icons,' replied Mr Pipkin. "Just a little hobby!" I'm sure I heard Mr Drufus let out the slightest involuntary snort of amusement.

Mr Pipkin beckoned me to follow him to a table, where he showed me some of his paintings on wooden panels, his 'icons'. They were objects of deep yet vibrant hues; lucent and inexplicably unfathomable. The closest I can get to describing them is to say that they were not portraits, but blurs of colour and texture which, by some alchemy, seemed to suggest their subjects. In the first, I saw three hares chasing each other in a circle, and somehow sharing just three ears, though all had two each; in the second, a smiling sun with great, crooked rays; in the third a Green Man like a briar-festooned bush on legs; then a contemplative silver-blue moon riding a frosted hilltop; next, a sloe-tree, radiant with snow-like blossom; and finally a creature half in and half out of a thicket, so that it might have been a stag, or there again it could also have been an antlered man. Also, each icon produced a different emotion within me, and as I described my responses to Mr Pipkin, he just smiled slightly, and nodded, and said quietly, "That's right, Kip." The countryman's enthusiasm and reverence for his 'hobby' were instantly captivating to me as he explained the painstaking procedures, which I will pass on here since I found such fascination in their meticulousness. Many skills go into Bill Pipkin's craft: he selects his own wood, which he cuts and planes into smooth panels; to these he fixes hardwood struts to prevent early warping; then he adds the underlayer of liquid size and linen ("This will bind the ground to the panel more firmly, and it protects against splitting and flaking"); next, he prepares the ground itself with a mixture of alabaster and fish-paste, applied in several layers ("Now each of these layers, Kip, must be as thin as possible, for better binding"); each coating he dries and cleans so that they are all evenly matt white and of uniform consistency, utterly smooth and without cracks. Only then can he begin his picture: he draws an image, then scratches it out with a stylus and gilds it. "You must do this before you paint, or your gold will stick to the paints," he explained to me, with as much care as if I were an apprentice.

Now the painting; and I record as much verbatim as I can Mr Pipkin's recipe for his paints, which he makes up for himself:

"Ah, well!" laughed Mr Pipkin. "This is almost a meal in itself! Eggs are very important." He lifted down a jar of viscous, brown liquid. "This is my jar of stuff for binding the pigments. Egg-yolk and water mixed together in equal measure, then add a spot of strong ale to help it keep, especially if there's a drop gone sour in the barrel. Not that that happens too often in this house!" he guffawed. The finely powdered pigments are then stirred into the egg-yolk mixture, using great skill to achieve the correct proportions. The icon is then painted, and when complete is left for several days to dry completely; but even this does not complete the process. "Finally," said Mr Pipkin, holding up his forefinger for emphasis and fixing me with his eye to hold my attention, "I makes up my oliver!" ('oliver' is how he pronounced 'olipha', and indeed his Tyner accent was more marked as his enthusiasm for his art glowed through his explanations).

I have since discovered that it requires (like the rest of the process) a rare skill founded on long experience to properly mix the boiled oils and resins that comprise the olipha, which coats the icon and protects it from damp and light. "Ah, but that's not all that it does," Mr Pipkin impressed on me portentously. "It's the oliver that makes the picture deep."

I cannot describe the effect with any better word, simple though it seems. I gazed with a feeling of privilege on these 'deep' icons with their strange, otherworldly images, and colours as exotic and sheened as enamel, beetle-wing, mother-of-pearl, gentian violet. I knew that both they and their creator were special: simple, yet deep.

"Thank you," I said to Mr Pipkin.

He placed a hand on my shoulder, looked intently into my eyes as if he could see straight to my innermost workings... and winked! Then I, who had considered myself such a man-of-the-world compared with rustic Bill Pipkin, felt like a child before him.

******

Mr Pipkin brought a tray when we had regained our comfortable fireside places in his parlour. On the tray were a small glass for each person and a green bottle full of some dark liquid. "A little something to aid digestion and sleep. My own receipts. Picked all the blackberries myself," he said matter-of-factly as the liquid glugged into the delicate glasses. He beckoned me confidentially with his forefinger and added in a stage whisper, "Bought the cloves from a spice-merchant for an exorbitant price!" He glanced at Brag with raised eyebrows and a twinkle in his eye, and chuckled.

The liquid warmed my lips and mouth, then my throat, then my whole body with a slow glow. It was like an ember or a ruby, or perhaps a combination of the two.

Mr Brag spoke. "So, Bill, what do your books and charts and constellations tell you?"

"Well, Brag, you're into something this time, and no mistake!"

"Aye! Whoever's tracking us seems to know my changes of plan before I do."

"Strangers," whispered Maddy.

Mr Pipkin nodded to himself. Mr Drufus looked at nothing in particular and I could hear his regular breathing. "I see," he sighed after a while, as if a profound foreboding had been confirmed. "So this is it."

"This is it, Brag." I became aware that I was sitting motionless and tense, staring at the faces of the interlocutors.

"What's your advice, Bill?"

"The stars tell of a ship. And the words 'white water' are in my thoughts. I believe a voyage is in the offing."

"Why?" I found myself asking.

"What do you think, Kip? To find something? To deliver something? To meet someone? Time will tell you. It's for you to discover for yourself. It's your journey."

He turned to Mr Drufus. "But be warned, Brag, there is great danger."

"Aye, Bill. I've been aware most of my life of a shadow awaiting me." I was beginning to realize, amid all this strange talk between a packman and a farmer, that I was caught up in some very long, serious, slow-moving event; had been caught up since the Old Dame had given me the carved spheres, and for who knows how long before even that! This event involves, apparently, many people over many years in many places.

Rowanmoon 17
We have been resting at Mr Pipkin's cottage for some days. He said that it was 'not propitious' to leave till after Candlefair, and, as that was good enough for Mr Drufus, who was I to argue?!

Rowanmoon 18 (First Quarter Fire) *from Kip's notes*
The people of the hill district of Tyner gather at the circle known as The Old Uns on this night to celebrate the resurrection of the land. Outside each huge stone a fire is built. No-one steps inside the ring at this time of year, as the circle of ground within the stones is covered in snowdrops: a cool, white fire of awakening, 'a delight to the eye'. This tradition symbolizes respect for the Earth, and the ground is considered sacred until the flowers have finished flowering.

The bonfires are lit and, from them, torches are ignited until there are hundreds of little fires bobbing and dancing, as the people holding them aloft move and jostle. Then the procession leads off from the hilltop singing a song used for the occasion since time out of mind, towards the market town of Lolsdun, the capital of the district of Tyner. From a distance, the procession appears as a tidal river of fire, boring down a channel of dark; or a necklace of flame threading round the neck of the black hill.

All the way, there is music and singing: but although joyous, it is all enacted with a dignified solemnity, for it is an encouragement to the growing sun; a rite of faith in the returning light, in the lengthening of days. The fun and frolics are saved for Candlefair, which begins on the following day. On arrival at Lolsdun, there is singing of the rowan-carols in the market-square; candles are lighted in all the windows, as are lamps on street-posts erected for the fair's duration. Everywhere, the town glows.

Then, everyone sleeps, but rises early for Candlefair Breakfast, a vast communal event. The Great Hall on the square is filled for several sittings to the rye bread, cheese, thick ham, a late-keeping apple called 'Rowan Queen', and specially prepared vintage cider and apple juice: all local specialities.

By late morning, the fair is in full swing.

Rowanmoon 19 *11 a.m. A coffee house*

After last night's joyful solemnities, today has been a cascade of noise, a tumult of impressions: aromas of food and drink; rags and strains of music rising from street corners or inns over the general hubbub and then weaving back into obscurity; the scent of pipe tobacco from a passer-by or of spices from a stall; the bustle of the crowded streets and the stallholders' shouts and calls; the colours of the street entertainers' fantastic costumes: jugglers, magicians, dancers, acrobats. I wandered through all this explosion of colour-and-sound-and-odour in a daze. Maddy exclaimed continually and ran back and forth like a five year old as we passed yet another attraction among many. She was captivated by the Lolsdun Stilt Dancers, who perform only on Candlefair Day: each dance is executed on taller and taller stilts, representing the lengthening of days, till their final dance is a weird, lightly lumbering, slow-motion affair performed twelve feet above the watchers' heads!

******

We are now sitting in this shop trying a new drink called coffee, which some of the spice merchants have brought to the main towns, though Mr Drufus remains unimpressed, and says he prefers good ale. Haven't seen him since breakfast: he went off 'to do some business'. Mr

Pipkin went with him.

Rownamoon 19 *11.30 a.m.*
Maddy and I have just had a shock. Our table is in the window of the coffee shop, and we were enjoying watching the endlessly varied stream of people passing by, an entertainment in itself, when who should appear but the companion of the bully Bob Nixon, from our confrontation at The Buzzard way back north in Hawkby towards the end of Birchmoon. He was talking and joking with a friend, but when he noticed us, he stopped dead, the smile dying on his face, and then he hurriedly moved off, pushing his friend ahead of him. I wonder why they are here. By the look on his face, our presence in the town was as much a surprise to him as his was to us.

Rowanmoon 19 *7 p.m.*
Unfortunately, Candlefair is being dampened by the elements. Well, one of the elements, at least. The rains came shortly after midday and have continued in sheets ever since.

Rowanmoon 19 *Just before retiring to bed*
"My guess," mused Mr Drufus, when I told him about our sighting of Bob Nixon's companion, "is that he was just careless. He'll have known we were here, alright, but I bet he wasn't supposed to let us see him. Low profile, you know. He must be a worried young man: his master has a strange knack of finding out the smallest error, and he doesn't suffer fools, gladly or any other way. And the lad didn't seem bad at heart. Just got in with the wrong company."

"You know his master?!"

"Depends on what you mean by 'know'. But my suspicions have been confirmed by my consultations here this morning. We'd best be off tomorrow."

Rowanmoon 20 *6 a.m. At Mr Pipkin's house*
A filthy morning! Rain cascading from the sky, and a cold wind blowing it aslant. And disturbing news. In fact, a huge, thumping shock of news! Mr Pipkin told us when we rose for our breakfast that a body has been found lying in the snowdrops of the old stone-circle. It is Bob Nixon's companion. Not only murder, but sacrilege, too.
The strange thing is that none of the snowdrops have been trampled. There is no indication as to how the body was placed in the centre. The only flowers flattened are those directly under the corpse. Also, there is no mark on him, but a frozen scream on his mouth and a fixed stare in his eyes that both betray terror.
Mr Pipkin has advised that we split our party to continue the journey, and has proposed that he take Maddy to 'someone he knows'. I was alarmed at the prospect of relinquishing my unsought stewardship, and I darted a concerned glance at Mr Drufus, who immediately gave me confirmation of assent with the slightest lowering
of his eyelids and head. I suppose it is best for Maddy to be out of harm's way, and harm is certainly about this way: you can sense it in the air.
Mr Drufus and I are to proceed 'incognito', myself as a journeyman tinker, and Mr Drufus as a smocked old shepherd. "No comments about the hat!" he remarked dryly, seeing my amusement at the shapeless, stained object he'd been given to wear in exchange for his own familiar garb. "I'll be glad of a broad brim in this rain, anyhow!"

******

It is now 7.30 a.m. We are packed and fed and leave imminently. Mr Pipkin and Maddy have been gone an hour, by a secret passage from Mr Pipkin's workshop. Mr Drufus was at the farm sorting out his mules when old Miss Dapplethorne called round.

"I'm just taking advantage of this break in the rain. I've come with some upside-down pear cake for Mr Pipkin."

"I'm afraid he's gone to see a friend." She looked disappointed, and I felt sorry for her. She'd obviously been up early especially to bake it for him, so I offered to put it in his larder and leave a note.

"I'll carry it, if you don't mind, young man," she declared, possessively hugging it to herself. I hesitated, unsure about letting a stranger into someone else's house, but then my more reasonable self pointed out that this was his neighbour, so I relented with a smile to myself at the maternal care she took over her gift. On the way back out, she noticed Mr Pipkin's walking sticks, a pot of which stood close to the front door.

"Oh, Mr Pipkin does love a stick! But I never saw this one before." She lightly stroked one which had a rounded handle carved in filigree. What was it: some inflection in her voice? A feeling in the atmosphere? An intuition? I don't know, but suddenly I felt a sense of unease about letting Miss Dapplethorne into this sanctuary of a house. I tried to bustle her out with, perhaps, too cheery a tone of voice.

"Oh, Mr Smith. So abrupt!" How can a voice be gently menacing? Yet, somehow, her light, mocking tone seemed to carry a hidden threat.

"I'm sorry, Miss Dapplethorne, but I need to be going."

"But Mr Drufus isn't back with his mules yet," she continued with a firm, quiet insistence, seeming to know a surprising amount about our business. "And this walking stick is so interesting, don't you think, Mr Smith? The way the handle is carved into this fine tracery." She turned her head up, like a small bird, to face me with a sweet smile which discomfited me with its hidden meaning. Perhaps my imagination is playing tricks with my anxiety. It's possible that all this supposed threat is in my own head. "Mr Pipkin is a dark one,' she said, in a village-gossip way, and I felt an animal wariness take hold of me.

"What do you mean?" I asked, in as breezy and innocent a way as I could muster.
"Oh, he's a man for secrets, our Mr Pipkin. Carries on quietly, you know. But there are few secrets in the country. It's not like a city where a person can lose themselves! Oh well, I must be going. So much to do! And I see the rain has already begun again." And with that she flitted away, without so much as a mention of the sensational village news of the discovery of a murder. Strange sort of gossip, wouldn't you say?!

Rowanmoon 20 *8.30 a.m.*
Well, what a morning this is! Maddy gone who knows where with Mr Pipkin; Miss Dapplethorne's unsettling visit; and now Mr Drufus has returned without his mules and informed me that our plans have changed! He says that we must at least 'do the best we can' to confound whoever or whatever has a malign interest in our journey. The 'best we can' in this instance is that he has arranged for someone to lead his mules-string to Cloveport, a small subsidiary port across the bay from Fiskemouth, and that we are to travel separately and meet up again in the main port at the anchorage of a ship called The Goodheart, belonging to a merchant friend of Mr Drufus. We shall slip out secretly some time in the next few hours, and in disguise. It's like an exciting game, except that Mr Drufus keeps reminding me that there is deadly danger. He seemed alarmed, then depressed, then resigned and philosophical, when I told him of Miss Dapplethorne's visit, and the fact of my letting her in. "Oh well, it's done now."
What is this object I carry that causes such a rumpus, and seems to involve so many people?

Rowanmoon 20 *Evening*
I watched from a rain-smeared window after making this morning's last entry as Mr Drufus returned to the farm

where his mules were stabled. He has arranged to give our travelling garb so far to the hired man and help who are roughly our height and colouring, and paid them well to see the mules safely to the depot at Salt Quay in Fiskemouth. They were recommended by Mr Pipkin for their physical likeness to us, and for their trustworthiness. I must confess that, as I watched them plod off down the road it was unsettlingly like spectating on a scene from my own life. I'm sure that any spies or observers down the way will suspect nothing awry.

About an hour ago, I watched a bent old shepherd in a floppy felt hat hobble off through the dusk-shrouded village in a southerly direction, making for the village of Elms Curney. His crookedness was partly acted, and partly to shield himself from the sheets of rain.

ASHMOON
(February 18 - March 17)

'The weeping Pleiades wester,
And the moon is under seas."
A. E. Housman

'Time held me green and dying
Though I sang in my chains like the sea.'
Dylan Thomas

'The Moon Under Water'
George Orwell

The ash is the tree of rebirth; the tree of the power of water (and this is the moon of floods). Oars were made of ashwood, which was acknowledged as a charm against drowning.

A spiral ash-stick was considered to have magical properties, and in many mythologies the ash is venerated as sacred (e.g. Yggdrasil in Norse mythology).

Chapter 3/ ASHMOON

Ashmoon 1

A little canvas-covered wagon, two miles out of Elms Curney, heading south. Tom Bussell, carrier and pedlar, dozing on the driver's seat; slack in his hands, the rope that serves as reins, but the two donkeys know the way, and plod on regardless of the torrential rain that sleeks their hair, as does another donkey tethered to the back. The gentle clank of dangling pots and pans which decorate the side-boards of the cart does nothing to disturb the old man, being so familiar an accompaniment to his travels, and even the persistent rainfall, which hasn't ceased for long over the last week or so, doesn't interrupt his dozing. As Kate, his lead donkey, passes a wayside cottage that announces the northern approach to Elms Curney, she brays her master awake, and he breaks into his automatic call: "Pots 'n' pans 'n' wicker baskets; wicker baskets, pots 'n' pans. What I haven't got, I'll bring another day." The second donkey, Emma, placidly ignores all the disturbance. After passing several orchards, a row of thatched cottages and a cider house, the wagon pulls up by the village-well at the edge of a small green, where several inhabitants sheltering beneath an oak await transport to Broadhemp ('Broddum') for the weekly market. Upon stopping, the carrier-pedlar breaks into his well-worn announcement: "Pots 'n' pans..." etc. as he pushes down the steps fixed to the side of his cart. One villager who isn't going to market delivers a saucepan for fixing.

Two old dames, a cottager's boy with a piglet for market, a young woman with a baby, and an aged shepherd in a battered felt hat, using his crook as a walking stick, are his pick-ups in the village. Whilst these climb into the depths of the wagon, the child thrilling to the mysterious-seeming gloom of the canvas-enclosed cart and the rapid tattoo of rain on canvas, 'Wicker Tom' unhitches Sarah, his spare donkey, and fixes her by an extension of the shafts of his own contrivance, so that she will walk ahead of Kate and Emma to share the added load of village inhabitants.

The child sits absorbing the muted light of the wagon's interior, and the vibrant impressions of a first drive to market; the two old dames sit opposite one another and chat ceaselessly; the young woman sews some repair to a blouse so as not to waste the journey time; the wheezing, ancient shepherd sits in silence, apparently taken up with his own thoughts, beads of water dripping from his hat-brim.

******

A young tinker, his toolbag announcing his craft, plods with a tired step down the steep lane which drops into the fishing village of Todenhay ('Todney'). Occasionally he skids and almost loses his footing, as the constant rain of the last few hours has made the lanes slippery with mud, and this is yet more treacherous on the steep gradient. He is directed to the quayside cottage of Cedric and Eliza Lanyard in answer to his enquiry after accommodation. As he makes his way, the lane drops ever more steeply into the cleft where Todenhay's cottages cling, and rivulets of rainwater have formed in places. He knocks on the door of the quayside cottage and waits, his drenched clothing clinging to his drenched skin.

Ashmoon 2   *Early morning*

"Course you can't walk to Fishmuth!" exclaims Eliza Lanyard as she serves Kip with a breakfast of mackerel, rough bread and homemade cider. "It's rained hard all night! The floods are out."

"But I have to get to Fiskemouth, Mrs Lanyard. I'm meeting someone. It's important."

"Well, it'll just have to wait, won't it, my love. You can't swim through a raging flood!"

Cedric Lanyard, a very quiet man, speaks now, though his

words are almost missed in the general breakfast bustle. "I'm going out later to empty my crab-pots and do a spot of overnight fishing. If you care to wait a day and join me I can take you round to Fishmuth. I'll be dropping off the crabs at the fish market tomorrow morning first thing."
"Well, that's very kind of you. I can't get much wetter at sea than walking in this rain, after all!"
Between Todenhay and Fiskemouth the coast is a labyrinth of creeks, most splitting and multiplying before reaching a tranquil, lapping end in the serene, green quietness of the oakwoods that cover the whole promontory right to the water's edge, where the high tides browse a straight line along the lower branches of the trees. Kip spent a busy evening and night on the level, rain-pitted waters of the creeks around Dawcombe, helping Cedric to haul in the wicker pots, and sorting the different species of crab ready for the market, as the fisherman had demonstrated to him at the first stop. Dark and early the following morning, he was delivered into Fiskemouth via the fishmarket.

ASHMOON 3 *from Kip's journal*

Here are my first thoughts of Fiskemouth, in which I have tried to create the effect of the barrage of impressions which hit my senses. Mr Sloethwaite always did say that I had a tendency to use 'somewhat flowery' language when I wrote. Oh well...

PORT LITANIES

Fiskemouth is like a cut diamond that flashes unexpected colours as you tilt it against the light. At first sight, the port is a homely fishing haven, folded into the maternal headlands. But then you notice that many of its lanes and alleys, which all inevitably tumble steeply to the waterfront, have strange and exotic names echoing faraway places, and when ships are docked at the quays, you often as not hear foreign tongues conversing or cursing or calling in languages you cannot fathom. The port is a meeting place, a meeting of places, an intersection of cultures, a town with its feet in the earth (or at least in the sand) but its eyes on the sea's horizon.

The waterfront comprises three main areas: the Fishquays, used by the town's fishermen for landing their catches, and the site of the Fishmarket; the Boatyards, where boats, ships and other watercraft are built; and the Wharves, where all the traded goods arrive and depart.

THE FISHQUAYS

cod, herring, skate, bass, gurnard, bream, sole, mackerel, gilthead, pollock, eel, hake, whiting, squid and crab:

silver-mailed; wings of wafered armour; rainbow-links; shifting light on a backbone; spined dazzling:

sheen of oil on water; mother-of-pearl; lustre like old Eastern silks; fish-heads and squabbling gulls

THE BOATYARDS

Here the nostrils are tanged with brine and pitch, for there is a constant coming and going of boats bringing barrels of tar from the Yewich tar-pits, on the island's east coast, for the caulking of ship's timbers to seal and preserve. All day there are the sounds of sawing, hammering, drilling, planing; all day the nose of the sea and the redolence of cut wood, mingling with the pungent aromas of pitch and tar.

THE WHARVES

A simple list of some of the varied products arriving on the ships at the wharves tells of the magic pervading the air of this bustling port.

AT THE FRUIT-WHARF: oranges, limes, lemons, figs, dates, olives, pomegranates, mangoes, bananas, avocados, juniper berries, pistachios, almonds, cashews

AT THE SPICE-WHARF: ginger, clove, cinnamon, orris root, angelica, coriander, cassia bark, liquorice, cloves, galangal, star anise

AT THE GOODS-WHARF: cinnabar, resin, alum, lamp-oil, cotton, silk, flax, southern wines & northern salt

ASHMOON 3 *Afternoon On The Waterfront*
I have met Mr Drufus, and we are wandering on the quaysides. We have left off our disguises, feeling that if we've shaken off our pursuers, well and good; and if we haven't, then there's no point walking around in costume. Occasionally, the packer glances at my dropped jaw wide eyes and he almost smiles! But it's all so strange! All these sights and sounds: I'd be a little nervous if I were not accompanied by him. He shakes his head and murmurs good-humouredly that I'm a 'queer fish.'
He is well known, and often a merchant or mariner will hail him, receiving a slight nod in return, for Mr Drufus (as I may have already said!) is not a demonstrative man, as with most Scalla Fells men.
We drift between the barrels, baskets, boxes, bundles and bales, as he allows me to wander and soak in the experience of the quaysides. The air is marbled with odours of tar, sweat, citrus, brine and ginger; blotched by shouts, accents and curses in foreign and dialect tongues, though the laughter sounds the same, whichever throat it erupts from. Harbour cats sniff round baskets of fresh and dried fish, often receiving a bellow or a boot. An old tan-skinned sailor plays a squeeze-box and sings with gnarled, briny voice: a sad tune about loss at sea, reminding everyone of the true cost of these cargoes. Many of them come from islands in the Southern Ocean with which this island does much trade, and it seems appropriate that they are known as The Aromatic Isles, because the ships seem to unload as much invisible odour or fragrance as solid cargo.

******

Ashmoon 3 *Dusk*

A sliver of moon hung over the evening sea. Some early reflected lights were like molten gold on the gently rippling waters of the inner harbour. As they walked, Kip became gradually aware of a familiar feeling of being watched. It made his heart sink into a desperate frustration that the tricks to elude their pursuers had, if his instinct was true, proved useless. He glanced furtively about, trying to appear as nonchalant as he could. No-one seemed, from his glimpses, to be concerned with him in the slightest. He kept a weather-eye open, without mentioning anything to Brag. A few minutes passed, and he had begun to relax, when his attention was, for some reason, drawn to a seagull sitting on the yardarm of a ship from which quaymen were unloading bales of tobacco-leaf and spices. Trying to hide the fact that he had noticed the bird, he snatched occasional glances towards the ship's rigging: the seagull was undoubtedly following their progress along the quays. A voice inside Kip's head said: "Here you go again! You are becoming mad with suspicion." Another voice within him retorted, "And with very good reason! You must talk to Mr Drufus."

"I'm just going back to The Goodheart," Brag's voice abruptly interrupted Kip's self-questioning, as the packer indicated the ship being unloaded of its cargo of tobacco and spices. It belonged to an old friend of Brag's who was a merchant from El Ilam-Coram, one of the Aromatic Isles in the Southern Ocean. "I'd like to fix a deal on some of that Dark Braxil leaf with my old friend, Madji. That'll make sure it's ready for my return trip."

As they approached the ship's captain, and Brag began to enquire of Madji the merchant's whereabouts, the seagull jumped from the yardarm and glided over the busy wharf and the heads of bustling mariners, merchants and quaymen. It sailed towards the wharfside houses, shops, inns and harbour offices. Kip was deaf to Brag's conversation: he was transfixed by the seagull, and soon found that his instincts were well founded. The bird landed on the cobbles outside The Angel Inn, at the foot of a steep street of steps called Angel Stairs, which climbed from the waterfront to the market square. Then, to his utter dumbfoundment, the gull hopped up the first couple of steps beside the inn, changing shape as it did so! It morphed before his eyes into a ragged human shape, and just before it disappeared up the shadowed passage, it looked back across the wharf directly at Kip, and the malevolence in its eyes startled him, so that he gave an involuntary cry.

This seemed to break a spell, for the busy wharf, which had been silent to Kip for the last few moments, suddenly opened floodgates of noise.

"What is it?" asked the packer, after thanking the captain for his directions.

Kip told Brag what he had seen, or thought he had seen, and of how he had dreamt the night before of a seagull changing into a man.

Again, as once before, Kip waited for the down-to-earth merchant to prick his fancies by telling him that his dream had coloured his imagination, and that his fears were making him over-anxious, only to be surprised as last time by Brag's response. "The fell wolf which attacked the mules..." muttered Brag to himself. "Come on!" he said briskly. "We must return to our resthouse and talk. This is every bit as bad as I feared."

******

Mr Drufus sighed. "Pipkin was right. There's extreme danger. It's time for you to know, lad."

They sat in their room at the packers' resthouse. Kip swallowed nervously.

"The followers who've been ahead," continued Brag, "the

strangers knocking at the door, clawing at the pane; shapeshifters who watch as you pass and then give chase: all these will resist you if they can. They are one and the same."

"Who is it?" asked Kip, not sure that he really wanted to know.

"He is, so to say, the outward face of The Dark Ones, but as he keeps changing it let's say his name is Falseface. He is your chief adversary. No-one will ever threaten you more than he will. He wants what you carry. The Dark Ones want it. The only reason they don't just kill you and take it is because you have secret friends who help to protect you... and the fact that you have more resources in you than you know or imagine. But make no mistake, they want it."

"But why?!"

Brag Drufus took a portentously deep breath.

"The strange object you were given is a precious artefact, imbued with ancient power. It was created back in the mists of time by the twelve Wise Ones: they were craftspeople, magi, watchers; in short, they were sorcerers who discovered what was required to put the off-set Vibrations Of Equilibrium back in alignment. As you know, our year is divided into thirteen lunar divisions, rotating round the hub: one special day which belongs to no moon, no tree. Each sorcerer carved a globe to represent one of the moons, using the wood of the tree that we assign to each moon. Then, by some secret knowledge and skill, they put each wooden moon-globe inside another so that when completed they shared a common centre. The first moon, Birch, was the smallest and was set inside the second moon, Rowan; the Rowanmoon went inside the third, the Ashmoon, and so on, until the thirteenth, the Eldermoon, contained all the other twelve moons. They then imbued it with a beneficent energy. Many years before, this vital source of equilibrium had been taken by the Dark Ones after a long and dreadful struggle. In its proper place, its influence for good could emanate into the world so that its energy could harmonise with the Earth's to the benefit of all that was good and true. Immediately, another great struggle followed, and the object was eventually recovered, though not before conditions were laid on it that meant that the attempt to return it could only be made at a certain time, by a certain person, and from a certain location. All the conditions had to be in place before the task of attempting the return could begin. No-one knew the details of time, place and person, not even The Dark Ones who had set the conditions. This element of the conditions was under the aegis of cosmic law, and could not be gainsaid by either side. The Wise Ones had to work ceaselessly in the meantime to keep The Moons safe and secure, until the preordained conditions were achieved. This moment would be indicated by the positions of stars and planets, and so The Wise Ones (and, undoubtedly, The Dark Ones) had to use their knowledge to track the alignments of the sky. After a vast period of Earth-time, the preordained positions were reached, and The Wise Ones brought The Moons to the place indicated by the alignments, and sought whoever was destined for the task. They then handed over the precious, vulnerable cargo to the person whose task it was to attempt the home-bringing of The Moons." Brag looked at Kip admiringly and pityingly. "That's the job you've been born for, lad."

A period of silence followed, while Kip pondered all he had just been told.

Then Brag sighed and said, "We must quickly seek those who can help thee. "

"But, Mr Drufus, you are with me. With you-."

"I can assist thee so far, of course; but *you* are the carrier; you alone can act. This is your task, Kip. It'll be difficult, cos they can take any shape -human or animal- or no living shape at all. But, by the same token, there are secret friends who can keep an eye out for thee.

"Early tomorrow morning we shall seek the 'whitewater ship' that Bill mentioned. Tonight, however, there's nowt to do but relax. We'll go and sup at The Monkey Tavern; both their shark chowder and eel pie are not half bad!"

******

A line of venerable buildings faced the harbour across the broad passage of the quay. There was a pleasing mix of rich merchant's homes, harbour offices, store-houses built with thick stone walls and stout oak doors, and no less than four inns: The Mermaid, The Old Cat, The Jolly (a type of boat), and The Monkey (a ship's cannon). Some of the fronts and gables were faced with slim, old brick the colour of terra cotta, lichen, rust and paprika. Others were plastered and washed in various shades of pink, white, mustard or blue. The Monkey was a building of creamy, plastered panels between silvery oak timbers, and towered high overhead- this overhanging effect amplified by a jetty protruding at first and second floor levels, where the newels and enormous supporting beams were richly carved, though the detail was much worn down by the weather.

Entering The Monkey off the quay Brag and Kip were hit by a wall of scented tobacco smoke, the smell of cooked fish and seafood, and a hum of conversation punctuated by bursts of laughter or raucous but good-humoured shouts. However, it was not (Brag assured Kip) such a riot as The Old Cat or The Jolly would be, for they were the haunts of the hands and quay workers, whereas The Mermaid and The Monkey were favoured by merchants and officers. Also, The Monkey was the one tavern run by a woman, and Mrs Brock would take no nonsense. Brag told Kip that at the first sign of boisterousness she was wont to say, "This may be The Monkey, but I'll have no monkey business here!" No-one argued with Mrs Brock!

A few heads turned their way and not a few voices hailed

Brag, who acknowledged them with small twitches of his head and raised eyebrows. Kip having lived a quiet country life had never witnessed a scene like it. Barely a piece of furniture or square foot of floor was visible, so crowded in were the patrons. And such an eclectic mix as had certainly never graced the parlour of Kip's local alehouse. The nearest Kip could recall was the crowd when the mummers visited his village each year. The romance and colour those strange actors brought was echoed in the variety of people here: merchants and ships' officers from his own island, and also from distant islands in the Southern Ocean. Dialects from all over the island, and languages from the isles wove together into a salty and convivial hubbub. There were pink faces of local officers' wives, tanned faces of local mariners, packers, farmers, black and brown faces from the various Aromatic Isles; round eyes, slit eyes, almond eyes; clothing of strikingly contrasting fashions: muted earth browns, charcoals, olives in simple country fabrics, as well as robes in vivid vermilion, emerald, saffron, aquamarine. And they all leaned against one another and draped themselves over tables, counters, sills and each other. The whole scene was well lit by lamps suspended from hooks in the ceiling timbers. An aged sailor entered the bar-room carrying a birdcage which housed a parrot with scarlet and turquoise feathers, so that it made its own gaudy splash of colour. He opened the door of the cage and the parrot hopped out onto his shoulder, freed for a while by the old salt from its ornate cage, which then swung slightly from a hook above the bar counter, upon which a cat curled at one end, asleep and apparently oblivious to the jostle and clamour. People sat at the tables were packed shoulder to shoulder and were variously spooning in mouthfuls of food, slurping from tankards, smoking clay pipes and/or chattering, joking, bargaining or quietly discussing business beneath the continuous noise. Emerging from the general barrier of sound, Kip heard a single deep voice calling Brag's name. A very tall man pushed through the crowd towards them. He was black-skinned and wore a large moustache, a little multi-coloured, peakless cap and an ankle-length robe of vivid scarlet. "Brag, old friend! How are you, man? Not seen you in ages." They shook hands vigorously.

"Let's go to the back room," shouted Brag. "It's less well-used. We'll be able to speak more easily!"

The rear parlour was a small, polished room of oak-panelling and brass candlesticks on walls and tables. Mrs Brock was very house-proud. Within the twelve foot square room were just a spice merchant and his sea captain quietly discussing the trip to the isles, and an old woman sat alone at another table on a wall-bench.. She had skin the colour of tanned leather and teeth dark as pickled walnuts. Her ilk-blind eyes wandered around the air and her hands in their fingerless mittens lifted a small, straight-sided porcelain cup of dark rum to her mouth at regular intervals, though she seemed only to wet her lips each time. "Keeps out the cold, my lovers!" her voice crackled out, sensing the arrival of newcomers, and raising her cup towards them.

Brag introduced the man in the red robe to Kip as Madji, the tobacco merchant with whom the packer did all of his 'leaf business', as he called it. While the two men discussed their present deal, Kip sat back and soaked up the atmosphere of the ancient place. Although the inn seemed something strange and new to Kip, he warmed to it, especially when it served him the most delicious 'fish stew' he had ever tasted (what Kip called 'fish stew' being the shark chowder recommended by Brag). The meal was accompanied by a strong, black winter ale redolent of liquorice, cloves and treacle, which made his head swim pleasantly. A little later, when the old woman had stubbed out her miniature, black cigar and begun to play dance-tunes on her fiddle, the small room attracted other people, including the old salt and his parrot, so that Brag, his business done, suggested that they move over to the wall-bench, and Kip was crammed between the fiddle player and the packer, feeling a relaxed, warm contentment at being part of this convivial evening.

He leaned his head to Brag's ear. "She plays well. Do you know her?"

"Alison Tudge? Aye! Years and years. She's Fishmuth through and through. Born sightless after a diphtheria epidemic. Hence her nickname."

"Nickname?"

"Blind Ali."

Kip jerked his head to look at Brag, but the packer's face was still and straight.

A few tunes later, Kip noticed that even the sleeping cat had removed itself from the noisier and more bustling main room, and was now curled on the hatch-counter, dozing but with one eye following proceedings.

A fisherman sang a song about a whale, and you could hear the salt-crystals on his larynx seasoning the melody.

Two mariners played tunes on a wooden flute and a concertina, managing to create a mellow sadness in their laments and slow airs, though they contrasted these with nonsense songs:

'I saw a mouse chase a cat,

Fie, man, fie!

Saw a mouse chase a cat,

Who's the fool now?' etc.

'Life is good' was Kip's feeling, as he drained his tankard for the second time, and the blind fiddler offered him one of her cigars, making him feel an accepted member of the Monkey's clientele, despite politely refusing the offer.

It was then that he noticed that the cat's one watching eye was fixed on him. He spontaneously looked away quickly, with a sudden thudding heartbeat in his chest, and tried to behave as if he hadn't noticed, but the next time he submitted to the temptation to steal a glance, the cat was still staring at him. In his discomposure his throat went dry: he looked down at the table in front of him and carefully examined a knot in the wood, then pretended to finish a drink from his empty mug.

"Bring the young man a fill of 'broad'", called the old woman next to him, taking his mug and passing it via other folk to the counter.

"Give us a tune, Ali," someone called.

"I will - as soon as you fill my cup with some of the dark stuff!"

However, Kip was not concerned with drink or fiddle tunes. His sudden rush of alarm, of panic, sped through his nerves, and his veins seemed for a second to carry acid instead of blood, as some ultra-quick sense of combined emotion and thought linked the snoozing cat with the memory of the shape-changing seagull he had seen on the quay. With this sense of a nearby threat, Kip turned towards Mr Drufus to confide in him and let him decide what must be done. Another shock awaited his reeling senses. Brag's eyes were unfocussed; he grinned stupidly.

"S'matter, Kip? Having a good time?"

Mr Drufus was drunk! This must be a bad dream. He felt like a small boy in a strange city who turns for his father's hand, only to find himself alone, deserted. The cat on the bar stood up, arched its back, yawned, stretched legs, paws and claws.

Kip swallowed hard and braced himself for an attack. He looked again at the packer, but he was lolling with his left shoulder draped round the blind fiddler's shoulders. Kip was hemmed in by the table in front, the wall behind, and companions on either side: he couldn't think what to do. So he did nothing.

The cat sat down, and Kip kept a wary eye on it, until he eventually persuaded an increasingly somnolent salt-and-spice merchant to go to bed.

Ashmoon 4   *Before breakfast*   *from Kip's journal*
This morning I am confused. The world is a different place to what I thought it was. And I am not the person I

thought I was. Let me humbly relate the early morning's experience:

We were supposed to be up betimes. I awoke to a light-filled room and found Mr Drufus snoring soundly in his bed. I remembered with a start that we had to find a ship; that it was urgent; that we had planned to be up and off to the quays early. I recalled last night: Mr Drufus drunk and staggering from The Monkey to the resthouse with me attempting to support his drink-heavy frame.

I jumped and woke him with a rough, angry shake of his shoulder. "Mr Drufus, what are you doing?"

"Well...," with a scratch and a yawn, "I *was* sleeping!"

"We're supposed to be up! We're on urgent business! At all times we must be alert: we are being watched and are under constant threat!!"

Mr Drufus sat up and stretched. "Good! That's very good!"

"Don't patronise me, Mr Drufus," I snapped. "Last night, whilst you were quietly getting yourself stitched, we were being watched. How could you be so casual? How could you miss the spy? What if we'd been attacked?"

"In a crowded bar!?"

His nonchalance was exasperating. "We still had to get to the resthouse. What if something needed doing?"

Mr Drufus knitted his brow in mock seriousness. "I said before: I can assist thee, but it's you must act!"

"Ha! Some assistance you'd have been last night," I retorted hotly. He simply raised his eyebrows and smiled slightly.

"Did you notice," I continued, "before you let the ale get the better of you, that cat on the counter?"

"Of course."

"It slept with one eye open."

"Cats often do."

"It was watching me."

"Perhaps it liked the look of you."

Mr Drufus was being unprecedentedly trying. "You're very

down-to-earth this morning," I observed, "very pragmatic," with an emphatic edge of irony.

"Anyway," I rejoined, "that cat must've been Falseface, or some sort of shapeshifter in his pay, I could feel the presence of it in my bones; and you......in your state you might've blurted out anything!"

Mr Drufus sighed and, for the first time, looked genuinely serious. "Not the cat."

"What?!" I exclaimed abruptly at the unexpected remark.

"The parrot."

My mouth opened in astonishment, and stayed open.

Mr Drufus winked at me.

At a quick breakfast, Mr Drufus said that I should stop calling him Mr Drufus. "Brag'll do from now on."

Ashmoon 5

Mr Dru... I mean 'Brag' has found the ship. It is called Tariqa. I asked what that had to do with Bill Pipkin's clue about 'white water'.

"The captain's name is Aquablanca. Bill does love a little puzzle!"

Ashmoon 9

We are still in Fiskemouth. Constant heavy rain, and winds in the wrong direction.

Ashmoon 12

A big storm overnight. The mast of the Tariqa struck by lightning. More delays while repairs are done.

Ashmoon 19

Repairs to the ship almost complete. Still raining!

Ashmoon 22

Still here!! Gales blowing constantly. All shipping at a standstill. Who knows if it's natural or the work of Falseface.

Ashmoon 27
A week of gales, but they have blown themselves out. Brag considers them natural. "Typical of the Ashmoon," he said. We set sail tomorrow for The Aromatic Isles and El Ilam-Coram. I wonder what awaits us.

Ashmoon 28
Finally, on this last day of the Ashmoon, the Tariqa was towed out this morning by twelve-oared longboats through the narrow havenmouth. We have been cast off half a mile from the shore. Looking back, the long hills around Fiskemouth seem to lie at anchor in a bay of mist.

******

So here we are, late in the moon of the ash, my home island a small blemish on the low, straight horizon. Ploughing through open sea seems to iron out time: have we been travelling an hour? Two hours? I can't tell. I've lost track. But we're away, headed for El Ilam-Coram of The Aromatic Isles, about which I've heard tales since I was a boy; but now these skeleton names are soon to be fleshed out by sights, sounds, landscapes completely new to me. Lucky that Brag will be with me, as he knows these places from many business visits with his friend, Madji. I can barely believe it, after all this waiting. We're off. Only a three moon voyage ahead!

ALDERMOON
(March 18 - April 14)

'From the molten dyes of the water
Bring the burnished nature of fire'
                    Ezra Pound

The alder is the tree of fire. Although it is poor fuel, it yields the best charcoal.

It represents the power of fire to free the earth from water, and withstands the rotting power of damp, so that alder-piles were used as foundations.

Green alder makes excellent whistles & pipes.

It is renowned for its use in dyeing: green from the flower, brown from the twig, and red from its bark; indeed, when it is cut, the white wood appears to bleed, which might be one reason why it was always held sacred.

In Greek mythology, it is one of the trees of resurrection, and this month includes the Vernal Equinox.

Chapter 4 / ALDERMOON

5th Aldermoon *from Kip's journal*

These ships that ply the ocean between the north and south with their various cargoes also serve as passenger ships, and carry a few people, albeit in cramped and very damp conditions. Mixed bags of humanity: merchants on trading trips, civic dignitaries keeping open diplomatic channels, travelling entertainers, fortune-hunters, sometimes women and children voyaging to join the man of the family whose work has taken him far off.

A list of passengers' names is posted, which I was reading earlier. As we often eat in our cabin, there are many of our fellow-travellers that I haven't yet seen. It might be of some interest to share the list in order to illustrate my point about the mix of travellers. Each name is accompanied by a short note connected to the 'reason for journey' that we are obliged to give when booking our passage, even though a phrase as potentially evasive as 'On business' is perfectly acceptable to the port authorities.

COLIN BRIGHTSTONE: Cloth merchant. On business.
DANIEL CAYFORTH: Harbour official. On business.
BRAG DRUFUS: Salt & tobacco merchant. On business.
WILLA FYNCH: Itinerant musician.
CLAUDE GREENHILL: Itinerant musician.
EDMUND & MARCUS OLDBURY (twin brothers): Emigration.
KIP SMITH: Apprentice to Mr Drufus. On business.
TAMSIN TALISMAN: Itinerant musician.
BLANCHE WHITEBROKE: Wife. Travelling to join husband (Walter Whitebroke, recently established by Merchants' Guild as their representative at the port of Miyan in El Ilam-Coram), with children AUDREY (aged 5) GILES (3) and AGNES (1).

I do not envy Mrs Whitebroke her journey with three small children, though they are cheerful enough so far. Brag and Mr Brightstone have talked 'shop' on several occasions, having met casually on deck. I haven't seen the others.

7th Aldermoon

We have been sailing for about a week, and I find that I enjoy sea-travel! My body is invigorated. The salt-clean air, pure as garlic, makes me dizzy as it purges my blood, cleanses my lungs, distills my senses.

I am, however, pleased to be a passenger, rather than one of the crew: Captain Aquablanca drives his men hard, though not mercilessly; he is at heart a kind and fair man, but he will tolerate no slackers on his ship. His reasonableness and even-handedness prevent inevitable mutters ever turning sour, let alone getting anywhere close to mutiny. Members of the crew grumble (out of earshot!), but they respect him, his fairness and his knowledge of ships and the sea.

8th Aldermoon

It must be close to the Equinox, for the light and dark now seem of equal duration. I have been able, with my enforced leisure, to spend many of the hours of dark studying the night sky. I sit on deck gazing at the stars, planets and constellations on still, clear nights, the rhythm of the swell rocking me, the chatter of the prow cutting the water, and, somewhere within the ship, one of my fellow travellers playing on a green alder-whistle haunting tunes that tell of a sad heart.

Captain Aquablanca reads the stars in a different way to Mr Pipkin. He uses them as guides and signposts to steer by. He helped me initially by pointing out some marker stars and prominent constellations. I shall use this page to put down what I know so far, in order to consolidate my knowledge.

THE DANCERS: a randomly spaced group of the most iridescent stars; they flash blue, white, green and yellow so strikingly that they seem to dance

THE HUB STAR: around which the heavens turn

THE MILL WHEEL: six stars that form a circle around the Hub Star and revolve slowly like Miller Thorndale's wheel at home

THE FIREFLY: a lone star that winks orange and red

THE TRACK OF THE WHITE COW: a glaze of incomprehensibly distant stars visible immediately overhead on brilliant, crystal nights; the eye can span galaxies in a split second

THE SENTINEL: the brightest star in our sky, and crowning star of the Watchtower constellation

THE SHEPHERD AND HIS FLOCK: a constellation formed of the bright star, Athel, which is the shepherd, surrounded by a cluster of about a hundred small stars (the sheep) and on the edge a star twice as bright as the sheep stars, but faint compared to Athel, which is Pozle, the shepherd's dog

11th Aldermoon
No stars to study for several days- just heavy rain. Cooped up below deck like fowl in a hen-house, only emerging in desperation to gulp fresh air.
Food repetitious and uninviting (sea-biscuits and gristly stew). Passengers are expected to eat the same fare as the crew. Maybe we'll be invited to the Captain's table one night. He must eat something better! I wonder if Brag might be considered worthy of the distinction.

13th Aldermoon
Constant strong breezes and drenching spray; regular nets of water cast over the vessel by the trawling winds.

15th Aldermoon
Everywhere is dampness: the wooden handrails, the ropes,

and-worst of all- clothes and bedding.

When I think of that grinning fool of a week ago, standing at the prow with his nose in the air like a figurehead, drinking in the experience... How the crew must have been laughing up their sleeves at my childish enthusiasm for the novelty of it all. Certainly now they make no use of their sleeves when they see me mooching about the deck, walking as if I've wet myself in my spray-soaked breeches.

"Mornin', Master Smith. Too late to piss over the rail, were you?!!" General mirth and ribaldry.

I just have to grin and bear it, unless Captain Aquablanca overhears, as he did this morning, when he set his men back on task with a sharp word and a wink at me.

23rd Aldermoon *A letter fragment from Kip to his parents*
My dear Mother and Father,

Although I know that you cannot fathom these scribblings of mine, I also know that someone in the village will kindly oblige and read it to you. The Captain says that we shall pass a homeward ship tomorrow and will make exchanges, so I am writing this now to have it ready.

Mercifully, I am well. I say 'mercifully' because last night we had a fire on board. It seems that one of our fellow passengers left a candle unattended by his bunk, and it tipped over and set fire to his blanket. He was in the Boarders' Room (the crew refer to us passengers as 'boarders') drinking with someone. (The captain has banned him from having a candle or drinking in the Boarders' Room for a whole week. He says everyone on board must keep to Ship's Rules, as it can be a matter of life or death. An example of his stern but reasoned justice.) Anyway, on board a ship (which is just a load of floating wood) fire can easily mean an end for all. Luckily, the Yardwatch* was vigilant, but the cabin was already well alight, and there was understandable panic among the landlubbers, most of whom had been in their cabins asleep, but some of whom were throwing up because of the heavy seas. Lieutenant Palmer herded the passengers into the Boarders' Room, well away from the burning cabin, but we still had to cover our faces to keep the mounting smoke from our eyes and breath.

******

* BELLWATCHES
(pronounced 'belches' by the crew)

0000-0400 **Yardwatch** *('yard' from graveyard, an allusion to midnight starting time)*
0400-0800 **Dawnwatch**
0800-1200 **Grogwatch** *(the crew's grog is served at 11 a.m.)*
1200-1600 **Noonwatch**
1600-1800 **1st Loblolly** *(from a mariners' term for food eaten with a spoon; the 2 x 2hr watches allow for main meal)*
1800-2000 **2nd Loblolly**
2000-2400 **Last Watch**

******

Up to this point, we had been riding up and down the thirty foot swell- an experience, Father, that makes an unmannerly shire-horse seem a trifling thing!- but Captain Aquablanca now ordered the ship to be turned '90 degrees West', so that we should be travelling up a trough between waves, and the swell should come at us 'broadside from port'- you see that I am learning the sea-speech! Certainly the sea was roaring like innumerable cannon!

There had even been a hint of hysteria from some of the crew (there is nowhere to run from a fire on a ship) and this seemingly suicidal manoeuvre was too much for one or two of the mariners. The steersman shouted against the wind half questioningly, half defiantly, "But, Captain, the ship will be swamped if we turn ninety! We'll be sunk!"

The captain, though, was well aware of the grave threat, but realized that even this slim chance was greater than what a fire offered. So when the steersman repeated his fearful opinion of the consequences, Captain Aquablanca replied, "Exactly, Johnson." (He addresses all his crew by name. Officers he prefaces with 'Mister' in order to show a distinction.) "Carry out the order!" he yelled through the wind and wave. Then he turned trying to catch sight of someone through a deluge of sea and rain. He sensed that the crew needed to be kept on a tight rein at this critical juncture.

"Coxen!?" he bawled enquiringly, for he had lost view of this officer in the acrid, black smoke that was now issuing from below. "Mr Stowe! Keep the men to their stations at all costs!"

"Aye, aye, Captain!" came from somewhere.

By now, the oakum was smouldering, and blisters were erupting here and there on the tarred planking.

We steered into a trough, and very soon the inevitable occurred: the vessel was stunned as an almighty wave crashed against its port side. Everyone in the Boarders' Room was sent hurtling against walls and furniture. Women screamed, children sobbed and squealed, Mr Cayforth roared from a dark corner on the floor. (We subsequently discovered that he had a broken leg.) I seemed just to stand still whilst the whole room, its contents and occupants, were sent spinning around me like a giant wheel-of-fortune from the travelling fair, though in truth I was flying, too! When the wheel came to settle, I found myself slumped against a door in a daze and my head filled with pure pain. Inexplicably, Maddy was bent over me.

******

I remember asking a silly question, "Where am I?" and Maddy, who was tending a cut on my forehead, replying soothingly, "Don't worry. It's alright. The fire and the water are one." It didn't occur to me in my pain and confusion to ask what on earth she was doing on board the Tariqa, or how she had got there. Somewhere in the back of my mind, I was aware of an irony that I, her self-appointed and supposed guardian, was being looked after by her.

It is one of the vicissitudes of sea-travel, dear land-lubbing parents, that if a wave breaks over the ship, as happens often in rough seas, the water rushes through the lower decks, giving the passengers and their belongings a regular dousing. It was this occurrence in an exaggerated form that the Captain sought and achieved by his apparently reckless manouevre. A huge heave of seawater pulsed through the Tariqa's cavities and passages, and spewed out steaming brine from every gap and orifice in a fevered, dragon-like hiss, but the fire in her belly was quenched, and she remained upright. An echoing throb of pain passed through my skull, and I passed out to the sound of crewmen from above shouting three cheers for their captain.

A few minutes later I recovered consciousness, the dream of Maddy's nursing me still very vivid to me.

So, dear parents, we have survived that little adventure, with ship not too badly damaged. A cracked yardarm from the wave, and some fire and smoke damage, but not as serious as the smoke had made it seem. Also, just one of the crew washed overboard, but even he was fortuitously recovered, as the next wave washed him back on board! There are cuts and bruises to almost everyone in some degree, as well as several broken limbs. Mr Cayforth moans and complains about his broken leg to anyone who'll listen. "Call himself a captain?! I could've been killed."

The ship's doctor had little sympathy. "Without him, you undoubtedly would have been. You'd have preferred roasting or drowning, I suppose?"

Anyway, today we had a glorious day of unseasonably hot sun, a hint of advancing Spring, and so the ship has been

bedecked in passengers' clothes: hung, tied or draped everywhere to dry! It looks quite festive, which represents the spirit on board, because everyone is quite heady with relief, as you can imagine. The lacy bunting which comprises some of Mrs Whitebroke's more personal garments has caused a good deal of interest and comment among the crew, though they are very careful to ensure that the Captain isn't anywhere in the vicinity at the time.
Now to amaze you once again, dear parents! My dream of Maddy was no dream!! She is here, on board ship. It is a great d..........

At this point, the letter paper has deteriorated to such an extent that no further writing is distinguishable.

WILLOWMOON
(April 15 - May 12)

'And in the warm hedge grew lush eglantine,
  Green cowbind and the moonlight-coloured may'
    Percy Bysshe Shelley

'Tell me not here, it needs not saying,
What tune the enchantress plays'
    A.E. Housman

'Hal-an-tow, jolly rumble-o!
We were up long before the day o,
To welcome in the Summer,
To welcome in the May-o!
For Summer is a-coming in
And Winter's gone away-o!'
    Traditional May Day song

The willow is the tree of enchantment, and as such was worshipped by witches; indeed, the words witch, wicked, willow and wicker are all from the same etymological root.

In the middle of this month, the second of the year's four fire-festivals falls, most popularly known as May Day or Beltane, when the Summer was welcomed in.

The moon was said, in ancient times, to own the willow, so this month is known as 'the moon of moons'.

Chapter 5/ WILLOWMOON

1st Willowmoon *A second letter fragment*

My dear Mother and Father,
It is nearly a week since the last letter 'exchange', but tomorrow one is scheduled with a ship from the Aromatic Isles.

I am now pretty used to the conditions of constant movement, though it is hard to acclimatize myself to the dampness of my clothes and living quarters. Also, the food is a little monotonous, and not within a country mile of your stews, Mother! Imagine a constant diet of lumpy porridge (breakfast), an indeterminate soup mixed with broken ship's biscuit which the crew members call 'Crackerjack' (lunch), and a salt-meat hotpot mixed with a little onion, potato, the ubiquitous sea-biscuit, and occasional spices (supper) which is known to the sailors as 'Lob'. On lucky days, this daily menu is varied by a supper of 'sea-pie', made up of layers of salt-meat, vegetables and pastry crusts. Also available is a pudding known to the crew as 'Dandyfunk', which is merely broken ship's biscuits mixed with some molasses. I tried it once; but as it threatened either to break my teeth on the stone-hard biscuit, or to pull them with the viscosity of the black treacle, I have since declined.

The discomforts and repinings are, perhaps, heightened by a particular nostalgia in this landsman's heart of mine as I think of the countryside during this lovely moon of the year. Were it not for the kindly, if blunt, support afforded me by Mr Drufus (Brag, as he insists I now call him), I should be a sorry creature, I know it. Also, the renewed responsibility I feel for young Maddy, though she does seem to be thriving under the constant uncertainties of our travelling life. Although she still often speaks in cryptic phrases, she seems healthy and happy and, at times, grown-up! Indeed, the longer I know her, the more difficult I find it to assess her age.

I have discovered how she came to be aboard. Mr Pipkin took her to a friend of his, Prunella, who is a dealer in herbal remedies, and also something of an apothecary-physician: she jokingly refers to herself as a healer-dealer! She was in Aphambold, and brought Maddy to Fiskemouth to meet up with us, but not openly. She was listed among the passengers as Tamsin Talisman, a musician. I discover that she can, indeed, play the......

(The rest of this bundle of letters is indecipherable or ruined, the seal on the container's lid having perished, allowing the ingress of damp and ants. However, from notes and references in others of Kip's papers, I have been able to reconstruct the rest of the Tariqa's voyage. All the descriptive phrases and pieces of dialogue are ones used by Kip in his papers.)

******

One evening, about seven days into the Willowmoon, Kip was on deck enjoying the mildness of the air as they sailed ever further southwards. Drufus and Maddy were with him.

"What a fine evening, Mr Dru-, er, Brag!" exclaimed Kip, slowly inhaling and exhaling delicious lungfuls of the salt-clean air. "It makes you feel privileged to have life, to be sentient, to... to be alive and know it, do you not agree?"

"Aye," assented Brag, laconic as ever.

"Just the sound of the waves on the prow," ploughed on his young companion, "the sough and rustle of the wake, the creak of the timbers, the...the..."

"The voice of Kip...," added Brag, with a straight face but a twinkling eye.

The young man looked startled; Maddy giggled.

Looking abashed, Kip stammered an apology. "Sorry, Brag. But it's so... so... oh, I can't find the words."

"I'm sure you'll give it a darned good try!" replied Brag

drily.

Maddy laughed again. "Don't tease him, Brag. He's just a boy."

The packer gave her a significant but barely discernible glance, and looked thoughtfully out to sea.

"Boy!" cried Kip. "Well, you are no more than a girl yourself! What age are you? Seventeen? 'Boy' indeed. Sometimes, Maddy, you- What is it, Brag?"

Kip interrupted himself because the merchant had suddenly leaned forward, peering intently out over the starboard rail to the sea beyond. He indicated a point halfway to the horizon, but all the young blacksmith could see was a glittering of small waves criss-crossed by a breeze which etched a million facets into them.

"Ah! It comes," Maddy exclaimed softly, with a hint of trepidation in her voice.

"Tantrum Bobus."

Brag looked grim.

Kip wasn't sure whether to look out to sea, or at this strangely composed and mature-sounding Maddy, but his eye was then caught by movement above the waves. Dolphins were breaking through the liquid cut-crystal of the rippling sea.

"Now, that is a beautiful sight!" he asserted.

"Beautiful, but deceptive," whispered Maddy, not taking her eyes off the dolphins.

Kip was still frowning at the perplexity of her words and manner when a whale surfaced, blowing a silver spume of broken moonlight into the air. Such was his confusion of simultaneous emotions, linked with the ethereal beauty of the scene, that he was unsure whether or not he was dreaming.

"What do you mean, 'deceptive'?"

"Shapeshifters," murmured Brag.

"It feels like a dream," said Kip.

"It'll be more like a nightmare soon," replied the packer.

The enchantment of the scene suddenly acquired an edge

of sorcery. Kip forced himself to stare unbroken at the curved dolphins as they leapt and dived, stitching together the sea and sky by their motion; and each time they performed their easy parabola, the arrangement of light and shadow seemed different: the shapes shifted! This was no parallax; no dream, no trick of the moonlight. Kip sensed evil in the air, in the vicinity, as when you wake from a nightmare and can still smell the malice close by, before it gradually drifts and fades like an invisible mist.

"I'm going to the captain at the wheel," announced Brag. "Be on your guaaar___!

His final word was transformed into a cry of surprise and alarm as they were all thrown across deck by a huge jolt. The helmsman was sent spinning through the air to crash against the planking, which pushed out his breath and knocked him senseless. The wheel was left to its own devices, revolving wildly and erratically. Captain Aquablanca jumped forward and grasped it just as Brag struggled up.

"What's going on, Brag? I saw nothing!"

"From starboard and below, Peter. A whale!"

A cloud of gulls appeared, seemingly from nowhere, and began to attack them both, pecking at their heads and eyes, while the men hit out, ducked, and danced about, avoiding the gulls' lunges and protecting themselves as best they could.

******

Kip recovered his composure and orientation to find himself alone, and immediately called for Maddy. No reply. He ran to the rail and looked over the side, wondering if she had been thrown overboard by the violent collision. He saw strange-shaped shadows on the side of the ship, like men but not like men. What his brain interpreted from his eyesight seemed impossible.

"Apes?" he murmured to himself, incredulously.

By now, all hands were on deck; there was a melee of noise and movement as crew-members strove to assist Brag and their captain to fend off the gulls. Then there were baboons everywhere, jumping onto men's shoulders and backs, biting, kicking, screaming. Many of the crew carried makeshift weapons- fish-spears, knives of all descriptions, hooks, whips- which they jabbed and swung and flailed, often aimlessly but sometimes injuring or even killing a creature, though an injury only enraged the baboons and made them twice the adversary they'd previously been. One or two sailors, whose hearts failed them, began to scamper up the rigging, but the baboons were even more agile than they were, and soon the errant mariners were sent, sprawling and screaming, to land on the deck with sickening, crunching thuds.

For some reason which he could not fathom, none of the creatures had come near him. He was about to run to someone's assistance when, to his dismay, a huge, ferocious, snarling male charged at him. He froze in terror, not knowing what he could do, when suddenly, round the cabin-house with a heart-stopping roar, appeared two tigers! There was a storm of shrieking from the baboons, and their simian screams turned into the sniggering squawks of gulls as they flew up from the deck in a sudden panic of wings, but not before a dozen or so baboons lay dead on the deck. The tigers sprang up after them, morphing into a pair of sea-eagles which fell upon the gulls, knocking them to the deck of the Tariqa. Caws and whinnies of terror accompanied the blizzard of beak and claw and feathers, which resembled a child's snow-toy in its glass miniature dome when it is shaken. The cloud of surviving seagulls made off, folded their wings and, diving into the waves, disappeared. Kip did not see whether the eagles followed them.

Now, everywhere, there were the moans and screams of injured mariners. It resembled a battlefield: the deck was littered with bodies and puddles of blood. Kip was bleeding from a head-wound that poured a red veil over his eyes, but he just brushing it clear and ran to help. The first sailor he approached was on his knees with his arms folded across his front, bent forward and rocking back and forth in a daze. Kip put his hand on the man's shoulder and pulled him gently upright, still on his knees. With a shock of revulsion, he saw that the thumb of the sailor's left hand was missing, the side of his hand just an open wound. He felt pity and helplessness mix with his shock, murmured a comforting word, and stood up to see the ship's surgeon, Mr John Appleyard, running about to assess the injuries. He called the doctor over and indicated the sailor.

"That's a nasty wound you have yourself in your head," he observed.

Kip's reaction was to tear off his shirt-sleeve and wrap it round his head. "It looks worse than it is. Can I help?"

The physician replied with the immemorial words of all medics in emergencies.

"Boil water- as much as you can!"

******

After several hours, some semblance of order was restored. Captain Aquablanca had some severe gashes to his face and head, but insisted on Mr Appleyard first tending 'the people', as he referred to the crew. However, the ship was only capable of limping along, as the crew was so depleted: of the thirty general seamen, nine were dead, another three missing, and five confined to their bunks or the sick bay with injuries; of the twenty officers and skilled men (carpenter, cooper, cook, boatswain, sailmakers, etc), a quarter were indisposed or missing. Most of the rest bore relatively minor wounds which variously hampered, but did not preclude their being able to execute their duties. The passengers were called upon to assist where possible, in order to leave the remaining crew as free as they could be to carry out the jobs which were beyond the knowledge, skill or strength of the 'boarders'.

Prunella, the spice and herb dealer, proved herself very useful to the surgeon, as she was so well versed in the applications of the herbs in which she traded, and of which she had a large supply in a chest! Without her support and expertise, the mariners would have been an even sorrier lot than they were. Kip had been kept busy boiling pans of water, or being part of the chain that passed the pails to wherever they were needed.

Now, he wandered, exhausted, into the Boarders' Room, looking for his companions. Neither Brag nor Maddy were present, so he left and went on deck, where he saw Mr Appleyard, Prunella and Captain Aquablanca engaged in quiet but earnest conversation. The captain caught sight of him and hailed him. Kip noticed that the captain's right arm was in a sling, and that his right cheek was a lattice of livid scratches.

Aquablanca smiled ruefully. "I'm pleased to see that you are not too badly injured, Kip," he said, not realizing the extent of the head-wound beneath Kip's makeshift bandage and his cap. The cap was stained with blood, but the darkness hid it from notice.

"I'm looking for my friends. Have you seen them?" enquired Kip. "I've looked in the cabins and the Boarders' Room."

The captain gave a self-conscious half-glance at his two interlocutors and approached the young blacksmith.

"I'm sorry, Kip. Mr Drufus is missing. I've already instigated a search for all missing people and boarders. The last time I saw Brag he was at the rail, attempting to shake one of those devilish creatures from his shoulders and into the brine."

Kip snorted out a single mocking noise which carried incredulity, shock, self-calming: "Ha! That doesn't signify. He'll be somewhere. I'll go and find him. What about Maddy?"

"She's fine," Prunella assured him. "She's sleeping in the sick-bay."
"The sick-bay?! Why? What's wrong?"
"She only has superficial wounds, but she was extremely tired."
Kip immediately went with Prunella to reassure himself as to Maddy's condition, which her peaceful mien effectively did. He was not so successful in his search for Brag. Though he scoured the whole ship- and Captain Aquablanca sensitively allowed him access to places not normally open to passengers- there was no sign of his companion.
An hour later, he found Prunella and the ship's surgeon in the sick-bay. There was a desperate despondency in his eyes.
"I cannot find him," was all he said, and then the shock of growing realization, added to his hours of strenuous physical effort and emotional strain, as well as his concealed head-wound, became too much. He simply passed out, crumpling into a senseless heap at their feet.

HAWTHORNMOON
(May 13 - June 9)

'... that which purifies us is trial'
    John Milton

*'I am the shadowed, the grief-stricken, the inconsolable,
The prince of Aquitaine at the ruined tower.
My lone star is dead, and my starry lute
Bears the black sun of melancholy.'*
    Gerard de Nerval

'Clean out your ears! Don't listen for what's already known.'
    Rumi

The hawthorn is the tree of self-denial, and was considered to be unlucky.

In classical times, this was the month of preparation for Midsummer, so it was characterized by chastity, asceticism, propitiation, washing & cleansing, all aimed at the purification of sacred places and of oneself. As one symbol of this, people would wear only old clothes during this month.

In mediaeval times, the tree had a different significance, connected to rites of the goddess, Flora, and so we see the connection with gathering branches of may, May Queens, maypole dancing, etc.

Chapter 6/ HAWTHORNMOON

from Kip's journal   (He gave no dates for the first few entries)
I will not let them get them. They live in the knot-holes of my cabin walls. I've seen them growing out of the grain of the wood. They fly over and prick me. I will hide in the folds of sleep.

******

A woman with a vaguely familiar face came into my cabin and bathed my head with cool water and gave me a drink, but I quickly realized her game, for the water began to burn, and I knew that it was acid. The last laugh was on her, however, for it was her face, not my mouth, that began to corrupt, right before my eyes!

******

6th Hawthornmoon *Surgeon's Log*
Kip Smith still in a high fever, but I know that the herb-woman is knowledgeable. Her infusions of sorrel are helpful. I am happy to leave the young man in her care whilst I deal with the wounds and injuries of the crew.

******

I have come to a room at the smithy, looking for my father. It's beyond the furnace and, somehow, I've never noticed it before. I open the door and, by the glow of the furnace, I see Brag. He is sitting, propped up in the corner like a sack of wheat. I cannot tell whether he is asleep or *(It seems Kip could not bear to write more)*

******

It is a dim dawn. I have just been disturbed from my sleep by a man who came into the room speaking so loudly that it hurt my ears. I called to him to stop, but he laughed, and the reverberations made my skull explode into pieces. Fortunately, I managed to find all the shards and fragments and fit them together again.

******

10th Hawthornmoon *Surgeon's Log*
The boarder, Kip Smith, is wandering in a fever as deep and labyrinthine as any I have ever come across. We manage to reduce the fever with borage, and the infusions of sorrel cause a temporary respite, but then he strays back into his maze. I fear that the loss of his companion has unhinged his mental capacities, at least for the time being.

******

I was sailing on a jollyboat this morning, no ship in sight. I was lying on my back in the bottom of the boat, eyes closed, enjoying the sensation of the dip and toss of the ocean. I then had an angry altercation with some flyingfish, they considering that I was trespassing, but I told them that I had to because I was looking for someone. Anyway, the waves became stiller and stiller until the sea was so calm that I was unaware of any movement at all, no matter how much I concentrated on it. The shadow of some passing bird across the sun caused me to open my eyes, and I find that my boat has turned into a bed, the sun is a lamp, the shadow is no albatross but a young woman who is mopping my brow with a cool cloth. I know that face... where have I seen her before?

12th Hawthornmoon
It has all come back to me, but I wish it hadn't. How can I continue, unprotected, unadvised? How do I decide what to do? How do I know who to trust? How do I assess where to go? In whom can I confide?

To me, this noble, exciting and mysterious quest on which I was engaged now seems a forlorn escapade. Only the fact that I am on board ship keeps me from turning back, as I have no power to turn it round.

13th Hawthornmoon
O, what ill luck this is. What a hopeless sigh it is that issues from my heart. Mr Drufus, dear Brag, was more like a father to me than my father. I looked up to him, I respected him, trusted him from the start; and suddenly something becomes obvious to me that I have not previously put into words, even inside my head: I loved him. I thought that I could achieve practically anything if he was there to guide me, and I was so anticipating this foreign adventure, side by side. And now, he's dead. Only desolation extends before me.

14th Hawthornmoon
I feel so weak. Merely to sit up in my bed exhausts me, so that I immediately lie down again, ready to sleep.
I was attended by Prunella today. She says that I was very silly to hide my wound, as it did not receive the early treatment it warranted. However, she has helped me to feel much stronger, reducing my fever with borage, and tending my cuts and wounds with yarrow, lady's mantle and marigold.

16th Hawthornmoon
Maddy visited. She amused me with the story of how she and Prunella came on board the Tariqa as travelling musicians: they were Willa Fynch and Tamsin Talisman on the travellers' list! What a jape! Not that it helped. Falseface has eyes and ears everywhere, and Brag is gone.

18th Hawthornmoon
Maddy is coming nearly as regularly as Prunella to tend my wounds. Mr Appleyard is run off his feet, and has

gratefully accepted Prunella's offer of assistance with the injured sailors, so Maddy is now devoted to my care under instruction from Prunella.

A strange thing: she seems different. Not so childish. Her words make more sense; I really believe she is getting better. Something on this journey is making her more whole.

I say she seems less 'childish', and certainly she keeps smiling at me with an indulgent, grown-up look, as well as seeming to have the advantage on me. For example, this exchange, which I record verbatim:

Me: I cannot go on.

Maddy: You have no choice.

Me: What do you mean?

Maddy: Captain Aquablanca will not turn round.

Me: But I have no heart for the journey. We will return by the first passage, I'll make up with my father, we'll find you somewhere in the village where you'll be kindly treated. Everything will fall back into place as it was before.

Maddy: Nothing is ever the same as before. You may travel in any direction you choose, settle where you will, but you cannot escape your destiny. (The room is suddenly alive with silent significance.)

Me: (after a pause to consider her words) It's strange. You seem different.

Maddy: Have I changed?

Me: Well yes, becau-

Maddy: (cutting through my words) Or have you?

Me: There! You see! You are saying things that are beyond your years.

Maddy: Maybe you are hearing things beyond yours.

This didn't seem to be the Maddy I had become familiar with. She spoke nonsense before! Everyone said so at home. I scrutinised her closely, but she gave nothing away, and her eyes just laughed kindly at me. I fell asleep to the silent sound of her laughter, and a voice within me saying how lovely this sound was. Like a healing.

20th Hawthornmoon

When I think of Brag, a huge cavern, dark and bottomless, opens up before me. But when I recall Maddy and her laughter, or Prunella, or indeed Bill Pipkin and Mr Sloethwaite, then the way ahead isn't a black pit, but seems to be green, rising ground. I am up and down by turns. But at least, unlike a week or two ago, I now remember that I do have friends in the world, albeit young and inexperienced or distant and out-of-reach. Prunella, of course, is neither young (50ish) nor distant. Perhaps I could share some thoughts with her. After all, if she is a trusted friend of Bill Pipkin...

21st Hawthornmoon

Really, I don't know where I am with these women! Maddy and Prunella, I mean. Just because I am a weak and recuperating invalid, they take advantage of me and rule my every move. I am too feeble to resist. Maddy has quite come into her own. It will be the making of her, this travel and this nursing. Experience is making a woman of her.

And as for Prunella, she quite bosses me about; and so dismissive, as if she were speaking to a child! For instance:

Me: Maddy is growing up quickly during this voyage.

P: Is she really? Do sit still, Kip! (This as she dabs some violent, stinging lotion to my poor head.)

Me: Yes. She tends me like a mature nurse.

P: Well now!

Me: I believe her quite altered from the young girl who left my home village with me.

P: And you're not, I suppose. Oh, do be still! (More stinging lotion.)

Me: Ow!! What is that supposed to mean?

P: What is what supposed to mean?

Me: (giving up this line of questioning) I was telling her that I considered her changed; saying things beyond her years.
P: (with heavily ironic tones) More than you know, Master Kip, o knowledgeable and seasoned traveller!
Me: Now then, Prunell- (At this point, she rudely sticks an evil-tasting liquid into my mouth so that she can escape my countering).
You see what I have to put up with?

22nd Hawthornmoon

Today I got up and walked for the first time since the second week of the Willowmoon. Prunella has been a strict nurse. I wobbled to her cabin. It was a calm day and the ship was steady. Her cabin is something between an apothecary's shop and an alchemist's den! "And this," she said, indicating her bottles of herbs, powders, potions and tinctures, "is only my travelling set!"
She told me that the worst aspect of my wounds is not the physical damage, but the poison of malice in them. It is lucky she was aboard, for I don't think that Mr Appleyard, for all his medical knowledge, can fathom how Prunella's treatments seem more effective than his own in combatting these wounds. I say it was lucky she was aboard, but perhaps, on reflection, 'luck' doesn't come into it. When I asked Brag, at one of my low points, why Falseface didn't just turn himself into some shape that couldn't be dealt with and take The Moons from me, he said that there representatives of 'The Good' who were ready to assist me, and their gathered positive force prevented the shapeshifter from doing all he would like to do. It was a battle of forces. Well, Prunella isn't on the Tariqa by mistake or by chance, I'd say. Anyway, she says that the important thing is to 'purify the wounds', which she is doing with the contents of her bottles, and who knows what else?

24th Hawthornmoon

I am sitting up all the time now, and have even tried a couple of short strolls, which were exhausting. Prunella and Mr Appleyard say I'm recovering well, but my brain seems to me to be in a muddle. Maddy continues to confuse me. Prunella shakes her head and always seems to be laughing at me. Even Captain Aquablanca smiled and whispered to her something about 'obtuse' after I said something about Maddy.

More importantly, he said that he estimates from his chart-readings that we shall 'put into' the port city of Miyan in the next week. This is the chief port of the island of El Ilam-Coram, which is the largest of The Aromatic Isles. Indeed, it is a vast island, much bigger than home; practically a continent!

Maddy was tending my head-wound (which is much improved) and was chattering in happy anticipation of the sights and sounds of the island, and I was musing on how, when I have regained my strength, I shall be free to move about this new land, when I sighed, more to myself than anything, "But how shall I know where to go? Now that Brag has gone I feel hopelessly lost and inadequate."

"The Inward-Looking Houses," replied Maddy solemnly, without faltering for a moment from her ministrations to my head. Then, catching my look of surprise and enquiry, she just laughed merrily and put a final dab of the stinging potion on the wound.

She comes out with the strangest things, but somehow they seem now to strike a chord in me, whereas they used to just seem...peculiar! All the same, chord or no chord, I can make no sense of it... Oh well!

OAKMOON
(June 10 - July 7)

'Death opens unknown doors.'
John Masefield

'As when, upon a tranced summer-night,
Those green-rob'd senators of mighty woods,
Tall oaks, branch-charmed by the earnest stars,
Dream, and so dream all night without a stir.'
John Keats

The tree of endurance and triumph, the monarch of trees.

'Oak' means 'door' in many languages, and in this month was the threshold of the year, for the oak-king in the ancient world ruled the waxing year, which ended after the midsummer month.

June 24/Oakmoon 15 is Midsummer Day, the day of the oak-king's sacrifice, when he became the Corona Borealis or Northern Crown constellation (cf. Osiris/Orion).

The midsummer fires were always fuelled with oak.

Chapter 7/ OAKMOON

1st Oakmoon *Mid afternoon* *from Kip's notes*

No venerable romance of the chivalrous olden times, no salt-tanged yarn of oriental splendour related by a returned mariner, could have prepared me for the beauty and strangeness that I beheld on our approach to the port of Miyan. I had already been astonished, on reaching Fiskemouth, at the mere hint of faraway places which permeates the homeliness and harbourliness of the town, but those accents, aromas and attires were as nothing compared with this shimmering vision of a city.

Instead of lying on land and meeting the sea on a shoreline like any normal city, this fabulous place grows from the ocean's margin like a forest of exotic water-plants, and it isn't clear where the ocean ceases and where there is a beginning of the waterways, channels, basins, and other aquatic features of the city. Miyan mingles with its ocean.

I have been to fairs and feasts at home, but there seems in this city to be a natural atmosphere of festivity. Flags and banners fly from poles which rise from the water or the rooftops, making the city a place of air and light as well as water. To my parochial gaze, all the buildings appear to be pavilions or palaces.

As we sailed into the harbour earlier this morning, some of these buildings lined either side of the main channel, many growing from the water on slender legs, and displaying row upon row of pointed arches. At these structures, strange-shaped boats with long, pointed sterns and prows were tied, and men were busy unloading baskets of fish into the open-arched edifices, which seemed to double as covered jetties and market-houses, for people were already haggling over the catches. I saw fish of all shapes, lengths, colours and sizes: some I recognised, many were unknown species to me. I saw the largest prawns I have ever seen, a good nine inches long, and extraordinary crabs: rose-pink, purple as plums, green like seaweedy rocks at low tide, yellow as mustard.

As we slipped deeper into the harbour, I could see no actual land, just buildings magically rising from the waters on stone pillars or plinths; and then channels running away to form side 'streets' between receding edifices. Some buildings straddled the channels so that the seawater lapped right through their bowels. Most of the structures were whitewashed, so that, however high the facades rose around you, the atmosphere was always light and airy, though it was dark and green-slimed in the forests of stilts beneath the buildings. There are narrow paths alongside all the channels, and these walkways are linked by little footbridges, so that it is possible, the captain told me, to walk about the whole city. It is, it seems to me, the loveliest man-made thing I have ever seen.

Immediately, my impression is that Miyan's essence is water and light, although Captain Aquablanca advised me that this was only its outward face, and but a partial glance at that. Inwardly, something else made its heart beat. I caught just a hint of what he might be alluding to when we passed a particularly delicate and graceful building, all white stucco walls with pillars and arches and pointed windows. It was set back from the main channel, thus forming a piazza with the building enclosing three sides. It was called The Hall of Thankfulness, and between its pillars I discerned people sitting cross-legged, eyes closed, silent and still- not just bodies free of fidgeting, but a tangible air of tranquillity surrounding them, like an invisible cloud or halo.

A 'Kip Smith' that I never knew existed has arisen within me and fills me with eager excitement and anticipation at the unfamiliar delights and discoveries that must await me. Then I recall the fact that Brag is gone, and I am overcome with regret and guilt.

OAKMOON

1st Oakmoon *Evening A lodging house near the quay*
I have just had a very serious, very salutary talk with my two friends. We have taken lodgings a few minutes walk from the quay where our ship berthed, but Prunella says that, though our ways converged on the Tariqa, now they must separate again. She explained- and I have to admit that it made perfectly good sense to me- that we must not make ourselves too obvious by sticking together. The bitter experiences of the voyage have doubled her resolve to be cautious and prudent. So she and Maddy are to slip away almost immediately (in local dress which they had with them by admirable foresight, and with faces covered), judging that any observers will be least wary of us just after we've booked into our lodging-house.

The strangest thing is that... I don't want Maddy to go. Now can someone explain this to me? Bill Pipkin? Captain Aquablanca? Prunella? Mr Sloethwaite? It seems that I left home full of bravado, the great adventurer, with a child under my protection, a ward. And now... now, in a foreign city, I feel like a lost orphan, a little boy far from home; and Maddy seems to me something like a protectress. Something very strange has gone on.

We have made no plans for meeting up, judging that the less we know about our own plans, the less Falseface the Shifter might know. This does somewhat frighten me, but Prunella- and Maddy!- are insistent that we should have trust. "We shall meet again," said Maddy with an uncanny certainty that made me believe she was right.

2nd Oakmoon
Today I slept very late. Prunella and Maddy left during the bustling late evening, about half an hour apart, looking for all the world like local women. They had even thought to bring some men's robes for me. It helps with my disguise that on this island, some of the men, the ones who Prunella says hail from the desert, go with their faces below the eyes covered, just like the women. Also, I shall

be rubbing on my hands, arms and face (just in case!) some of the plant dye that Prunella had brought with her, anticipating far better than I what might be needed once we were here. Despite the fact that Falseface the Shifter seems to have extraordinary knowledge of our plans and intentions, we still consider that it does not do to make life any simpler for him and his servants than necessary. Prunella quoted a rather piquant local saying which translates as: 'Trust in God, but tie up your camel!' I shall also be fine with the local tongue, as it is one of the languages that Mr Sloethwaite so ably taught me; and the thought occurs to me now that I have been, and continue to be, given help in this task that has come to me. Mr Sloethwaite, Brag, Mr Pipkin, Prunella, the Old Man-Woman Mummer, even Maddy, seem to have appeared when necessary and provided me with what I needed at the time, even though unaware of it at the time! Anyway, I shall try to continue tying up my camel: a careless minion of Falseface's could miss one of our moves which might, at some point, provide vital time for who knows what?!

So I slept late, and then hung about the lodging-house, resting and recuperating from the voyage and its vicissitudes, and eating olives, dates and bread which I purchased from a street-seller who came round the courtyard.

3rd Oakmoon

What a city this is! Everywhere it glitters with music and water: these comprise the heartbeat of the city. Apart from the channels which form the byways, there are fountains in the squares and courtyards, and miniature conduits rilling through the public buildings, and forming little waterfalls beside any steps, so that, wherever you go, there is the song of water. The citizens of Miyan are musical people, and often the voice of the water is but a background chorus to the music and singing in which they constantly indulge.

Today, as I walked the hot streets imbibing the character and spirit of the city, I heard singers on street corners, in squares, outside the numerous teashops or within closed buildings. Also, the music of instruments such as flute, and a stringed something like a fiddle or rebec, and a sort of portable harmonium.

I listened, entranced, to a woman singing near a teashop: there was the passion of lament and longing in her voice, and the people who were seated cross-legged at the low tables outside the teashop listened in enthralled silence. I was captivated by the haunting melodies, by her voice and her appearance: she wore loose robes and swathes, and in such colours! Emerald, aquamarine, kingfisher blue, saffron, vermilion.

I moved further along to the central square of the city, called The Maidan, where a turbaned man sat beneath a tree, playing a stringed instrument like a lute: it had a slightly pear-shaped body, like an elongated half-melon, and an extremely long, slender neck. The man was, like all the locals, robed, but unlike the mass of city men I had seen, he showed himself to be one of the desert people, as his lower face was wrapped in cloth so that only his eyes and brow were visible. His tune was proceeding slowly and meditatively when I arrived, but it gradually built to a frenzied crescendo, with occasional whoops and screams from his appreciative audience. Another man, close by, who was similarly veiled, was moved to accompany the crescendo on his hand-drums. What impressed me most of all, though, were the eyes of the two musicians: as the music gained more and more in tempo, their eyes seemed to remain calm and still, as if reflecting a serenity and containment that they felt inwardly, and which was accentuated by the fact that their eyes were all I could see of their faces. I sat on the sandy ground in the dappled shade of one of the many trees in The Maidan which made it such a delightful place to be: sunlit and dapple-shaded, full of bustle and music and the aromas of street-vendors cooking, yet restful with water-song as it leapt in glistening arcs and fell tinkling into the stone basins of the numerous small fountains...

It was with a sudden shock that I realized that I must have dozed off, and that the music was over, the musicians gone. My eyelids snapped open and presented me with a second shock. A camel was snouting into my shoulder-bag, where I always kept my precious bundle of rags secreted.

"Hey!" I shouted, thankfully alert enough to use the local tongue. "There's no food in there. Be off!" The camel spat at me. Some bystanders smiled, and one of them made his companions laugh with some observation in a language or dialect that I didn't understand.

The insolent creature lumbered off across the square, its bright, red saddle-cloth flashing like a warning through the quivering air beyond the shade of my tree. It seemed not to belong to anyone, and was about to trot down a narrow alley off the dazzling square, when it stopped in it tracks and looked back directly towards me with a familiar malevolence that made my stomach lurch. Then the creature was gone in a moment, as I reeled in the memory of that look from a seagull, and of Brag's recollection of a fell-wolf.

So. Falseface was here, and had already seen through my disguise. The shock reminded me that I wasn't on a jaunt, but that I had an urgent task: I was here to seek The Four Inward-Looking Houses.

I needed time to compose myself and to consider my situation in an undisturbed atmosphere, so I walked to one of the teashops just off The Maidan and entered its shadowy interior. Even when my eyes had adjusted somewhat, the place was still dim. Low tables of decoratively carved wood were lodged in their own private spaces, divided from one another by wooden partitions, also carved in elaborate designs, but the carving was into solid wood screens, not open fretwork, so that privacy was not compromised. Just one of the tables remained vacant, and at this I sat cross-legged on one of the four low chairs, in imitation of the resident drinkers. Although Mr Sloethwaite's tuition had equipped me to converse fluently, the written language was more opaque to me, but I suddenly recognised the words 'lime' and 'lokum' in one of the items and asked for that, receiving a pot if lime tea and some cubes of rose lokum as a result. Although the teashop was almost full, everyone was speaking in low voices, with just occasional bursts of laughter, so it was ideal for my present purpose.

However, I had been sipping my refreshing infusion and nibbling the fragrant jelly for only a couple of minutes when I saw the singer and musicians from earlier enter together. One of the men was speaking in a private, though sonorous, voice as they entered, and the woman in bright robes laughed merrily in response, though her interlocutors remained silent: only their eyes laughed. Many of the tea-drinkers stopped their muted conversations: the musicians arrival had caused an intrusion, firstly because the singer's laughter had hit a different note to that which had hitherto prevailed in the place, and secondly because she now constituted the only female presence. Perhaps, also, itinerant musicians were looked down on and would not normally have entered this teashop, but these three people did not seem to recognise conventions: she with her gay and charming abandon, her companions with a quiet aura of self-possession.

Noting that all the tables were fully occupied, the trio was about to depart when I found myself, to my own surprise, standing and indicating with a slight bow that they were welcome to share my table. The two men, one young and the other old, with wrinkled crowsfeet radiating from the corners of his eyes, bowed slightly in response and, coming across, apparently thanked me in a foreign tongue that I did not recognise. Absent-mindedly I replied in my own tongue, "You're welcome." Tucking their robes behind their knees, they sat, and the woman gave me a confident, open, friendly look. The teashop conversations resumed.

"So, you are from The Northern Isles, am I right?" she asked in the Miyan tongue as she sat opposite me. "That is so," I replied, reverting to Miyan speech. "So much for my disguise!" She laughed again, and I noticed for the first time little silver badges, wrought like shells, studding her braided hair.

I was glad in this situation for Mr Sloethwaite's thorough language lessons, though often at the time I complained that the language of El Ilam-Coram was irrelevant to a blacksmith. I am beginning to wonder if he knew all along.... but no, how could he foresee a child's future?

We spoke for a while, and I immediately felt at ease in her relaxed company, and admired the quiet dignity of her companions. I learned that they were in the city only for a short while, picking up some supplies, as they were nomads. They were camped with their tribe just beyond the city walls, and had been earning a few coins with their music to buy their teas, and just because they enjoy singing and playing!

And then I had a great stroke of luck, if luck it was; I begin to wonder. She asked me my business in Miyan, and the same inner resolve of trust that I had felt on first meeting Brag now made me speak openly, though I had learned some caution from my late mentor, so my voice was lowered, and my eyes repeatedly scanned the nearby bays.

"I seek the Four Inward-Looking Houses."

The nomads glanced at one another, obviously impressed. There was nothing furtive in their glances, just open surprise.

"We know where they are."

Now it was my turn to be surprised. My look of astonishment turning to eager enthusiasm made the singer's laughter bell around the room for a third time, though on this occasion it only caused a few casual looks.

"But, my friend," she added, "knowing where they are and

getting to them are two very different things. They are in the most remote and inaccessible part of this great land. It is many months journey, with constant hardships and dangers which could put a stop to your search for ever. And, even so, we could not say exactly where they are."

I must have looked so crestfallen that she laughed again.

"But I must find them," I said with something of desperation in my voice.

"Why must you?" she asked.

"I don't know why. I simply must."

The three nomads leaned close and, in a strange tongue of clicks and murmurs, discussed with quiet earnestness for so long that I began to feel as if I was intruding at their table! Eventually, they straightened their backs again and the woman said (always it was her who took the lead, the men sitting watchfully behind their veils): "You are a kind young man, and showed hospitality to strangers in a strange land. If you are really determined, then we can lead you much of the way, and also give you some directions to The Fortress and the Houses when you have to leave us for the final part of your search."

I looked closely at them, scrutinizing these new companions, and they returned my gaze without any apparent discomfort: the two men with open, penetrating steadiness, the woman with eyes that glittered and danced.

"I should warn you," I said in a whisper, "that I have enemies. At least, there are those who would see my mission fail." My voice became the ghost of a whisper. "I have been told the name of....Falseface."

For the first time, the laughter and light drained from the singer's face. She turned and spoke again with her friends in their tribal tongue in low tones, heads bent together. After a minute or two she looked at me and spoke seriously.

"We don't doubt your words. We know the Legend of the Houses of Sahada, passed on by our bards in the flickering flamelight of desert campfires, and we know what forces

are at large in the world against The Houses. It is a solemn and holy journey we have stumbled on. We are honoured to assist you. What is your name?"
"Kip Smith."
She smiled at me, like the sun coming from behind a cloud, and the two men placed the palms of their right hands over their hearts, like saying a prayer, and bowed their heads briefly to me.
"We are delighted, Kipsmith." She inflected my name as one word. "My name is Fadouma, and my friends are Ussa and Akhman."
I copied the men's greeting and they returned my gesture. We arranged to meet by the Desert Gate in the evening.

3rd Oakmoon *Late afternoon*
I have collected my belongings, and I'm about to leave the lodging-house, but I have been in a torture of indecision.
I spoke into the air as I gathered my possessions, and it was Brag to whom I addressed my questions: "What should I do? Should I go with them? Are they as they seem? What do you think?"
"Well?" I heard Brag's voice in my head, familiarly perfunctory, and throwing my questions back at me with one word.
I replied with some exasperation, "I don't know! On the one hand, I think they may know where the Houses are, but on the other, I consider—." Brag broke in.
"Think! Consider! Pah! What do you *feel*, Kip?"

3rd Oakmoon *Evening*
Leaving the last buildings behind as I walked out of Miyan with my new companions, and passing through the arched, stone gateway, I saw palm-groves ahead of me. These trees shaded the vicinity close to the city-walls, but once beyond them there was visible, in the last orange-gold glow of late evening sun, a flat, sandy, scrubby landscape, stretching in tones of ochre as far as I could see into the purple

shimmer of distance.

Half a mile away, I descried an encampment: tents, bivouacs, camp-fires, herds of goats and camels, as well as special riding-camels used by the tribe. As we walked towards the camp, Fadouma began humming a melody which she embellished with clicks and rolls of her tongue; the two men soon began to accompany her with a rhythmic grunt, and the whole song formed an irresistible beat, which I was enjoying immensely when I stopped suddenly in my tracks, the shock in my face bringing a peremptory finish to the song.

"What is it, Kipsmith?" asked the singer.

I pointed to the riding camels, all resting with their legs folded beneath them, and still clad in their backcloths of black or purple or white or red. I told the nomads about the camel which had taken an interest in me, and its malicious stare, and about the shapeshifter who dogged my journey.

For the first time, I heard Akhman speak aloud, and it was just a single word, the meaning of which I did not comprehend, but with which I would be painfully familiar before my journey's end.

"Mauhin!"

Ussa and Fadouma nodded in sombre agreement.

"We must be vigilant," said Ussa. "But we know the life-history of all our camels; I'm sure he could not be hiding here."

******

After a supper of goat-stew and black bread, I was taken to a tent, the nearest name for which that I can suggest in translation is the Digestion Tent. It seems that these people have separate tents for distinct purposes, rather as we have rooms in a house; so there are 'day tents', 'reception tents', 'dining tents', 'sleeping tents', 'conference tents'. The 'Digestion Tent' is the one to which the men sometimes repair on the only occasions I have seen so far when the men and women spend time separately, the women having their own after-supper tents.

The men who chose, on any particular evening, to forsake the after-supper activities at table, dozed, read, or played a game of strategy, cunning and intelligence at boards resembling chequerboards, except that these squares are alternate crimson and purple rather than black and white, and the strange, carved pieces (coloured saffron yellow or the green of ripe limes) depict different figures which, like chess pieces, all have their own distinct and peculiar ways of moving about the board. I noted twelve pieces: phoenix, gallows man, fishing boat, camel, lute, palm tree, scimitar, pomegranate, shaduf, scorpion, rose and snake-charmer. Their arcane properties and ruling governances I have yet to ascertain. There were at least a couple of dozen games in progress, and many more men who were not playing, but standing about, or sitting, or lying on couches and cushions, deep in murmured conversations. I watched Ussa and Akhman as they played, aiding their concentration by taking turns to draw smoke through the tube of a narghile, the water bubbling in its base of blue glass, and its tobacco and charcoal glowing in the canister which topped the brass tower from which the sucking-tube emerged. The air was full of pungent tobacco scent, as it seems to be the custom for everyone to smoke whilst playing this game, either hookahs or long-stemmed pipes that the herdsmen call something like 'chibbuk'. They also drink green tea, poured from tiny individual teapots. All this smoke, strategy and tea constitutes their way of aiding digestion after supper, hence the name of the tent. After the game (which is called, for no reason I can fathom, 'mongoose') we repaired to the largest tent in the encampment, the 'Assembly Tent': a huge, silken pavilion, where all the people of this Tu Darshaq tribe had gathered: old women, babes-in-arms, everyone- except those whose turn it was to guard the herds from marauding wild beasts.

It was a riot of colour, as the Tu Darshaq people love to dress in a kaleidoscope of hues- brilliant to subtle, but always strong- and, in contrast to the Digestion Tent, there was a loud hubbub of conversation, shouting, bursts of song, tuning of instruments. Now, the evening was devoted to music...

4th Oakmoon *Early a.m.*

Dawn has come and gone after a bitter night of stars flashing above the desert in a way that seemed to me both motionless and frenzied. Fortunately, I slept through most of it, snug in sheepskins.

Already, as my eyes stirred, I heard sounds of activity. Sheep and goats bleated, camels coughed and bellowed, men shouted and called, children called and laughed at play, babies cried, a woman sang a song which sounded natural enough to have grown out of the desert edges like a tamarisk.

When I poked my head out of my guest-tent a little later, I was astonished to discover that mine was the only tent still standing! The camels were loaded; the whole tribe almost ready to move.

"Good afternoon!" called Fadouma with heavy but playful irony, a smile playing along her lips. She was at a small fire tending some water which was approaching boiling point.

"You have time for some flat bread, goat's cheese and tea before we leave. Be quick! Your new friends were... what is it you Northern Islers say? 'Up with the lark'!"

(So Kip fell in with the rhythm of the days and nights of these proud and dignified people, whom he found so joyful, so serious, so attuned to their world. From here, his journal becomes a monthly account of his life with the travelling desert-people, the Tu Darshaq.)

❖❖❖❖❖❖

KIP'S MONTHLY JOURNAL

'Listen, lay your head under the tree of awe.' Rumi

Oakmoon

I soon discovered just how far these nomads are from being simply a tribe of rustic camel-traders. I had been tortured with uncertainty about joining them. When I thought over my decision, it seemed very rash, not to say foolhardy. 'Once well into the desert, these yokels could murder me at leisure and... No! Will I never learn?! Maddy. Mr Pipkin. My tendency to feel superior always leads me to subsequent humiliation. These people I am now travelling with are very cultured, and inherently honest, utterly trustworthy. Also highly hospitable: they always speak in the Miyan tongue in my company so that I am included, which is very gracious. I must keep listening to that small voice inside me that said, "Trust Brag", "Trust Fadouma".

******

Ussa is a scholar; he reads from a 'book' of loose-leafed, unevenly hand-cut pages, copying passages in the singularly bizarre script of the Tu Darshaq. This script is nothing like any writing I have ever seen, being something between hieroglyphs and mathematical symbols, without actually resembling either.

One evening I was with him as he wrote, and I tried to make something of the writings.

"Why do you copy these papers, Ussa?"

"It is a task," he replied without a moment's pause in his labours.

"Who set you this task?"

"I did," still intent, as if he had the ability to split his attention without the least detriment to either portion.

"What is the writing? Why is it important for you to copy it?"

Now Ussa stopped and put down his quill. He looked at me closely, and then smiled. His mouth was hidden by his veil, but his eyes smiled with twinkles and wrinkles. I'd never realized before how important, how revealing, the eyes are in a face.

"This, Kip," he replied, laying his hand gently and reverently on the rough-cut parchments, "is a collection of writings sacred to my people." And that was the sum of his reply!

He gazed at me with steady intent, awaiting my next question. As always, he was spare with the spoken word. Most of the men seem that way; it appears to be a cultural characteristic. The women are quite different. Chatty, laughing, easy-going. It's how these people are, it seems. In his company, I feel that my own speech is flabby, meandering, full of dross. But this feeling comes from myself; he does not judge me. Indeed, he is always patient and forbearing with me.

"Am I allowed to hear?" I asked.

"If you listen, you will hear."

"What does your sacred writing tell, Ussa?"

"It says, o my friend from the North, that he who truly seeks for a treasure will surely find it."

"Does it mention the Inward-Looking Houses?" I enquired, thinking of my task.

"What do you think a house is, Kipsmith?!" he asked after a few moments' pause.

This stumped me. I thought. I thought hard. Nothing came, except the obvious.

"I cannot think of the answer. I'm not sure what the question means. It's a place where you live... but that's too obvious to be the answer you're looking for."

"I wasn't looking for an answer," he replied quietly. "When you are journeying to a place, do you sit down with a feeling of arrival as soon as you see its name on a signpost?"

My mind laboured for a connection between houses and

signposts. Ussa smiled sympathetically at my perplexity, and came, as it seemed to me, to my aid.

"When I see the prospect of an oasis, my heart always rejoices," he said. "Not for the word 'oasis', but for what 'oasis' means."

"You mean fresh, cool water?" I thought I had caught on to what he was telling me.

"Yes, but then why does my heart rejoice for water?"

"Well, the physical pleasure of slaking your thirst."

"Yes. What else?"

"The idea of survival." Then, just as I thought that I had mastered his line of questioning, he came up with:

"Yes. But why survive?"

I began to stammer an attempted reply.

Ussa held a finger to his lips, and whispered: "No, don't try to answer. Let the question sparkle like water in the well of your being."

Ussa is a true scholar. I have much to learn, despite Mr Sloethwaite's schooling.

******

I must mention the meals we have eaten, as they are so different in nature to any I ever ate in the Northern Isles, due to the fact that they are eaten in silence. Not a silence bursting with suppressed anger and parental domination, like some I've had at home, which is not really silence at all, so loud are the underlying animosities. This was an easy silence, which allowed obvious necessary speech such as "Would you please pass the cactus conserve." (No, no. I jest!) But yes, conversation is considered by Tu Darshaq convention to be an insult to the food and the preparers, to the meal's quality. However, after the meal: well then there are stories, genealogies, poetry, music, tribal history, songs, laughter...

******

OAKMOON

On our first extended encampment, I was surprised to witness the skill of my hosts as metal-smiths, working for utility or decoration: making hinges to mend the lids of teapots and coffee pots, or using silver to fashion the intricate shells and brooches that decorate the women's hair and the men's turbans.

About a fortnight ago I came upon one of the tribesmen working on these hair-embellishments. His name is Agouti, and he and I have become good friends because we both love words, and, of course we simply like one another! He is much more like the women in that he laughs a lot, and is always ready to joke; as I am, perhaps, a little too earnest, this is good for me, and maybe we balance each other when we are together. I also discovered that my friend is a poet, a storyteller, historian for the tribe: the Tu Darshaq bard, in fact.

Agouti does not write, as Ussa does. He has his ballads, rhymes and histories in his head and heart. What he does with his hand is not to scribe, but to work metal. He is a skilful smith: dextrous, nimble-fingered.

He also creates luminous enamels to decorate some of his metalwork, especially the men's turban badges, in strong desert colours: burnt orange, turquoise, vermilion, orpiment. When he works, he works in silence. But when he finishes or pauses, he sings refrains from his songs, tells his stories, chants bits of his histories.

"You are very silent when you work your metal, Agouti," I observed one day. "You don't even hum a tune."

He laughed, slapping his thigh.

"Think what my work would look like if I did not concentrate my skill on the silver. And you, Kipsmith!" he hooted, clapping his hands loudly together and showing his white teeth as he laughed and pointed his finger at me in mock accusation. "Are you seeking silence, or fleeing it?!"

Always these people are asking questions! Questions that seem to defy answers. In one way I find it exasperating: it's as if I'm constantly being put on the spot. Yet, strangely, part of me feels that this has brought a deeper gratification than mere answers would have given, and a sort of echo of stillness and inner rest.

These people will not hurry, and to them answers seem to be hurry, and a conclusion. The Tu Darshaq have an air of awaiting, always expectant, though for what I haven't the faintest idea.

******

Agouti was very interested to learn of my trade and has promised to instruct me in the skills of working with his delicate metals, in return for me sharing some of the secrets of my trade.

HOLLYMOON
(July 8 - August 4)

'Of all the trees that are in the wood
The Holly bears the crown.'
The Holly-Tree Carol

'"Gawain," said the green knight, "may God guard you!
You are welcome to my dwelling, I warrant you,
And you have timed your travel here as a true man ought.
You know plainly the pact we pledged between us:
This time a twelvemonth ago you took your portion,
And now at this New Year I should nimbly requite you.'
Sir Gawain and the Green Knight

The holly was known as the 'holy tree', and 'bears the crown' because, upon the sacrificial death of the oak-king at Midsummer, the holly-king assumes the king's mantle and rules the waning year. This seasonal coronation is reflected in the fact that the holly blossoms in July (cf. 'the holly's Autumn falls in June' - Edward Thomas).

Historically, this month could be ruled by either the holly or the evergreen oak; the two trees share many features, including the botanical name, ilex.

The immortal Green Knight carried a club of holly, and was, without doubt, a representation of the holly-king. He and the oak-king appear in the traditional mummers' play as St George who is killed (as oak-king) and rises again (as holly-king).

This is the eighth month, and eight is the number of increase.

Chapter 8/ HOLLYMOON

from Kip's notes

I have found out a quite a bit about the island, and particularly about the way of life of these new companions of mine.

El Ilam-Coram has no national government, no organised state power, but comprises independent city states and tribal domains, with occasional alliances according to need.

The economic life of the desert is built round the supply of camels, and this is the business of the Tu Darshaq. They trade camels, and as these are best bred on the upland pastures of nutritious thorns, the camel-trading peoples of El Ilam-Coram revolve through the rota of seasonal pasturage and camel-markets.

The heart of this vast island is sandy desert, a great ocean of dry swells. This is ringed by the sea to west and south-west, and by mountainous lands to north and east. Within these mountains are scrubby uplands which support the occasional 'pastures' of thorns upon which the camels thrive. The camel-traders orbit the desert, 'hopping' from pasture to pasture, with diversions into the desert itself for short-cuts or to trade at the desert markets. The Tu Darshaq herd is prospering, and all looks well for the next market, I'm told. Their animals are highly prized on the island market, as they are always in such fine condition.

******

Today, Fadouma showed me how to milk a nanny-goat. I watched, and she handled it with such assurance that it did not fuss, but stood browsing a prickly bush, placidly chewing whilst she deftly drew milk from it. It looked easy enough! I took Fadouma's place on the stool and, as soon as I tentatively put a hand on the creature's back, it bolted, leaving me on my chin in the dust. This seemed to be a source of amusement for, after several attempts which led to similar results, quite a large and jovial crowd had gathered! However, their laughter was not in the slightest bit malicious, and I confess that I had to join in. Fadouma, though, persevered with me, and I did eventually manage to draw about half a pint of milk.

These creatures seem less co-operative than the horses I'm used to in my trade, but I'm sure that my experience in the forge at home helped to cut down my training time!

I am keeping a suspicious weather-eye on all the animals, especially the camels, but a month has passed now without incident regarding Falseface the Shifter. Perhaps I allowed my imagination to run away with me in Miyan, and the camel was just that: a camel! Perhaps Mr Drufus- Bragwent to his death finally seeing off Falseface after the attack on the Tariqa.

HAZELMOON
(August 5 - September 1)

'The salmon-trout drifts in the stream,
The soul of the salmon-trout floats over the stream
Like a little wafer of light.'
  Ezra Pound

The hazel is the tree of wisdom, its nut being a symbol of concentrated sagacity. In ancient lore, the flower and fruit of the hazel represent beauty & wisdom, and eating the nut was said to make one erudite in all the arts and sciences.

Divining rods were always made of hazel, and were used to identify the location of water, buried treasure or people guilty of serious crimes.

The third of the year's fire festivals marks the third quarter on the fourth day of Hazelmoon: Lammas or Lughnasa, the thanksgiving for bread at the wheat harvest.

Chapter 9/ HAZELMOON

I got to know Akhman a little better today. He is a taciturn man; makes Ussa seem garrulous! And he is quite a man with water. There are wells and water-holes known to the tribe: either shallow pools left inexplicably in a slight depression, or deep wells lurking down echoing chimneys of stone to which access is gained only by climbing down the sheer sides, using hand- and foot-holds. But Akhman can also find water where no-one has an inkling about it, not even his fellow Tu Darshaq nomads with all their desert experience.

Today I watched him: the expected water-hole had been fouled by some wild creature drowning in it. Akhman was summoned. His first act was to take the creature's body respectfully in his hands, bury it a hundred yards away, and make a chant "over its being, to assist its return to the Desert Spirit."

That done, he crouched on his haunches, threw some handfuls of dusty sand into the breeze, and intoned a few phrases indistinguishable to me as words. Next, after ten minutes of complete cross-legged silence and stillness, he suddenly stood up, turned a few degrees on his heel, and walked rapidly away for two or three hundred yards. He stopped abruptly, turned a single, slow revolution with an acutely listening aspect, and then called, "Here!"

Some men ran up with various wooden implements resembling mattocks and shovels, and began digging and clearing a pit. Sure enough, within a couple of feet's depth, they had uncovered dampness in the sand, then as they proceeded a little lower it gradually turned to sandy sludge, and at several feet down water bubbled up from grainy mud. Soon, there was a small pond which, within a quarter of an hour was full of clear water!

As well as replenishing the water-bags, the people drank deeply, much more than I could stomach. I asked Akhman the reason why.

"For the thirst of yesterday and tomorrow," he replied, which I sort of understand, but when I try to really fathom it clearly in my head I find that I couldn't say what he meant!

He also warned me never to drink too much if ever I found myself in the situation of discovering water when in a critical state of dehydration, as this understandable response would almost certainly result in my death!! "Sip, and gradually ease your body back out of thirst, no matter how much temptation rages."

"How did you know the water was there, Akhman?"

"To find water in the desert, you must lose yourself," he replied in the usual oblique Tu Darshaq fashion that I was becoming accustomed to.

"How do I do that?" I persisted.

"In your body, become as motionless as a rock. Invite the Desert Spirit to immerse itself in you, just as you immerse yourself in it. Let your mind become a still pool. I am emptied of Akhman so that the Desert Spirit has room to enter. It uses my body as a channel to show where it hides water."

Suddenly, all I wanted to do was fold my hands and bow my head, Tu Darshaq fashion, and tears filled my eyes. What is happening to me?! Recently, my eyes seem to water at the slightest provocation. It must be the sand-grit and constant glare of the sun...

******

Today, we rode from the peripheries into the desert proper, heading for a camel market at an oasis-town. This was hard going: leaving behind the familiar scrub and tamarisks of our valley of shingle and light, sandy soil, and a sea of pure, white sand from which the ruthless sunlight reflected with a glassy heat and painful brilliance. Ussa told me to cover my face, allowing the camel to follow its own way, as hour after hour of this glare can cause blindness, even to seasoned travellers.

******

Mid-day rest stop
We have been travelling for two and a half days, and the last vegetation I remember seeing is the woody wafers of a cactus-skeleton the day before yesterday, when I briefly succumbed to the temptation to escape my veil. It was weird to witness the caravan of faceless riders: it resembled a dream-like funeral procession.

Tomorrow, we arrive at the oasis-town, but there are many more hours yet of that relentless, unrelieved heat and dazzle, which with the concomitant boredom, becomes loathsome. It is the most tedious, most trying part of my journey so far. The pattern of our expedition is to rest at noon for a few hours while the sun is at its peak, then set out again in the late afternoon and, finally, stop for supper and sleep at about three or four hours from midnight. Then up again just before dawn to begin the cycle again with a short break at mid-morning. My admiration for these nomads has grown as my romantic view of their life has diminished on this stage of the journey. I see where they get their patience and fortitude from!

******

Because the air in the hollows is stifling, I walked up onto one of the nearby crests, where it is comparatively fresh- at least, the air seems to stir very slightly!

From my vantage point, I could see most of the camp set out as bright spots of fire and black shadows of tents and animals; also, up high out of the firelight, the stars are sparklingly evident.

Stars overhead, campfires crouched low like desert

blossoms; they reflect one another, whispering some deep connection between above and below.

******

At one point of today's passage, Ussa suggested that I remove my eye-veil, and, though he wouldn't say why he had made the suggestion, I was only too ready to comply. After a short while, we came over a dune, and there it was! It took some moments to register, to drag my stupefied senses from their sun-baked torpor, to shake my consciousness and rouse it from its numbness. It was like waking to a dream! After the unforgiving hours of white glare from the vitreous sand and the blank fuss of the inside of my veil, here was colour: a shimmering relief of green and earthy pink. Now I saw why this oasis is called 'The Rose of the Desert'.

Coming closer, sight of the town was lost as we dipped into a trough of the dunes. We encountered first some scrub and a few tamarisk trees, and it is a measure of the inhospitality of the white desert that, by contrast, I had a feeling of homecoming at seeing a resemblance to Qasaba's outskirts! Next we came to high acacias and thickets of oleander. The viridescence was like a food, the verdant cool of the shade a balm. We came to the town-gates: heavy, studded, sun-bleached cedar doors, which opened at a call from Ussa. All the buildings within were the same colour as the blank walls: a dusky pink clay, and there was a scent in the air. Not overpowering, but as if you had passed close to a flowering shrub. I commented on this to Agouti, who explained that when the inhabitants mix the clay for their buildings, they stir in oil of rose-petals, in honour of the flower to which their town is dedicated.

******

Simple pleasures! O, just to sit in the shade of an oleander beside a spring of clear, bubbling water, listening to the melodious gurgle and tinkle of its falling into a stone trough. What a splendid treat for the senses after all that time in the pitiless desert conditions!

We have been here for several days now, my nomad hosts involved in their camel deals, and I just resting or sightseeing when not helping with camp chores.

The camel-market is held outside the town-walls, between the oleander groves, in the shade of the tall acacias.

Within the walls, at least away from the bazaar, it is quiet, except for the sound of dancing water from the spring-heads, which does not disturb the oasis' tranquillity. I generally keep away from the bazaar, because the stallholders keep trying to engage me in transactions, but I cannot understand the oasis dialect, and there are no set prices: everything is haggled over. So I just wander about the town. The most amazing discovery I have made so far is a building that seems more like a natural formation- something made by giant ants, maybe- than anything constructed by man. It is of the usual earth-pink clay, but is a fantastic assembly of spirals, whorls and pinnacles ascending wildly into the blue endlessness above, like a miniature range of mountains almost; organic, rather than man-made. And yet, it was built, centuries ago, and is a deeply respected place, housing as it does the history of the oasis, recorded on various leaves of parchment, papyrus, fine leather, strange vegetable papers, not unlike Mr Pipkin's document. And not only the history, but venerable wise sayings, poetry and song, philosophies, sacred writings, and so on. For this is none other than a place of learning, a university, a library, a confluence of the arts and sciences and ancient teachings.

******

We headed back towards the desert edge, where the surroundings are relatively private, compared, that is, with the oasis, because there is an important Feast Day for the Tu Darshaq approaching early in the new moon.

26th Hazelmoon
Early today, a stranger arrived: an old man with a silver beard, neatly trimmed. At first I thought that he was royalty, so fine and elaborate with gold thread were the cloths and trappings on his camel. He had a little string of four camels, like Brag's mules: there was the camel that he was riding himself, and three with supplies and equipment.
It turns out he is a merchant (a very rich one, obviously) who is returning to the north-west after visiting relatives in Muchaa, El Ilam-Coram's second city. He came at us from a tangent over to our left as he was cutting a corner to save time, and he was welcomed by the hospitable Tu Darshaq, and invited to attend the feast as a guest of honour alongside me. He has accepted graciously, offering gifts in respect of their feast day, and agreeing to travel with us for a while.

******

The merchant, Eqbir, and I have spent much time together. His stories are fascinating: he has been to many exotic places, buying and selling the rugs and carpets in which he deals, and has an apparently numberless number of tales to tell!

******

Today, unexpectedly (to me, at least!), the sky darkened from the west and, for just over three hours, it rained! My hosts laughed at my astonishment, but I had imagined that, as deserts are said to be hot and arid, they *never* had rain.
The landscape was transformed within the first hour of precipitation: where before there had been emptiness and dust, stars and rosettes of flowers blossomed as if they

were a vision, and jewel-like insects ran and flew everywhere. The Tu Darshaq call these 'ephemerals': those desert flora and fauna that are only released into their quick, brief life-cycle by a rare rainfall.

For the previous week, it had been a monotonous, dry landscape of grey shingle, very little sand, the only plants being pale, lifeless twig-bones: apparently dead, but only apparently, it now seems.

Eqbir and I continue to spend a great deal of our time together: we talk as we ride, and at camp, often long into the night. Something about him fascinates me.

******

A strange incident today, which I found embarrassing at the time, and disturbing afterwards. I was talking with Akhman when Eqbir came up and greeted us. When he held out his arms to hug Akhman and kiss his cheek in the traditional local manner, my Tu Darshaq friend stayed his ground and stared directly into the merchant's eyes with a concerned and searching expression. Then, with a grunt, he turned on his heel and walked away!

VINEMOON
(September 2 - September 29)

'But still the Vine her ancient Ruby yields...'
  Omar Khayam

'O for a beaker full of the warm South,
 Full of the true, the blushful Hippocrene,
  With beaded bubbles winking at the brim,
   And purple-stained mouth'
    John Keats

'Think, in this battered Caravanserai
Whose portals are alternate Night and Day,
How Sultan after Sultan with his Pomp
Abode his destined Hour, and went his way.'
  Omar Khayyam

The vine is the tree of joy, exhilaration and wrath.

It is the first of the pair of trees which symbolize resurrection; the vine because its wine symbolizes preserved strength. In northern climes, the bramble was used as a substitute, blackberries making a strong and delicious wine.

This tree-moon includes the Autumn Equinox.

Chapter 10/ VINEMOON

1st Vinemoon
We are camped for a few days now, in order to prepare for a feast to celebrate a special day to the Tu Darshaq: the third day of the Vinemoon. They call it The Day Of Rubies.

3rd Vinemoon *'The Day Of Rubies'*
All day, preparations were in hand: goat and sheep roasted, the preserved meat of boar sliced, black bread baked in ovens of stones like little cairns; a circle of tents erected forming a large enclosed area where a campfire was built. Everywhere, a bustle of activity. I helped as directed on various chores, and Eqbir threw himself cheerfully into useful labours too.
One of my jobs was to help Ussa fetch goatskins full of some liquid to the tent circle.
"Is this extra water, Ussa?"
"No, Kip. It is wine."
This surprised me. Until now, all I had seen the Tu Darshaq drink was water, tea and goat's or ewe's milk; never strong drink. I voiced my surprise.
"This is a special day," Ussa explained. "It is 'The Day Of Rubies'. On this day we drink the liquid ruby as a reminder of the treasure we all seek, which is greater than gold or precious jewels. However, Kip, we respect the power of its essence." There seemed a gentle warning in his accompanying look.
"And what is this great treasure, Ussa?"
He indicated some Tu Darshaq folk preparing food. I looked at the figs and dates being sorted by some women, ready for the evening's feast, and vats of large, green olives being spooned into huge bowls, at pomegranates being distributed around the tent-circle.

"And this,' he added, before I could ask why these fruits were greater than gold and jewels. He raised a goatskin of water high above his head.
"Water?" I questioned.
"And this," as he poured it in a silver, twisting rope to the dusty sand, where it seeped away.
"Ussa, you're wasting it!" I cried out, having had it drummed into me by my hosts how valuable a resource it was out in the desert.
He stared at me for a moment and then shook his head slightly, a movement and a look in which it seemed to me there was something of the indulging of a child, and wonder at perceived foolishness, a little sorrow.
"Come, Kip," he sighed. "We have tasks to complete."

******

For people who seem so self-possessed, the Tu Darshaq certainly know how to enjoy a celebration! What an evening!

The desert stars were as brilliant as ever. Fadouma pointed out a line of seven stars which were stretched in a procession across the black dunes of the night sky from horizon to horizon during the passage of the year. Her people refer to it as 'The

Caravan', and a bright cluster at their eastern edge as 'The Caravanserai', which is the desert's equivalent of an inn.

The tents of the circle were filled with fruits, goats' and ewes' cheeses, breads; and people ate, drank, jested, chattered, laughed (all contrary to the normal practice of eating in silence).

The inevitable music and song followed the feasting: rhythmic clapping, chanting and drumming accompanied the imzad, tinde and tehardent instruments.

It was all so exhilarating: the leaping fires, the driving, insistent rhythms of the music and the wild yet earthed and earthy singing, the deep-hued robes, the acute tastes of the food, the wine! My head was spinning with the joy of it all, and I clapped and whooped with the best. I am unused to strong wine, but I had Ussa's recent warning to remind me to take care. Besides, the feast for the senses was indulgence enough. It was a joyful few hours.

******

'And when they that were in the tents heard, they were astonished at the thing that was done.' 'The Book of Judith', The Apocrypha

Many people had retired to their tents to sleep. Eqbir and I were walking together just beyond the edge of the camp. The air was cool, and some desert crickets were ratcheting the night away. Eqbir suddenly spoke, as if having just made an important decision. "I trust that you will forgive my impertinence, Kip. But already I like you.
You are honest and open. I never had a son, but- forgive me, please- you show me a little of what it might have felt like."
"You do me much honour, Eqbir," I stammered.
"Nonsense," he chuckled. "It is as it is."
We strolled on, contented in the ease afforded by having spoken openly, admiring the vast, quiet darkness of the desert, and the vaster quietudes of the night sky beyond.
"You know, Kip," Eqbir rejoined after a minute or two, "I have long searched for someone that I could trust to help me with my business. I am getting too old for all the travelling that is necessary in my trade. Of course, if I had had a son, it would have been easy and natural. But it was not to be... I should be most honoured and delighted, Kip, if you would consider becoming my apprentice, with a view to becoming my successor. Fate has brought me here at this time, and I see that it has been kind to me."
I was amazed, confused, elated, mystified.
"Why me?" I stammered. "You've only known me for a short time. I'm just a poor blacksmith."

"That is a shade disingenuous, Kip. A poor blacksmith who hasn't pulled a bellows for months, who is miles away from home with an ocean in between. From what I have observed, you have fine qualities. Your honesty and openness are obvious. And I have taken a natural liking to you. These feelings are inexplicable, but they are also undeniable. Please consider my offer, Kip. I'm sure I'm not mistaken about you."

I decided to be frank.

"Eqbir, you are very kind, but I cannot accept your offer. You see, I'm on a special journey. My new friends, the Tu Darshaq, are guiding me to The Fortress, where I will find the Four Inward-Looking Houses. It is a place I must go to."

"I know it," replied Eqbir in a disarmingly matter-of-fact way. "It is the subject of many tales."

"You know it?!" I exclaimed. "You've been there?"

"Four decades, I have travelled the length and breadth of this island: certainly I've been there."

"And...?"

Eqbir sighed and looked a little sorrowful. "I do not wish to deflate you when you are so alive with anticipation and hope, but....it is a place......it is a place which.....it does not live up to its legend."

It was my turn to sigh and, after a deep breath of preparation, I said, "Tell me, Eqbir. I am ready for what you can tell me about The Houses."

Eqbir suggested that we return to his guest marquee, as the night was rapidly cooling. His servants brought more robes and fleeces, and then retired to sleep at his dismissal as we settled on soft bolsters.

"Have your friends told you how hard the journey to the fortress is, Kip?"

"They said that the journey is long, that The Fortress is remote and inaccessible."

He gave a short, derisory snort of laughter. "They understate, Kip. The way there is so difficult, so dangerous, that few even attempt it; of those few, only the reckless persevere; of those most reckless, nine out of ten die in the attempt."

I was feeling a whirl of emotions: disappointment, panic, anger, resentment. And I was by no means sure at whom or what these feelings were directed: the Old Man-Woman Mummer, Brag, Bill Pipkin, Maddy, Eqbir, the Tu Darshaq, myself, The Fates...

I seized on a sudden idea, a gleam of hope. "But what is there at The Fortress that is worth these dreadful odds, Eqbir?" There was a tremulous dread in my question, for a part of me was aware that I was on the brink of losing something which had become very important to me, that I had begun to build my life around.

The rug-merchant looked long and sadly into my eyes; then he sighed heavily.

"That is the great sadness, Kip. For there is nothing there. Nothing." He bowed his head heavily. "I have been. There are old men worshipping trinkets, and trying to remember why. There are tricksters promising anything that guileless travellers desire, in return for whatever valuables they have to give. It is a palace of illusion and deception, Kip."

I was so distraught that I could not think. Had all this trip, all the hope and promise, all my faith in different people, my 'intuitions', been founded on a mistake, on self-delusion?

Eqbir tried to ease my hurt and confusion, which must have been all too clearly visible.

"O, Kip. I am truly sorry to bring you this news. But how much better that you hear the truth now, than to discover it for yourself in a few more wasted months; or, worse, to die in the attempt to reach for nothing but an empty dream. Fate has been kind to us both. It has sent me someone to whom I can confidently pass on my business and my wealth with peace of mind. And it has sent you a warning angel to prevent you taking a wrong turning in your life, as well as offering you a road to satisfaction, comfort and riches in the real world, rather than losing your way in illusions."

I began to see how foolish I had been. Such a callow youth, imagining that insignificant little 'I' had been chosen for some Great Purpose. Even Maddy, young and simple, had laughed at me sometimes; couldn't hide her amusement at my pomposity. I recalled with a humiliating shock that it was Maddy who had first mentioned the Inward-Looking Houses to me. She must have heard a story of them and innocently repeated the name when she thought I needed help.

"Well," I exclaimed with an ironic, self-deprecatory sigh, shaking my head in wonder at my gullibility. "How can I thank you, Eqbir? You have pulled me back from the brink."

"No thanks is due, my son," replied the old merchant softly. "Having you take on my mantle is reward enough. Tomorrow we shall set out for Muchaa and a new chapter in your life will begin."

"But what about the Tu Darshaq?" I asked. "They seemed so... so wise; they seemed to think that I was on a journey of deep importance."

"They are good people, Kip. Their intentions are scrupulous, but they are full of myth. It is all superstition. That Agouti fellow, for example. He has told so many stories, that he really believes them; he can no longer tell the difference between them and reality. Do not blame them, Kip. They have acted in good faith, as far as their limited understanding of the real world allows."

And then, abruptly, the real world was a dream!

I could not make head or tail of what was happening for, suddenly, Fadouma and Akhman were standing there, just inside the entrance flap of the marquee. Eqbir looked astonished.

"You evil man!" breathed Fadouma, with such contained anger that I was terrified. "You would lure Kipsmith from his sacred path with falsehoods and talk of riches." She turned her look to me. "Kip! Come over and stand next to me."

I was in a quandary, and swallowed hard; I was finding it difficult to breathe. The merchant's eyes darted back and forth between Fadouma's and mine; she alternately gazed earnestly at me, and then, with narrowing eyes, at Eqbir.

Holding his stare at Fadouma now, Eqbir spoke to me.

"It's your choice, Kip. Search in your reason. Who is really talking sense? Why should I lie to you? These poor, kind people simply don't understand. Don't throw your life away on a dream."

I was at a loss. I didn't know what to do, which voice in me to trust. Something deep inside me just cried out for help, and, as if in reply, I suddenly had a picture of myself in my sickbed on board The Tariqa, with Maddy tending me. My question then echoed now in my head and heart: 'But how shall I know where to go?' And the immediate, strange reply that Maddy gave before applying the stinging potion to my head-wound also came back to me: 'You must search for the Four Inward-Looking Houses.'

I can't explain how or why, but something resolved within me, and I found myself walking towards Fadouma. There was no reasoning, no consideration, no conclusion, no thoughts weighed in the balance. I was just walking, dream-like, to stand beside her, my back to Eqbir, head hung like a patient draught-animal, half-ashamed, half-bemused. Fadouma gently led me to the tent opening; all the while, Akhman stood motionless, his eyes unblinkingly fixed on Eqbir.

As soon as we were halfway through the exit, Fadouma let out a scream to waken the dead. Instantly, Tu Darshaq men were running up with drawn sabres curving from their hands. Fadouma pointed at the marquee and said just that single word that I had heard on first approaching the Tu Darshaq camp outside the walls of Miyan.

"Mauhin!"

There was a rush for the tent, but a great shout from within halted everyone simultaneously in their tracks, and awoke me from a mental torpor that even Fadouma's scream had not broken. I turned and lifted the tent-flap.

On the bolsters where Eqbir had been lounging, there was an enormous, rearing cobra, jaw wide-hinged, throat hissing, fangs and flickering forked-tongue glinting in the lamplight. Eqbir had gone! Akhman stood murmuring what sounded to me like some sort of incantation, half-speaking, half-chanting. I glanced briefly back outside at the sound of Ussa's arrival, and was confounded on looking straight back into the tent. I blinked involuntarily in my astonishment: Akhman was no longer there! A movement caught the corner of my sight and, turning my head, I saw a huge mongoose. All this was so fabulous a turn of events that I was not surprised to hear a loud and unaccountable tearing sound from the back of the tent. There was a great rent in the silken wall. The cobra had disappeared and I rushed to the gash in the fabric only just in time to see some winged creature disappearing into the desert night, its harsh cries filling the sky with threatened revenge.

IVYMOON
(September 30 - October 27)

'Who is it that cometh out of the wilderness like pillars of smoke...?'
Song of Solomon

'Oh roses for the flush of youth,
And laurel for the perfect prime;
But pluck an ivy branch for me
Grown old before my time.'
Christina Rossetti

The ivy is the second of the pair of trees symbolizing resurrection, partly because it grows in a spiral. It has a connection with strong drink, like its sister tree, the vine, because the ivy-bush is an ancient sign for an inn. Also, in mediaeval times, ivy-ale was a brew renowned for its intoxicating strength.

Chapter 11/ IVYMOON

from Kip's journal

It is the morning following the Day of Rubies. Earlier, I sat at breakfast with my special friends, so recently doubted: Fadouma, Agouti, Ussa, Akhman. Fadouma's face was strained with pent-up anger, and I avoided making contact with her eyes.

"How dare he?" she muttered. "Using our hospitality. Living amongst us. Trying to turn Kipsmith against us. How dare he?! She almost shouted the last three words, her repeated question.

"Calm yourself, Fadouma," said Ussa quietly. "It is, after all, his reason for existing: to deceive, to tempt. We must be vigilant. We had become too casual. Apart from Akhman, who was wary and watchful. It was he who said that you and he should go to the Guest Tent, because he felt uneasy." Ussa bowed to Akhman in respect, and Akhman tipped his head slightly in acknowledgement.

"And you, Kip," Fadouma continued, as if Ussa had not spoken.

My heart sank at her words, and I cringed. I had dreaded the question, but it was deserved.

"How could you doubt us?"

The reproach and the hurt in her voice were a bitter draught to swallow.

"I never doubted your goodness, your kindness" I replied in a low, penitent voice, my eyes fixed on the ground before me. "But even he never questioned that. That's what was so clever. He didn't say... he was so sympathetic," my voice trailed away to nothing.

"We cannot be too hard on Kip," murmured Ussa. "He is young. He has taken on a heavy mantle. Mauhin is endlessly cunning, endlessly ruthless."

"Mauhin will not let us be," added Akhman, almost to himself.

Fadouma's face softened, and relaxed into a sad smile as her spiral of anger, fear and resentment untwisted. She touched my arm.

"I'm sorry, Kip."

And, in an instant, there I was again! Those three gently spoken words, that look of understanding, the support of these true friends, the shock of events, the increasing use of the short Kip: everything welled up and burst out in a shudder of tears, and Fadouma was hugging me in her open, easy, generous, maternal manner.

At this point, a dreadful realization hit me and cut off my sobs. I grasped Fadouma by her shoulders and held her at arms' length: "I told him! I told him where I am going. I told him about the Fortress!"

But, yet again, my friends immediately came to my aid.

"It would not have been news to him," Ussa assured me. "His knowledge is great. His knowledge, but not his wisdom. His appetite for power is also great, and this means that he does not use his knowledge to wise ends."

Akhman raised his head and gazed at me with a curiously piteous look.

"He has trodden your path before you, Kip. It does not get any easier, and the higher up the mountain path you reach, the more dangerous it is to fall.

******

It is a couple of days since the Day of Rubies. Today I was speaking with Ussa as I helped him tend the camels prior to the tribe's departure from camp.

"What happened with Akhman in the tent?" I ventured. No-one had mentioned the scene, and I wondered if there was some sort of embargo on it. But Ussa seemed to have expected the question, for without hesitation he replied.

"Akhman has special powers. You saw him find water. We Tu Darshaq all know the desert and its ways, but Akhman can speak to its spirit in a way that is not open to many of us. If one of us is unwell or an animal is sick, and our normal remedies are ineffective, it's Akhman in whom we put our trust.

"So he is like your doctor?"

He shook his head. "Not just medicine. He is a wise man. He is more like our guide, our respected elder."

I'm not sure that I fully understand, but they seem to have utter confidence in him, and he certainly scared off the Shifter. For now, at least!

******

Two or three weeks have passed peacefully since The Day Of Rubies. We have followed a meandering route, which I am assured has saved us time, and thus is easier on the animals; this has involved us in tracking the courses of dry stream-beds, called by the Tu Darshaq 'owads'. Several days ago, we left the sands, and even the shingle, in order to follow, for most of the daylight hours, a great pavement of rock exposed by the winds (this natural pavement is called a 'hamdaa' by the tribespeople. Up and down we went, which was hard work day after day.

Agouti repeated today that we were making good progress. He has made up a song/poem called 'The Night of the Cobra', describing that awful event. Part of the horror, which he captures in one verse, was the complete plausibility and charm of the Shifter. A loose translation of what he sang to me:

'He smiles, he comforts, pledges rubies so fine,
Rubies of the Ancient Vine.
He's like a lost father come home in the morning,
But remember, in truth, it is only Mauhin.'

"What is 'mauhin'?" I asked when he had finished his song. "I mean in your tongue, what is its meaning?"

"Mauhin is utter darkness, the dead of night."

"Suddenly, Agouti, I feel a surge of courage. I feel like a warrior! I want to search out this Mauhin and slay him!"

Agouti opened his mouth, laughed through his white teeth, and instantly sang to the accompaniment of his handdrum:

'Look out, Great Mauhin!
Just one speck of light,
Like our Kip's naive courage,
And you'll lose the fight!'

I'm sure he could have chosen a better word than 'naive', but it was a spontaneous effort, and the right word escapes me just now.

Akhman, who had been sitting motionless a few yards away, gazing into the desert, suddenly spoke, without removing his sight from the distances.

"Agouti! Do not speak that name too lightly. Kip will not need to seek out his adversary. He will come again."

Agouti raised his eyebrows at me and winked, but then he did look a little shame-faced.

******

We had to cross an area of true desert for a day or two, desert as I heard about it in childhood tales: endlessly undulating dunes ribbed and ridged by the winds. It was a difficult time for the herds of camels and goats, but the knowledge and skill of the Tu Darshaq have brought them through to new grazing.

This evening I went walking with Akhman after we had set up camp. We sat on a high dune well away from the encampment, and as we looked back through the gathering dusk, the tents seemed to glow in the twilight. As so often in Akhman's company, I was happy to sit in silence, and we watched the dim shining of early evening fade with the tents into the darkness, after which he pointed out stars and constellations unknown to me, and showed how you could steer yourself even through a featureless desert by using the stars as your guides, much as Captain Aquablanca did when crossing the sea.

Suddenly a frown appeared on his brow, accompanied by an intent look of puzzlement in his eyes.

"What is it Akhman?"

His eyes scanned the low sky where the horizon rose and fell. He seemed to talk to himself.

"Samoom? It cannot be. Yet I feel it in the air. The spirit of the desert is troubled."

Akhman's alert yet worried eyes continued to scan the dark wastes; after a few seconds he leaned forward, peering into the horizon, where a relic of paleness remained from the sunset.

"It is not the season for the hot wind," he murmured. He turned to me. "Can you feel it?"

Now I could. The air was suddenly warm, as if someone had suddenly blown a draught from my home-forge towards us.

"This can mean only one thing. Mauhin!"

At this name, despite the sudden warming of the air, I felt a chill in my veins.

"What do you see, Akhman?"

He pointed to the far rim of the desert, but I could make nothing out, except a high dune dark against the dark sky. Or was it not a dune, but a cloud?"

"Is it going to rain, Akhman?"

"Much worse," he replied, shaking his head. "Come! We must warn the village and make preparations. The sandstorm Mauhin is approaching!"

We ran back as fast as we could, which I did not manage nearly so efficiently as old Akhman: he seemed to glide over the shifting grains, whereas I slipped and slid and sank, almost swimming in sand at times. By the time I arrived back at the encampment, there was already great activity as Tu Darshaq folk rushed about to cries and orders, these chiefly from Ussa. Great canvases were unrolled, from which were erected defensive walls in the shape of a 'V' with its point into the advancing storm. Akhman estimated that sandstorm would take an hour to reach us, so there was time to make many preparations.

Eventually, all that could be done in the time available was completed, and the women (who are, of course, normally unveiled) wrapped long, wide scarves around their own and their children's necks, heads and faces in one continuous bandage. Everyone then huddled behind the canvas screens and waited, except for Akhman and me.

"Come, Kip. As you are on a great journey, I will show you something."

We went beyond the 'village'. The first, tiny stings of fine, hot grit were hitting the narrow strip of cheek and forehead exposed by pulling apart a gap to see by.

"We must rise above the sandstorm, Kip. This will feel strange; just pretend to yourself that it is quite normal, like a child at play, and you will find that everything will come to you. Just keep close to me."

Suddenly, there we were: two falcons, gyring up into the air, further and further from the undulations of the dunes, and above the tidal wave advancing like a dark, threatening shadow towards what Akhman always referred to as the 'Village'. We hung, we glided, we dipped; and it was as the Tu Darshaq shaman had described. It was a sort of suspension of disbelief, a falling into trust, which led somehow to an experience of endorsement, of verification. It soon became apparent to Akhman, from his aerial observations, how he needed to act in order to best attempt to counter the effects of The Shifter's onslaught, for this storm was more intense than a natural one, and it was clear even to me that the canvas walls would soon be scaled by new formations of sand, and the whole village, with its people and animals, be obliterated. As we hovered there, I could just discern the sound of babies crying, a pathetic, baleful sound in these remote, strange circumstances. Akhman swept down and alighted by the tip of the 'arrowhead' formed by the canvas defences, where he reassumed his human form. I followed. I was anticipating some astonishing feat of wizardry, or an almighty battle as the magicians met in shamanic single combat. But nothing of that sort occurred.

We now had to turn our backs to the storm, and pull our veils, turbans and robes close round ourselves. Akhman called above the rising howl of the tempest.

"I saw from above that the sand-blizzard is illusion. Mauhin plays games with us. Deadly games, games that cause suffering and fear and distress. We must counter this with truthfulness.

Beckoning me to join him, he sat down cross-legged, facing directly into the storm, back straight, hands folded in his lap, head bowed slightly, and his face now blanked completely by his protective scarf. I covered my face and copied his posture.

"Do as I do, Kip Blacksmith," came Akhman's voice through the increasing moan and scream of the stinging gale.

He began to murmur a chant from which I quickly distinguished a rhythm and a pattern. I seemed to hear Akhman's words inside my head, underlying the pulse of the chant.

"Be like your hawk-self. Let Kip Blacksmith go and become the chant. Build a wall of true song against the lies of the black wind. Sing yourself into this moment of the desert's being."

Gradually, my past melted, the moment was all I knew: there was the cruel shriek of the black wind, the pitiless lashing of the sand, the small chant of two voices.

******

Ussa squinted through a slit he had pulled in his veil as he pushed himself against the gale, and passed between the huddled forms of the Tu Darshaq folk, adjusting an old woman's scarf here, comforting a distressed child there, reassuring a frightened young mother who gripped her baby within the folds of her robe. The wind rode the canvas walls and leapt like a wild beast among the terrified tribespeople, though for now most of the sand-grains were being deflected along the outside of the protective 'arrowhead'. For any normal sandstorm, these walls were always sufficient protection. This demonic hurricane was a more serious threat.

At one point, one of the poles supporting the protective canvas defences snapped in the teeth of a ferocious snarl of the gale, and it took many men to replace it, but not before a great buttress of sand had piled through the breach in the wall.

Soon, even the men had to take up huddled postures, as they could no longer stand in the increasingly frantic, malicious blasts of the tempest.

******

I was still aware of the manic blizzard, but its stinging ceased: it seemed that Akhman and I were inside the vortex, the spiral of malice. I struggled, but the struggle was not physical, or even mental. It was a struggle not to struggle; to seek myself in relation to the struggle; not to allow 'Kip Blacksmith' to push forward, but to remain at one with the chant.

At times, it felt that the protective diaphragm of song was being pushed from behind by Kip's (ie. 'my') desire to do something heroic, and from in front by the evil intent of Falseface/The Shifter/Mauhin. I felt like a tightrope walker, delicately balancing on a slender support. The blackness of the sandstorm seemed to kindle into a glow, a red shiver, snaking between the sand and stars. The ripple of its turbulence became my own pulse, thumping at my temples. It seemed like only a matter of a few moments could pass before I and the chanting resistance and the whole place would be overwhelmed by noise and chaos and death.

And then, there was silence! I was suddenly aware of being Kip again. I waited, my senses straining for some clue as to what was happening. Nothing stirred. The babies were not crying. Were they buried, interred within barrows of suffocating sand? Why did Akhman not do something? I was agonising over what to do when I heard a satisfied grunt.

"Hmm! It is done."

I pulled apart my storm-mask. We were facing a high bank of sand, where before there had been an expanse of flat desert, but the bank split a yard ahead of us and followed the line of the canvas walls, leaving a small, miraculous space where we sat in front of the 'V'. The stars blazed from a clear sky; the desert air was still. I had no sense of how long we had battled with the onslaught of Mauhin.

"How long was our struggle, Akhman?"

"A moment, a century, forever."

I should have known better than to expect a straight answer!

******

It has been a sad time since 'The Black Blizzard', as the Tu Darshaq refer to it. Although it was evil magic, producing an illusory storm, people still suffered the consequences of what they believed was happening to them. Even though we managed to dig out the couple of dozen people who were buried in the fresh swells of sand, an old man and a baby did not survive their ordeal. They were blessed by the Desert Spirit while old Akhman chanted, and then their bodies were left on a high rock for the desert scavengers to eat. The Tu Darshaq do not hold the dead bodies of their people in the same regard as we do. I was deeply shocked by this, and spoke with Fadouma about it as she showed me how to sew repairs in the torn canvas sheets.

"They are shells, husks. But we do not cast them away like litter. They are returned to the desert, just as their little souls have returned to the Great Desert Spirit."

I must have looked solemn, or at least thoughtful, because Fadouma broke into sparkling laughter, as she generally does if I seem unduly serious (which, according to her, I do quite often!)

"Besides," she added with a down-to-earth practicality which left me nonplussed, "if we did bury our dead, how long would they remain concealed in the ever-shifting sands?"

I have felt great guilt about the tribulations I have brought upon these tribesfolk by my presence, so much so that I suggested one evening to Akhman that I should continue my journey alone.

"It is very considerate of you, Kip Blacksmith. But Mauhin is not just your enemy.

He is against us all, and we must work together against him. Besides, you are not ready to face him alone. Not yet."

******

My prose translation of:-
AGOUTI'S 'SONG OF THE BLACK BLIZZARD'
A black wind, a red snake, a yellow shroud:
They came together, sharing a name.
The people crouched low and waited
Whilst their emissary flew into the storm's heart.
There, he saw that the name it brought was 'Death';
But his stillness and his song meant that
We only heard the name as a whisper. Then, once more,
Clear nights full of stars, and the great Desert Spirit
Refreshing as water from a deep well of silence.

******

I am still deeply grateful to Mr Sloethwaite for his lessons, the fruits of which have been invaluable to me on my journey, but these people make me see my learning in a new light. I thought that my knowledge from books made me somehow superior to my fellows who could not read. I see through Agouti that this was a very naive and oversimplified notion. He is illiterate, and I state this as a description, not as a judgement. His ground, his medium, is the oral world. After each significant phrase pleasingly turned, or view-shifting metaphor, he will pause o allow the words to resonate in a moment of silence, and be considered or appreciated by his companions in the oral tradition, who in their turn have learned to listen as well as to speak, and to recall from deep memory, and who acknowledge and respect the breathing spaces between people.

REEDMOON
(October 28 - November 24)

'I saw pale Kings, and Princes too,
Pale warriors death pale were they all.'
John Keats

'My lament of longing has lasted
Since I was cut from the reed-bed.'
Rumi

The reed used in thatching is emblematic of established power, since a house is not properly completed until its roof is in place. This sense of established power was recognised in ancient times, when the reed was a symbol of royal power and sacred to Osiris.

Reeds are ready for cutting in this month.

During the Reedmoon falls the fourth and final quarter day, known as Samhain: the last fire represents the Festival of the Dead, the honouring of ancestors.

Chapter 12/ REEDMOON

It has been a difficult month, as I have been assailed by waves of homesickness. Often, it has seemed to me that what I had with my home, and a family business that I would inherit, as well as the community I've known since as far back as I can remember, is all I really want, and what I desire most is just to go home. When the wave comes, that's all I feel. At other times, I relish the adventure, its new sights, culture, excitement, friends. The novelty of it all is invigorating, so I can cope with the bouts of yearning for my past life.

But there is another sort of nostalgia: a true nostalgia, if you like. It has increasingly pulled at my heart this month, as if brought on by the other pangs. I can barely describe it, except to say that this homesickness is every bit as sharp as the ordinary type, and that the place I feel the longing for is no place I can picture or describe, yet I somehow know it and yearn for it more deeply than anything. What is also strange is that some instinct seems to tell me that going home to the forge would take me away from this indescribable place that I cannot remember, yet miss so deeply; and that the journey I am on which is taking me further away from what I have known, is paradoxically the way towards this other place, this home that I do not know, that I cannot remember yet cannot forget. None of this makes any sense to me, but it's how I feel.

Anyway, looking back otherwise over the month, I am amazed at some of the sights I have seen. Amazed and humbled. This moon-of-the-reed, we made for the Winter Pastures, where the Tu Darshaq pause for several weeks and let their animals rest and gain condition, though it's a hard ride, and it culls not only any weak animals, but also tribespeople. This might appear criminally harsh, but it would take too long to skirt this arid land, beyond which the winter thorn pastures lie. Besides, the detour would be worse, through land which is fiercely inhospitable: glaring rock floors without any vegetation, steep inclines and fearsome precipices. So, the tongue of desert is chosen and, though painful, unforgiving and even, in some cases, fatal, it is an accepted element in their way of life.

Also, I am told that the desert way is eased by something like an oasis, but the tribesfolk seem very secretive about it, except to mention somewhere they call The Valley of a Thousand Thresholds.

After about a fortnight of relentless desert journeying, I spied an alteration in the landscape. Instead of endless dunes, the ground flattened out and became harder: more dust and fine shingle than yielding sand. Also, unexpected sheer granite cliffs appeared like a mirage out of the shimmering distance, and hemmed us in on either side, so that we were making our way through a gap about half a mile wide. However, the gap was not empty, but contained islands of sandy stone with their bases eroded by the desert winds so that they were sculpted into many fantastic shapes, like ornate staddle-stones. These formed a maze of blind alleys, a labyrinthine pass in which anyone but the initiated would become hopelessly lost. Agouti told me there were at least a thousand alleys, but only one passed right through, it being known as The Footsteps of Aramata, after the dry, hot, dusty wind which had gradually, persistently clawed its way through this closed door of sandstone between the granite walls. Annually, at this time of year, it takes about a week for the Tu Darshaq tribe to make its way through this pass, and somewhere in the middle of it, Agouti informed me, was a resting place. Traditionally, they stayed in one particular blind alley in which water rose in a spring surrounded by vegetation; one small, green gorge hidden from the sun's glare by its precipitous walls, in the middle of a stark, sweeping desert.

How they knew where to turn I do not know, for all the junctions wore the same aspect to me, and I could not even tell the difference between a forking alley and the main way! However, one day we turned into a shadowed cleft which jinked like a dog's hind leg, and there it was! The sudden, narrow, unaccountable greenness. It was backed by a granite wall which showed we had followed a tangent as far as the enclosing main cliffs, but the side walls were composed of the sandstone which formed the alley. This secret cell of moist verdure makes this route possible, which would otherwise be unthinkable, so it is called The Spirit's Well, in recognition of the bounty of the Desert Spirit.

In the middle of the space is a lake, fringed with reeds, and the bush-covered land around it slopes gently towards the cliffs, so the whole structure is like a gigantic trough. The sandstone cliffs are pitted with caves, and both these and the granite walls are covered in paintings, some of them centuries or even millennia old, showing many beasts which I have never seen, but only heard of: antelope, rhinoceros, giraffe, woolly elephant. Also painted on the walls was a strange script which Agouti could not read, but Ussa could; it seems that the Tu Darshaq written language is kept and studied only by the tribe's scholars. This is not considered 'fair' or 'unfair' by the tribespeople; it is simply accepted as the duty of those on whom it falls to maintain and deepen the written word, just as it is the duty of the oral bards, like Agouti, to foster and nurture the spoken and sung tradition.

Ussa showed me some flowing script, which he called Old Shaqi, and pointing to a piece at the end, which for all I knew might have been a word, he said, matter-of-factly: "That is my family name. This was written by my ancestors a thousand years ago."

The very air of this ravine, though clean and fresh, seemed undisturbed by the passage of time, and I thought of the pride with which my own family back at home told of our nearly three centuries of smithing at the forge in the village of Straight, and I smiled to myself, and bowed my head at the scale of things.

******

We eventually came through the maze and reached a small pasturage where the animals could feed and drink in preparation for the final effort towards the Winter Pastures. It was during this period of the journey that I began to feel the rhythm of Tu Darshaq life as a part of me, though I cannot entirely relax into it for fear of being caught off my guard when The Shifter makes his next assault, as he surely will. Even so, I readily acknowledge that I am no match for his guile and power, and he catches me by surprise despite all my efforts.

******

One day I was given the task of watching the flocks. We were settled for the grazing by some thin thorn pastures. It was very peaceful, sitting on the high ridge, overlooking the encampment with its activity and its campfire smoke-plumes drifting between the honey-hued desert and the silver-green shrubs where the scant vegetation grows. How the goats and camels find enough sustenance, I don't know. These hills are hardly the emerald pastures of the Donney Valley, or the verdant turf of the Cromber Downs, but the creatures seem to survive and, indeed, thrive!

There was very little sound: just occasional voices from amongst the tents below, clunking chimes from the bells on the goats, the echoing mew of a lofty bird of prey lazing vigilantly on a thermal.

After sitting for an hour or so, I found that I was quite relaxed, and there came to me the words of Akhman when I asked him how he found the water in the desert:

"Become still in your body." Well, I'd just spent an hour more or less inadvertently doing that! "Become still in your mind. Invite the Desert Spirit to enter you." I thought I'd give it a try. After all, there was nothing else to do, and it would be a couple of hours before anyone came to relieve me. As I was a little self-conscious, I found a hollow just over the crown of the rise where I could still spy almost the whole of the herds over the dusty rim, but not be in full view myself from the encampment.

I found that 'stilling my mind', as Akhman calls it, is much more difficult than sitting still. I kept thinking of things: what my journey held in store, how my mother and father were, how Maddy was getting on: all sorts of nonsense besides.

About half an hour or so had passed when I heard a sibilant whisper. For a moment I thought it must be a snake, but immediately knew that this was not the case. Then it came again, and this time I could distinguish a word, a name, but the recognition caused my blood to run cold.

"Kip!" Someone was whispering my name, a voice with which I was utterly unfamiliar. Surely this had only one explanation. I took a deep breath, gathering myself, and then opened my eyes.

A man sat just a couple of yards away from me, staring intently at me with wild eyes. He was impressively dressed, in cashmere robes and silken, embroidered head-cloths, and bore himself proudly.

"Go away, Mauhin," I sighed, with as much nonchalance as I could muster. "You do not frighten me, and I am not going to be diverted by your tricks," I asserted with what was a deal of false courage, since I actually felt stiff with terror!

He laughed at the sky, a big, open-mouthed laugh, full of glistening, white teeth, his head thrown back. Still he remained, slung between his legs in an easy crouch which told of a lifetime of campfires and nomadic life. He shook his greased, black plaits and they tumbled like dark cataracts about his jawbone, cheeks and temples. There was something of a wild creature about him, something almost elemental. "No, Kip. Even I do not claim the powers of Mauhin! I have other concerns, more immediate. Also, I have many spies, and what they have been telling me about you convinces me that you could be very useful, both to me and to yourself."

"So who do you say you are this time?" I questioned, sceptically.

"I do not know what you speak of, 'this time'. Do you mean on this turn of the wheel of life? I am Prince Qusah. I am a warrior."

"Are you Tu Darshaq?" I enquired, even though he looked different to anyone I had met.

"I shall forgive you that insult, since you are a stranger and know no better. I am a prince, and ruler of this region of desert; no-one has the right to pass through without my assent. These Tu Darshaq (he spat on the ground as if the very name carried an unpleasant taste) are impudent goatherds who treat the desert as if it were all their own. They will be taught a lesson; my patience has ended."

It was true, I knew from Agouti and Ussa, that there was no organised nation on the island of El Ilam-Coram, but independent tribes and settlements who made various and occasional alliances when a mutual need arose, and as quickly turned to curse and threat.

"But you, Kip. You interest me. You come from afar with knowledge, learning, contacts, courage, ambition. I could make good use of these attributes and, in return, a position of some influence could be found for you.

"Within a year, the whole desert region will be under my aegis. Following that, the mountains. Once I have control of the trade routes, the ports will soon bow to my authority. You see, Kip. It is a long-laid plan that is coming to fruition, and you could play an important part in its realization. If you do well, you could become....what? What would you like to become, Kip? Ambassador? Governor?"

He smiled a cold smile, but his ferocious eyes were unquelled.

"No," I replied, "my friends down there w-."

"IF!" he interrupted with a snarl which immediately altered

to a half-smile as he continued quietly, "If you agree, then we can, for the time being, leave the goatherds in peace. On the other hand, should you spurn this opportunity, then I might have cause to, er..." He searched for a satisfactory phrase, "... to remove a few obstacles." His sleek, sombre brow flickered with ominous meaning, and he turned his gaze onto the 'obstacles' going peacefully about their quotidian business in the thorn pastures below. "Consider well. Tomorrow I shall return with a few friends for your answer."

******

The following day, we sat at breakfast. I had kept my meeting with the 'desert prince' to myself, though I was in a torment of indecision. Something in me knew this offer to be just the latest bribe of The Shifter, albeit backed this time with a deadly threat, rather than sweet words: last time it was a merchant's wealth, this time a prince's power. Yet, simultaneously, something else in me longed after the ludicrous pictures of Governor Kip reclining on cushions, issuing orders, riding into Miyan on a white stallion in great splendour. I tried to persuade myself that I had as much right to these as anyone. At the time, it did not occur to me to question who within me was attracted by these temptations, and who within considered the grand pictures to be ludicrous; or who, indeed, was attempting the persuasion on whom? I glanced furtively at Ussa, who sat next to me, and then back at my hummus and flatbread. I was just returning to what I thought was my secret inner debate, when Ussa spoke.
"Something troubles, Kip."
I started sharply, but almost as soon as a feeling of disconcertedness and embarrassment welled up inside, it was superseded by a sudden resolution to speak what was on my mind, as if Ussa's perspicacity had released something in me.

"Yes, Ussa. I believe that Falseface came to me yesterday, whilst I was watching the herds."

"What! And you said nothing?!"

"I'm sorry, Ussa. He said he was Qusah, a desert prince, and promised-."

"Qusah!" exclaimed Ussa, with a contemptuous snort. "That is not Mauhin. Qusah is much less than Mauhin. Even a true prince would be much less than Mauhin, and Qusah is no true prince. Yet his name in your language means 'relentless', 'without mercy'. He fancies himself a warrior, a figure of noble desert blood, but he is no more than a vain, presumptuous bully. We call him Muta-Azim: 'The Arrogant', 'The Upstart'. His attack will be more conventional than Mauhin's, but we shall need to be ready in order to repel him. He has a large band of followers."

******

Understandably, I was sent to do some mundane camp jobs, whilst defensive preparations were made against an expected attack by Muta-Azim and his marauders, who took advantage of the loose-knit structure of the desert society to seek opportunistic gain. Whilst Akhman holds a position of respect and even awe in the Tu Darshaq tribe, to me Ussa seems to be their natural leader. He has organised everything, just as he took charge of arranging defences against the sandstorm.

He seems to hold no grudge against me for my spineless prevarications, which left so little time to prepare for the attack. As we watched the hills together from behind the barricade, he said:

"It is lucky that you mentioned your meeting with The Upstart, as we now have well-prepared defences to repel the false prince."

"I can see nothing but this barricade," I replied, thinking it a poor defence against an attack.

Akhman, who happened to be passing, raised his veil from

his chin and spat on the ground.

"Muta-Azim! He does not know the Spirit of the Desert. All he sees is Territory."

He twisted his sandalled foot on the place where he had spat, and walked on. I, for one, was glad that it wasn't my name associated with that maledictory gesture!

As the sun sank below the horizon and the land seemed to absorb shadow, desert birds began to call in the uplands, and crickets stirred into their steady, constant chirrup. I kept waking with a jolt of my dropping head to realize that I had dozed off, but when I glanced at Ussa he was always watching the hills, vigilant as a hawk.

Suddenly a whistle, a sigh, and a thud. Shimmering into motionlessness, not a yard from where we stood, was an arrow! After the first shock I noticed that a piece of parchment or rough paper was attached to the shaft of the arrow.

"Knowing what I know of the false prince," Ussa remarked, "that will be a message for you. If you care to remove it, I shall translate for you."

Having cast a cursory glance over the missive, he returned his scrutiny to the direction of the threat.

"Muta-Azim, may the Desert Spirit teach him humility and understanding, says have you reached a decision yet on the matter you discussed with him?" Ussa spoke without removing his eyes from the ridge.

"Go to Hell!" I screamed into the dusk air. This may have had more to do with bravado and a sudden flush of heroic idealism, because Ussa raised his eyebrows quizzically, as if I had not employed the most effective tactics, and nearby tribesmen sighed and murmured to one another.

A rider on a long-maned white horse appeared over the hilltop and rode to within twenty yards of our defences. He looked, I have to admit, very princely in his arrogance and self-possession, if a little rougher and wilder than you might imagine royalty to be.

"Kip!" called the rider. "It is I, Qusah, Prince of the Desert. I admire your youthful courage. I would expect no less of you. Join me now, and I will spare your goat-herding friends and allow them to pass freely through the island as they wish."

There was a significant pause in which the corollary of his statement hung in the air, ominous even while unspoken. However, he could not resist spelling out his point.

"Refuse... and I shall order my army to wipe out these impertinent rustics, before taking you to fulfil the role that awaits you. A great future, Kip. I look forward to making use of that fine, educated, Northern brain of yours. Best it does not drip with the blood of your friends, do you not agree, Kip?"

I looked at Ussa. He returned my look with expressionless eyes: no fear, no anger, no imploring. How, I thought, could I bring such a fate upon my friends? Death, destruction, misery, pain. These were peaceful herdspeople, craftspeople: artistic, sensitive, spiritual. I could not be responsible for bringing this upon them, so I began to clamber over the makeshift wall.

"Kip!" Ussa whispered urgently. "We are all on this journey. This is not something that you are bringing on us. Everyone is on it, whether they realize it or not! You are not on your own."

I looked deep into his eyes and I saw that what he said was true. I also saw that, besides his quietude and down-to-earth efficiency, there was also suffering, and I saw in that second that without this suffering there can be no understanding. How I understood this I cannot tell, but it made me step back and shout out again beyond the barricade: "I am not interested in your bribes and threats." Then a thought occurred to me, and I added, "Muta-Azim!" I used the name intentionally, and I saw it sting, though when he spoke, Qusah had recovered his composure.

"A pity, Kip," he called quietly. "I shall try and knock some sense into you later, after this next necessary business." He glared at us, and even over the distance of twenty or thirty yards, I could feel the power and animosity of his falcon eyes. Turning his white horse with its lilac and silver saddlecloth, he rode casually, nonchalantly, back over the ridge, as if he was to emphasize that he was in no hurry to despatch the 'obstacles' in his way, and would choose his moment.

"How do we combat the arrows, Ussa? You only have curved blades."

A few yards away, Agouti sang under his breath:

"Tu Darshaq warriors fear no enemy.
They fight with honour and courage
When the hour falls...."

"We are not as simple as the false prince believes us to be," replied Ussa in answer to my question. "You have seen that we are not just country bumpkins! We converse with the Desert Spirit, and we fashion silver; our silver is probably what 'The Impudent One' is worrying us for now. Also, we contain lightning and thunder, and release it at will. We can hold distance, and draw it close to our sight. We can draw in sea-mists and cast them about the desert hills. If, as you say, he is intending to try and draw the whole desert under his authority, then it is time that Muta-Azim was taught a lesson."

By now, hundreds of threatening, heavily-armed horsemen had appeared on the ridge, and they were joined by legions of archers, maybe a thousand.

"The Pale Warriors," whispered Ussa.

And I could see why they were so named, for their faces were smeared with a pale taupe-coloured paste which gave their countenances a deathly pallor, and they were all dressed in muted tones, and the horses were white or roan or grey.

I was just facing up to a sense of foreboding at the fate which must await my nomad friends when, in a line along the rough pastures, about halfway up the rising ground towards the ridge, there was a series of muffled eruptions like ocean waves exploding on a rocky shore from which there emanated growing plumes of mist, which spread

out and created a curtain between us and the ranks of warriors. There was a wave of consternation among the cavalry and archers as they disappeared from our sight in the mist. A further series of detonations told that the process had been repeated along a line between the mist-curtain and the prince's army, doubtless enveloping them in a swirl of blinding confusion. Then there was yet another series of explosions; from the evidence of the volume of sound, it must have been from just behind the line of warriors!

Already I could hear much shouting and consternation amongst Muta-Azim's troops; but then a huge single explosion occurred, like a thunderbolt hitting the earth just ahead of the clouded stumbling and shouting of the warriors. It was near enough to them to cause alarm, even panic, but far enough away not to cause any injury. Now there was fear: screaming men, horses whinnying and bolting.

After half-an-hour or so of the sound effects of mayhem, I saw some shadowy figures approaching out of the hanging mists. They were a group of Tu Darshaq warriors with scimitars in their belts, one of them leading a white horse. In their midst was the false prince himself, being led as a prisoner, and looking resentful and uncowed. Somehow, the Tu Darshaq had brought off a complete and effective victory without any fighting having taken place. Qusah's army had evaporated into the hills.

"Sometimes, wits can be more powerful than an army," Ussa commented.

I learned later that the little thunderbolts were caused by a percussive detonating powder, which the Tu Darshaq have knowledge of, but which is not generally known in the world, and certainly not on my home island. There is yet more to these new friends of mine than I ever dreamed of! We have travelled now for a week or more with the false prince as our prisoner. He is surly, and behaves like an untameable beast. It is intended to hand him over to 'authorities' in the next large town: a great prize for them, as he is an acknowledged threat to the peace and stability of the whole island.

******

I asked my friends about their strange thunderbolts and mists one midday rest-time as I sat drinking an aromatic tea with Agouti, Ussa and Fadouma.
"Was it Akhman?" I asked. "Can he control the weather?"
They laughed at this notion.
"No," replied Fadouma. "It is just the application of the mind. We are very inventive people."
She proceeded to explain about the thunder-and-lightning powder, and also the mist, which is some sort of ice-gas, I think: I didn't really understand all they told me. When this gas comes into contact with the air, it turns into mist and expands rapidly. So they developed a method of containing it until it is needed, when it is released by igniting their storm-powder. Truly, they are magicians!
Fadouma then showed me several objects which she had been working on.
"She is our cleverest inventor, perhaps the most imaginative on the island," Ussa told me with some tribal pride in his voice.
I picked up a tube she showed me. In response to her instructions, I pulled at each end, and it extended to twice its original length.
"That's clever!" I laughed, genuinely impressed by the idea, as well as the skilled crafting which enabled one tube to fit exactly within the other so as to slide out when pulled, and otherwise to sit snugly inside. The tube was made of a dark, smooth wood, decorated on the outside with carved,

intricate patterns. Each end was stopped by a glass disc, one about half the diameter of the other.

"Point the large end at the hills and look through the small glass," Fadouma suggested.

I did so, and immediately withdrew as is a punch had been aimed at my head. The hills had suddenly leapt at me, but I looked and they were now back in their proper position. I checked the large glass to see how the trick was done, but it was just a plain disc of smooth glass. With great caution, I brought the tube towards my eye. As it came closer, I could see the hills in their right relation outside the tube, but within the tube I could see hillside bushes as if they were a few feet away.

By now, my companions were showing signs of great amusement. In fact, Agouti was rolling on his back and kicking his heels delightedly in the air!

While Agouti continued his uninhibited display of mirth, and Ussa, more restrained, simply smiled behind his veil and shook his head occasionally as if to retain self-control, Fadouma tried to explain.

"Now, you two! It's so rude to laugh at our guest and friend."

"But he looked so startled when he tried to look...." Agouti lost control again, held his sides and thumped the ground. Ussa snorted briefly and hid his face: though more or less silent himself, his quaking shoulders betrayed the fact that he was also seized by glee at my expense.

"Ignore them, Kip," soothed Fadouma with a pitying look at them. "I got the idea for my 'farsight' (the closest literal translation I can think of) from noticing how things change shape and size in water."

Ussa and Agouti were recovering their composures.

"I performed many trials, and discovered that regular natural laws were at play. Then, in a flash- The Desert Spirit often comes to assist long and strenuous effort- I realized that if I used glass as a sort of solid water, I could control its dimensions, and make the objects observed through it whatever size or shape I wanted. It was easy then to proceed to the idea of a tube where two glasses could concentrate the effects. Then, when you put the tube to your eye-."

Another explosion of laughter occurred, as Agouti was reminded of my startled surprise.

Fadouma pursed her lips in mock severity. "When-you-put-the-tube-to-your-eye," she repeated emphatically, a word at a time, with a simultaneous stern but indulgent glare at her comrades, "you can draw distant objects close enough for inspection. This can be very useful. For example, when you were taking your turn to watch the herds, someone was watching you. A safeguard," she added to counter my look of consternation and astonishment. "You remember Ussa's words when you first mentioned the camel back in Miyan? 'We must be vigilant.'

"So... you saw my meeting with Muta-Azim?" She nodded. "One of our scouts came close by and listened."

"I wondered how you had put all those thunderbolts and mists in place so quickly! But why let me agonize, and then pretend that I had forewarned you of Qusah's imminent attack, when you knew all along?"

This question simply caused a burst of laughter and kindly song from Agouti, accompanied by a spontaneous rhythm on his hand-drum:

" Kip is on a path, but doesn't know where he's going.
Then he asks why his guides help to show him the way!"

ELDERMOON
(November 25 - December 22)

*'Love alters not with his brief hours and weeks,
But bears it out even to the edge of doom.'*
 William Shakespeare

'A fool sees not the same tree that a wise man sees.'
 William Blake

The elder is the tree of doom, and has a long association in folklore with death. In Britain, it was always the belief that a baby kept in a cradle made of elder would die, thus the opposite of the birch (the traditional cradle wood) from the year's beginning.

It was also part of British folklore that to burn elder logs in the hearth would bring the devil into the house.

It is no coincidence that this is the thirteenth month, and thirteen is still regarded with suspicion, even in our sceptical, scientific days.

This month includes the Winter Solstice.

Chapter 13/ ELDERMOON

1st Eldermoon
There is to be a great wedding at the end of Eldermoon, when the year completes its cycle. Fadouma and Ussa are to be married! She asked him some weeks ago, apparently, but they waited till this moon to announce the news. The ceremony will take place in the middle of the four weeks winter rest, when the Tu Darshaq make camp on the well-watered pastures near the Asira Pass, which leads from the desert lands into the mountains. That time is about a fortnight away, and after that I shall have to leave 'The Village' and strike northwards alone on the next leg of my journey to Sahada and The Inward-Looking Houses.

The wedding will be the occasion of the year for the tribe, and it will fall on the Nameless Day, as they call it here ('The Day of the Mistletoe' on my home island)*, when it happens that the brightest star, known on El Ilam-Coram as Raffaj, literally meaning 'flashing radiance' (at home, it's 'The Hunter's Hound'), sits in the Asira Pass when viewed from the main spring of fresh water where the camp, by tradition, is made. It is the only day of the year when it does so.

******

(*It's worth mentioning here, I think, that the local calendar on El Ilam-Coram is also ruled by the moon, and matches the one I know; but, of course, they have different names and lore attached to their calendar.)

14th Eldermoon
Today, at last, we arrived wearily at the Winter Pastures and released the excited goats and camels to the thorn bushes and tufts of thick grass.

It is a fortnight till The Nameless Day, but naturally it is the chief topic of conversation. Fadouma and her women friends are busy making special clothes for her to wear from fabrics always carried for repairs and renewals, but adding particular touches. Agouti is composing a wedding song. He has also kindly allowed me the use of his tools so that I can smith a personal gift for my dear friends, using the special skills I have been learning from him to augment my own blacksmithing craft.

28th Eldermoon

Although he is always fettered, Qusah is treated well, kept in food, drink and company (the latter being partly expedient, so that he is always under guard, but also from genuine considerateness that a man must have someone to talk to if he wishes). Not that he seems to appreciate the company, as his surliness does not dissipate with the passage of time.

Today, Fadouma took a break from her wedding preparations and went to the prison-tent with the captive's evening meal. She has visited him several times a week in the fond hope of persuading him to a more honourable way, but he just spits out insults, being particularly galled, it seems, by the fact that the Tu Darshaq did not dare "to fight like true warriors in open battle" but defeated him by "smoke and sophism".

"It was not trickery," Fadouma insisted when, as usual, the resentful prisoner began his outpouring of bitter accusations. "We needed to defend ourselves, and we wished to do it, if we could, without taking life. So we used our wits and ingenuity."

"Ha! Your camel-traders and goatherds were too cowardly to fight, you mean. There's not a single warrior amongst them."

"You know your desert history, Qusah. You know that isn't so. Your view is spoiled because you see the world in terms of territory, power, self-glorification." Qusah looked hard into Fadouma's eyes, as if ascertaining whether she was capable of understanding him. Then, with whispered ferocity, and still holding her gaze, he replied.

"It is a harsh world. My family was wiped out in one evening attack by desert raiders when I was a child. I have always had to look after myself since then. It is not for self-glorification, but self-survival- or say, if self-glorification and seizing power increase my chances of survival, then I will use them gladly."

"But is this life simply about survival? Are we here just to survive? What is the point of that? Eventually, we shall die; and if we only lived to survive, what achievement was that? What have we heard; what have we given; what have we served?"

"Ah, keep your poetic philosophy and your sentimentality and compassion to yourself, tribeswoman. I do not need any of them."

Fadouma sat up, a fierce, desperate fire dazzling through her tears.

"You equate poetry and philosophy with sentimentality, and compassion with weakness. We see in them Truth, and a connection with our fellow beings and the Great Spirit of the Desert. It's not an evasion; it is a way of seeing the world, of being in the world."

They were becoming so animated that the perpetual guard came and sat nearby as a precaution.

"I do not doubt your sincerity, Fadouma," and this was the first time he had ever used her name, "I can see that blazing in you."

For a moment, a look was cast back at Fadouma from those dark, ferocious, hunting eyes, a searching, yearning, lost and starving look, full of imploring. Fadouma stared back, feeling at last some contact with this wild desert tribesman.

Then, moving so swiftly and deftly that even an eyewitness could not have said with confidence how he had done it, he managed to snatch the guard's dagger and grab Fadouma in one lightning-quick manoeuvre.

With the dagger's blade at her throat, he ordered the guard

to cut his ankle rope, which the guard did with his scimitar, not doubting the ruthlessness of the false prince..

"Well done, tribeswoman. Almost....almost, you began to convince me." He exclaimed, as if realizing that he had just come to his senses. "Ha! You are a witch! I believe you could have milking goats if I spoke with you for too long."

Next, he ordered the guard to precede them, clearing a way through the camp, and to prepare his horse for him. Qusah then followed the guard, still with the terrified Fadouma held close to him, the last rays of the sun shining menacingly at her throat where they caught the clean blade.

The white horse was prepared, the Tu Darshaq people stood at an unthreatening distance in shocked silence, the whole scene frozen, like a tableau, in tense anticipation and anxiety, and old Akhman, looking distressed and tired, turned away into a tent as if he could not bear to watch any more.

"Now, Kip!" Qusah suddenly shouted, and my name sounded to me like a betrayal, coming from his tongue. "You see who is ultimately the cleverest. Not your beloved goatherds, but the Desert King, Qusah!"

I noticed that he had promoted himself in his grandiose sense of triumph. I expected him now to throw his hostage roughly to the ground, spring onto his white stallion, and ride away leaving a wake of dust and victorious war-cries. However, he had a metaphorical knife to twist into the Tu Darshaq, following the humiliation he felt he had suffered from his defeat and confinement.

"But wait! What a prize I can take with me," casting a covetous eye at Fadouma. "A worthy queen for the Desert King!"

At last, the tortured Ussa seemed about to lose his composure. He started forward, but the knife pressed Fadouma's throat and she let out a stifled scream. Ussa froze.

"If you make it difficult, Ussa the Goatherd," the hawk-faced bully warned contemptuously and ominously, "I can always leave alone, and you can prepare for a funeral."

"My motionlessness is love for you, Fadouma," said Ussa quietly across the space between them. "It keeps you alive even on the edge of death's precipice." Qusah spat with contempt. "Poetry even now! Pathetic!" He edged backwards towards his horse, closer and closer to his escape and the ruination of the joyous plans.

What he could not see, but many silent Tu Darshaq could, was that each step also brought his bare feet nearer and nearer to a deadly white scorpion which had just sidled out from behind a stone. His horse saw it and whinnied, snorted, and showed its alarm in a wild eye. "Even my horse anticipates my escape," laughed Qusah, hearing the whinny, but not taking his eyes from the tribespeople.

The idea of the funeral seemed to have amused Qusah, and he settled on his most spiteful, vengeful and bitterly heartless notion.

"Hah! What am I thinking of? A goatherd for a queen! I shall take my leave, and you can be occupied with organising a slightly different sort of event than you were planning."

Was it just an empty taunt? Or would he have drawn the blade across Fadouma's throat? Perhaps her visits to his prison-tent might have moved him to spare her at the last. We'll never know, for at that moment he stepped back and the scorpion stabbed his heel. With a startled cry, the self-styled king of the desert dropped his knife and stared in disbelief as the scorpion scuttled back behind the stone. He knew that a sting from the rare white scorpion was fatal in seconds; already sweating and breathing heavily in poisoned pain and panic, he jumped onto his horse, which immediately galloped away towards the Asira Pass; but in the violet shadows of the desert evening, we saw him drop to the amber-coloured dust a couple of hundred yards away. When we reached him, he was already dead.

MISTLETOE DAY
(December 23)

*'The day that is no day calls for a tree
That is no tree'*
      Robert Graves

'Call for the robin-red-breast and the wren.'
      John Webster

*'Joy, health, love and peace,
Be all here in this place.
By your leave we will sing,
Concerning our king.'*
      'The King', traditional British folk song

The thirteen months, each of 28 days, equalled a year of 364 days. Following the Winter Solstice, that left a spare day which fell outside the astronomical year, and was, therefore, not ruled by any of the trees.

Traditionally, in Britain and Ireland, on this day, the wren was hunted, as it was the symbol of the Old Year/the Holly King (cf. preface to 'Hollymoon' chapter). The wren was actually referred to as 'The King' in this context (e.g. British folksong 'The King'). In British folklore, the counterpart of the wren/Old Year is the robin/New Year.

Being the time of the birth of the New Year (or, anciently, the Day of the Birth of the Divine Child), it was naturally linked to a plant that was a symbol of procreation, the mistletoe.

Chapter 14/ MISTLETOE DAY

from Kip's journal

If these were going to be joyous celebrations before, then the previous evening's events and emotions gave them an immediacy which was intoxicating.

Ironically, given 'King' Qusah's taunts about taking her to be his own bride, Fadouma was like a queen in her robes and scarves of halcyon-blue, the centre of attraction with her vivifying laughter and easy manner, apparently fully recovered from her ordeal, though I'm sure it will take longer to settle within her.

Both she and Ussa did me the privilege of wearing brooches that I had fashioned for them as wedding gifts: she as a clasp to hold the cobalt and russet shawls of silk to her blue marriage-robe; he as a badge on the front of his head-cloth.

There was a great feast of roast camel with quince, honey, goat's cheese, dates, figs, and herb teas. And, of course, there was music and singing! Fadouma and Ussa sat on cushions, framed by an arch of intricately carved cedarwood, which will be re-erected at the entrance to their marriage-tent as a symbol of their union.

Akhman blessed them; Agouti sang his ballad, and his tears flowed as he sang, so happy was he for his friends. We stopped to watch the star, Raffaj, coldly flashing in the narrow mountain-pass to mark the passing of the old year and the approach of the new. Akhman murmured an invocation.

And now I am lying in my tent, knowing that, after tomorrow's rest day, planning and preparations will begin for my departure in a couple of weeks. What a blessing fell upon me that day in a Miyan teashop when I offered to share my table with three strangers.

THE SECOND YEAR

BIRCHMOON

It is nearly a year since Maddy and I left The Forge. I scarcely can believe it! I wonder where she and Prunella are now. I have not put this question into writing before, but I am assailed daily with doubts and guilt concerning the transference of my unofficial wardship. It might have been a grave betrayal, or it might have been the best thing I could have done. Even now I have no idea which it was!

Fadouma announced that she, Ussa, Agouti and Akhman have decided to accompany me as far as the rock-town of Kayya, which is apparently the closest settlement to my destination. They feel that it is 'proper' that they go with me that far, and I am grateful for their support.

"It is some months journey yet, and we became part of your journey when we met in the teashop."

"You do me a great courtesy," I said, bursting with appreciation for the way in which these people are putting themselves out for me.

Fadouma laughed her usual easy laugh. "It is because we love you, Kip."

"Besides," said Akhman, in that contained way he has that seems almost as if he is speaking to himself, "as well as it being your personal journey, it is also everyone's journey. We are all called home."

Agouti grabbed his hand-drum and burst into spontaneous song. There were the characteristic rhythmic clicks and exclamations, and a burden to which he returned several times, though with these extempore creations, he never makes any attempt to

to rhyme, or even scan!

"We are all seeking water in the desert;

The spirit calls us to the deep well to quench our thirst."

******

SECOND YEAR: BIRCHMOON TO HAWTHORNMOON

Early after sunrise, farewells were made and the five of us set off northwards on the ever-rising ground that cuts through the rock-face, creating the Asira Pass.

My four companions turned at the last minute and watched the herds of goats, the browsing camels, the families and friends. I noticed Ussa's hand go to the 'farsighter' at his belt, then pause and just pat it as if telling himself, "No, the parting is done." I could imagine what he was feeling.

Then we turned into the golden rocks to begin several hours of unbroken trudging, leading a camel laden with the 'few supplies' that were considered necessary.

******

I keep wondering what Falseface is up to. What tricks does he have up his sleeve? He surely has some. Why is he so quiet? Or did Akhman achieve something special which has driven him away for ever? Ah, but I thought we might have seen the last of him back in the Hollymoon, and that was before Eqbir and the sandstorm! I will talk with my friends about it.

ROWANMOON
6th Rowanmoon

My nomadic friends showed me a small tree growing amongst boulders which, by eating a few of its berries, has an astonishing property of satisfying the appetite and providing ample sustenance for many hours, even when the berries are shrivelled on the twig.

As well as this, my friends are very skilled, wonderfully skilled, in living from the land. They find herbs and water, succulents as sweet and juicy as the melons I tasted in Qasaba; and they hunt with an almost magical efficiency, as well as compassion. I witnessed Ussa, having just captured a mountain rabbit, speaking to it, before killing it with a quick blow to its neck. In answer to my question, he said that he was asking its forgiveness, and thanking it, and the Great Desert Spirit, for its sacrifice and sustenance.

We sheltered from a terrific storm last night under a ledge of rock, from which grew several of the trees which grow the special berries. The lightning tore the air, causing huge ripping noises whose echoes bounced around the mountains, to be drowned only by the cataclysmic roars of thunder which followed.

We remained safe beneath the protecting ledge, and dry because no rain accompanied all this remonstrance of the atmosphere.

13th Rowanmoon

Returning from a firewood-foraging expedition with Agouti and Ussa, we came round a promontory of rock to see that Fadouma and Akhman had a campfire burning in the small depression (concave, but not exactly a cave!) halfway up a low cliff-face, which is our resting-place tonight.

We stood and stared. The rose- and lemon-tinted flames dancing in the dusk were striking, as well as comforting. Everything was still and calm, and this tranquillity was deepened by the serenading of the desert crickets.

"It is a delight to the eye!" observed Agouti in a respectful whisper.

Ussa and I nodded.

Agouti began to hum a tune as we resumed walking, and this melody seemed as natural a part of the short desert twilight as the deep cobalt sky, the first stars, the shadow of high rock darker than the dark of evening itself, the quiet tread of nomadic feet.

ASHMOON

'Paracelsus was left alone. Before extinguishing the lamp and going back wearily to his chair, he tipped the fragile ashes from one hand into the other, and he breathed just one word. The rose reappeared.' Jorge Luis Borges

SECOND YEAR: BIRCHMOON TO HAWTHORNMOON

I spoke with Akhman about the desert. We are up in the foothills of the mountains, which are dry and scrubby; still semi-desert, but well away from the ocean of seemingly endless dunes. However, this separation from what we have been so close to for so long seems to have sharpened my awareness of it. It still baffles me how such a parched, barren wilderness can be the source of such richness of culture as the Tu Darshaq display, and how Akhman detects a spirit in it. This led me to speak of doubts about my journey, or, at least, my destination. I cannot deny that I have gained a great deal already from my journey, but what can there be at this fortress which seems so valued by Brag and all the others; which is of such worth and significance that Falseface is prepared to make profound efforts to prevent me from reaching it? What nature of expedition am I on? Do I want to find it, whatever it is!?

Akhman listened to all of this with silent nods of the head, and a look of kindness in his eyes. When I eventually fell silent, he sat motionless and silent for a long while, till I thought perhaps he was not going to say anything about my questions.

Then, suddenly, he spoke: "Do not try to judge the Spirit by the World's measure, Kip." I was pondering this, and wondering what he meant by it, when he took from a bag at his side a desiccated plant. It was silvery grey and had what appeared to be a network of roots at both ends, except that at one end the 'roots' terminated in what might once have been tiny florets. It fitted neatly in the palm of Akhman's hand, and when he moved it slightly its colour seemed to change to a sandy-beige. As I looked, his hand closed round it and crushed it to a fine powder which he poured onto the ground with a tilt of his wrist.

"It is dust. It is gone."

I nodded, wondering a little what this had to do with the 'Spirit'.

He then took an identical dead plant from his bag, but this time also a small, stone jar with a tightly-fitting cork lid. He placed the dried relic in the jar and poured in water from his camel-leather bottle, then replaced the lid. We sat in easeful silence, maybe for a quarter of an hour, perhaps more. Then he removed the lid of the jar. I was astonished to see some sort of lotus floating in the water, in full bloom: robust, delicate, fragrant.

"The desert lily," said Akhman. "But if this beauty, this vivifyingness, was also within the first dry plant you saw, where did it go when I crushed the flowerhead?

You saw dust. You agreed the flower was gone. Was it dust: just dead, dry particles? Life's meaning is more elusive than the constantly changing dunes of the desert, and Truth is a mystery deeper than the beauty of a desert lily."

He put his hands in the respectful praying position of his tribe, and bowed to me, and all I felt I could do was to return the gesture.

ALDERMOON

This evening we were sitting by our campfire. Akhman sat a little way off, vigilantly watching and listening, as it was his turn to keep a look-out.

"Sometimes," I ventured, "I feel I could live the rest of my life in the Tu Darshaq way."

Fadouma laughed indulgently, but with an obvious appreciation of the suggestion that I loved them and their way of life.

Ussa said, "We are all nomads, Kip, whether or not we live in tents!"

Quietly, yet abruptly, Akhman interjected.

"Build up the fire!"

Without the slightest hesitation or query, Ussa and Agouti were on their feet and had sticks on the glowing heap. We all gathered several each of the club-like stems from a shrub which was known to burn very brightly but slowly, making ideal torches when you ignited one end and held the other.

SECOND YEAR: BIRCHMOON TO HAWTHORNMOON

Once prepared, we all sat close to the fire, facing out into the darkness in a circle.

"What is it Akhman?" asked Ussa.

"Rock panther," replied the old tribesman, and by the look of concentration on his face you could discern that he had invisible antennae sensing the dark spaces around us.

"Rock panther...," he repeated, then, "...Mauhin."

No sooner was the name off his breath than a snarl gashed the darkness, and a savage mask of fiery eyes and flashing teeth showed on the borders where night-shadow and fire-glow mingled.

We pulled our brands from the fire and Agouti threw some bundles of dry sticks into the small flames, which immediately sprang into a sizzling, crackling tumult of light and heat. The rock panther backed away a few feet, and other eyes flickered in the night beyond it. An ordinary rock panther, Fadouma informed me, would have considered that discretion dictated a dignified retreat at this point; but this creature, being The Shifter, suddenly rushed, spitting and growling and yowling. It slashed at Ussa with its claws before turning tail and disappearing into the shadows.

"He is just reminding us that he is here," observed Akhman.

"But why doesn't he just become something so overwhelming and kill us all, and have done with it?" I exclaimed.

"It's not so easy, Kip. To change shape uses much energy. And to maintain the new shape for more than a few minutes is deeply exhausting. Even more so if you are pitting yourself against an adversary who can do likewise, such as Akhman. He is the only one in our tribe with this rare gift. It is lucky we have him: he has the rare combined gifts of shapeshifting and wisdom. Neither the powers of darkness nor the powers of light have unlimited strength."

******

Falseface has made several more forays into our camp as a rock panther, but seems to fear a full attack in the presence of Akhman. We have kept our fires bright during the evenings, and take turns to keep watch throughout the night.

WILLOWMOON

All trace of the storms, wet or dry, has vanished, leaving our days and nights a procession of alternating gold and silver.

Last night, under a full moon which gave the landscape an incongruous hoary appearance, I tried in vain to explain to my companions what I meant by 'frost'.

However, the talk of clear nights and the shining moon reminded Agouti of an old Tu Darshaq tale, which he told us as we sat at our campfire.

Agouti's tale of 'THE MODEST MOON'

Once, longer ago than anyone can remember, the moon rose over the desert and shone down on the sands with a cold brilliance. She saw an encampment of Tu

Darshaq near the oasis town of Yar Khill, and called to them: "Look at me! Am I not beautiful? How serene the desert looks coated in my silvery light."

The desert whispered to the Tu Darshaq to ignore the moon's boasting: "If I were not here," the desert pointed out, "her light would fall on nothing, and would be invisible."

The Tu Darshaq bard agreed. (Agouti held up his hands and grinned widely, with his eyebrows raised, as if to say, "No, I am not boasting; the story says it was the bard. I am simply passing it on!"

The bard made up a story about the moon, and the following evening, when he knew that the moon was listening, he began to tell his story ("A story within a story!" said Agouti):

There was once a beautiful princess who lived in a palace in the oasis town of Yar Khill. She always dressed in silver cloth and white jewels. She looked in her mirror every day, and admired her beauty endlessly. (The moon thought that this tale must be about her, and settled down to soak up the adulation.) The princess looked in her mirror every day, admiring her beauty endlessly, until one morning she found her mirror cracked.

"How did this happen?" she cried out, ready to admonish and dismiss one of her ladies-in-waiting.

"It was none of your servants," sighed the mirror. "The weight of your vanity was too much for me to bear.

She cast the mirror out of the window, and it smashed to pieces in the courtyard below. However, she had no more mirrors, so she began to visit the palace lake; everyone saw her there each day, gazing into the till waters, until one morning she arrived to find that the lake had gone: it had dried to one final drop!

"How could this happen?!" cried the princess, angrily.

"I did it myself," sighed the lake. "The weight of your vanity was too much for me to bear, so I asked my friend, the earth, to open a crack, and I slid away."

The princess ran to the palace, weeping petulant tears of frustration. She stayed in her room and would see no visitors. She continually questioned her maids: "Am I not the most beautiful princess this land has ever seen?"

And she would be angry with them if they showed even the slightest hesitation to assent. Her face became sour in her vehemence, and everywhere, in every encampment, every oasis, every caravanserai, tales were told of the princess's lost beauty. The Sultan of Yar Khill, her father, shook his head sadly, and decided to teach her a lesson. (The moon, still listening very closely, began to feel distinctly uncomfortable. The bard's story was taking a turn she had not expected.)

Soon, the princess noticed that she seemed to have no sense of taste: all her meals had become bland, and she sent angry admonitions and demands to the kitchen. All to no avail. She became more and more irritable and moody, until one day she slumped temperamentally into her place at the table to eat a meal with her mother and father without any sense of relish or anticipation. Eating had become a chore, a tiresome necessity, which she endured simply in order to stay alive. With lustreless eyes and heavy heart she took her first mouthful, and exclaimed with joy at the array of rich and subtle flavours that blossomed on her tongue. Observing her ecstatic countenance, the Sultan enquired after her welfare, and receiving her explanation, he explained that, for the first time in days and days, he had allowed a little salt to be added to her meal. The princess stood up abruptly the back of her legs pushing the stool along the stone floor with a jarring scrape. "What is the meaning of this indignity?!" she demanded of her patient father. He looked at her sadly before answering.

"Salt doesn't say, 'I am salty'. Yet we all appreciate its qualities," was all he said.

The princess who, although vain, wasn't stupid, immediately understood, and dropped her eyes in shame. There was a pause of at least a minute, which felt to both of them like a hundred years, during which the princess struggled with her pride.

Then she spoke in the quietest voice the Sultan had ever heard her use: "Father, I beg your forgiveness. I see that I have been vain and foolish. I must follow the example of the humble salt."

From that day, the princess turned her attention from herself to other people: she became courteous to the poorest beggar, patient with her servants, considerate to everyone she met. Her humility and kindness became renowned throughout the land, and lo! the amazing tale of the princess's restored beauty was whispered in the shade of every tamarisk tree and the flicker of every campfire.

The storyteller looked up at the moon. She, abashed, ran behind a cloud; but never again was she heard to boast. The bard composed a song in celebration of the moon's beauty and humility, and ever after, when the song was sung, it seemed that a yashmak of cloud was magically available for her to hide her face in modesty- which she always did!

HAWTHORNMOON
1st Hawthornmoon

Coming over yet another of a series of ridges in this seemingly infinite semi-desert mountain region, I saw this morning a gigantic outcrop of rock. My four companions walked ahead, zigzagging through a dry valley strewn with boulders, where grew sage-bushes, cacti and other scrubby plants that I had no name for. After heading towards the

SECOND YEAR: BIRCHMOON TO HAWTHORNMOON

towering rock-face for a couple of hours, with it looming ever higher before us, we came to a stop within a stone's throw of the blank wall. My nomadic friends just stood motionless, as if in silent prayer; but they were not praying, because after a minute or so of this, Fadouma snorted into a burst of laughter, saying something to her compatriots so quickly in their native tongue that I couldn't follow her words. Then she turned to me.

"Well, Kip, after you!"

I looked puzzled.

"It is well hidden, is it not?" she laughed.

She proceeded round a large rock which stood only a couple of yards from the cliff-face, and as I followed her I was astonished to see an arched opening. This led into a tunnel, and we entered the inky darkness and made our way cautiously till I became aware of motes of light, and then slanting rays. We emerged into a place which caused me to gasp with amazement, like a child.

The cliff turned in at right angles on our right and left to form three sides of a quadrangle; straight ahead of us, the fourth side was a grazed hillside which rose to a ridge about a mile away. The enclosed land was bisected by a stream (the first I have seen since leaving my home island), which was diverted into irrigation channels for watering rice and rye, though it still flowed strongly enough into the rock-face we had passed through to power a waterwheel, before disappearing into cavernous depths beneath the cliff.

The three cliff-faces are pocked with holes- no, 'pocked' does them a disservice, for the holes are skilfully carved into arches on four storeys. Each level's openings allow light into the recessed terraces which act as streets. Set back within these hidden streets are the rooms, workshops, dwellings, cells, halls and other places which comprise the rock-town of Kayya.

Despite the heat of the day, the streets remain just pleasantly warm, and, as I discovered, the rooms mercifully cool.

We led our animals to the ground-floor arches, through which there was stabling, and where men and boys could be hired to look after your camels, horses and herds. After Ussa had bargained with a man, we climbed some steps which took us to the first level above the ground floor. Everywhere was quiet because it was early afternoon, and it was the custom to sleep, or at least to rest, in the midday heat. We found benches outside what Agouti said was the best teashop in town, and sat to rest our legs and await opening time.

3rd Hawthornmoon

This honeycomb of a town is fascinating! Agouti and Fadouma laugh at my wonder, and I laugh with them because I amuse even myself with my amazement. But everything is here, concealed within this secretive rock: homes, markets, meeting places, tearooms...

Today, we had just finished drinking tea at our caravanserai, which is on the top floor of the town, with its courtyard open to the sky, when Agouti sighed and said, " Aaah! Banyo!"

Fadouma, Ussa, and even Akhman murmured their assent, but I didn't recognise the word he had used. In response to my questioning look, Agouti just made a gesture which suggested that here was something I should not miss, and we went down to the ground floor level of the town, and into an opening which turned out to be the town baths!

Until this experience, I had thought that a bath was just a practical and occasional necessity, a cleaning job that you performed (when conditions dictated) in a tub before a hearty fire; but my friends approached this venture (at least it was a venture to me!) not only with all the relish and anticipation that you would associate with an imminent treat, but also the quiet awe and respectful self-containment (at least on the part of Ussa and Akhman!) proper to approaching something ceremonial, even almost

SECOND YEAR: BIRCHMOON TO HAWTHORNMOON

sacred! I watched carefully and tried to follow their lead. Fadouma's parting words to me, as she went to the women's half of the building, were: "Let yourself go, Kip!" First of all, we were given thick, soft towels of a luxuriousness I have never previously encountered. Then we walked down a passageway to a room, the walls of which were lined with pigeon-holes where all patrons footwear was left, before continuing down another passageway to a changing-room, where we undressed and wrapped our largest towels round our waists to form skirts of a sort, draping the smaller ones around our necks. It was disconcerting to see Ussa, Agouti and Akhman with bare heads and faces revealed: they seemed like people I had never seen before, until I looked into their eyes.

Next, we passed through an archway that began a short, barrel-ceilinged passage which led into a room where I stopped short and stared, open-mouthed, such was its beauty.

The walls and floor were entirely covered in decorated tiles, forming intricate patterns in a forest of chromatic and harmonious movement. There were tessellations of stars, diadems, shapes reminiscent of the children's windmill-toy, with its three blades on a stick, that travelling tinkers would bring to the village on their rounds. In the floor were set a number of receptacles full of water: just rectangular pits reached by steps, but all tiled like the rest of the room. A heavy and pleasant perfume pervaded the air.

"This is the Hall of Fragrance," said Agouti. "You may go to the hot and cold baths as you wish. They relax and stimulate the muscles."

******

After some time, we proceeded through another open arch and along a further tiled passageway, which opened into a room of even more astonishing beauty. Again, it was completely tiled: this time the patterns were a dazzle of crescent moons, roses and chrysanthemums; never quite pictorial representations, but images suggestive of these natural phenomena.

A fountain of heated water bloomed continuously from a central pedestal, on the edge of which you could sit and be sprayed by its hot rain. All around the perimeter of the chamber were recesses set into the walls where men sat and talked, or just sat with head back and eyes closed, relaxing in the sensuous awareness of their body.

The atmosphere was so sultry and steamy that, at first, I could barely breathe, but eventually, after occupying a recess with my three friends, I became more accustomed to it. I seemed unable to relax to the same extent as the tribesmen, however, so I looked around the hall. At one end of the hall, the recesses were overhung by a gallery supported on graceful pillars. The gallery itself was not open to the hall, but rose as a fretted screen of carved arabesques.

I was just beginning to count the moon-shapes in a nearby wall, when I remembered Fadouma's parting words, so I leaned back, closed my eyes, and let myself go into the Hall of Vapours. Then it was as if the tension in my muscles poured away with the perspiration, and a relaxation came to me that I can hardly recall feeling since childhood.

So soon, it seemed, I was called from this happy state in order to tramp once more to a perfumed bath, and thence to a hall named The Chamber of Tranquillity. This room was decorated with tiles bearing acanthus and other leaf patterns, and furnished with couches where we were massaged with scented oils before resting, dozing and eventually stirring, relaxed and rejuvenated.

Akhman seems particularly to have taken me under his wing since our arrival in Kayya. We walk out amongst the cultivated areas and groves of trees, and I talk about my feelings, thoughts and experiences in a way I have never even thought of doing before, but he just seems to draw it out of me and I speak despite myself. He listens and replies, usually in the form of searching questions that enquire of my motivations, and seem to direct me into areas of my existence that I was not even aware of before. Today, at his bidding, we sat by some rocks adjacent to a rye plantation, and became so still that I had the feeling that I was a wild animal, or even a part of the natural, physical landscape of these desert-mountains, a rock or a shrub or something like that. But most memorable was the way Akhman gazed at me at one point: a look so brimming with love and understanding that I almost wept; and I had the clear impression, quite distinct and unmistakable, that he was nourishing me, like a parent bird feeding its young, giving without qualification or requirement.

******

We were in a coffee-shop today: A cool, shadowy room furnished with cushioned benches and low tables. Agouti and Fadouma fell into conversation with some local people. Ussa is more taciturn than either of these two, who are out-going and easy-mannered. Akhman rarely converses much in social situations, but makes occasional observations, and does not give an impression of stand-offishness at all.

According to Agouti (the Kayya dialect is beyond my comprehension), the local people were talking about rats, which have suddenly begun appearing in noticeably larger numbers than is normal. The residents do not understand it; there has never been a problem before, and it is not the time of year when an invitingly full harvest-store might encourage an increase in the rat population.

Immediately, I smell not rats, but *a* rat: Falseface.

6th Hawthornmoon
More and more rats. Akhman says it is undoubtedly caused

by 'Mauhin'; he says that he can 'smell' him! I asked the old shaman how he was going to tackle The Shifter this time.

"I am not," was his surprising answer. "Agouti has the power to stop the rats. They are not Mauhin. He has simply caused them to be here."

8th Hawthornmoon

Agouti has been working hard, but I do not clearly understand what it is that he has been doing. He has stayed in a quiet room for two days, and all he will say when, at mealtimes, I enquire is that he is 'preparing' himself.

9th Hawthornmoon

Today, Agouti went to the elders of Kayya and offered his services.

Rats can now be seen openly running through the crops, along the streets, and in the premises and living quarters of the town.

I hope that Agouti can fulfil whatever promises he has made: the local people are beginning to panic and becoming desperate.

10th Hawthornmoon

Agouti took me with to a storage cave where bags of rye are stored. As we opened the doors and light broke into the cavern, I saw a swarming movement which dissolved into stillness before my sight: rats running for cover.

Now, I'm going to relate something that seems incredible, I know; but I swear that I witnessed this with my own eyes.

Agouti stood with his feet apart and his arms akimbo, head slightly raised, looking strong, defiant, imposing, more solemn than normal. Then he began to... he began to... recite poetry! It sounded like nothing special to me, and if I give you an admittedly unworthy-sounding translation, I assure you that very little has, in fact, been lost in the

transference:
'Rats teeth are blade-sharp,
But they can't play the harp.
Rats snouts are acute,
But the can't play the lute.
Rats eyes shine star-bright,
But they can't play the light.'
However, hidden somewhere in that modest doggerel there was magic, because something like a hundred rats immediately poured out from their hiding-places among the rye-sacks, and slid, like the earthbound shadow of a cloud, out of the town and away into the mountains!

14th Hawthornmoon *Late morning*
Agouti the bard has spent nearly a week wandering the town rhyming rats away!
He is a hero, and we other four, as his associates, are radiant with reflected glory. He is like a paladin from folklore come to save the people. There is great rejoicing, and tonight there is to be a feast to celebrate.

14th Hawthornmoon *Late!*
I am about to put out my candle and sleep, but I am troubled. The feast this evening was a joyous occasion. I was participating in the general atmosphere of celebration and deliverance, but realized at one point that I had not seen Akhman. I asked the others, but they just said that it didn't surprise them as Akhman didn't like parties.
I went to search for him, and found him by the rocks near the rye plantation. He was sitting cross-legged on the ground, looking out towards the distant white peaks of the mountains and, beyond them, the empty spaces of desert and the night sky. He was as still as the rocks themselves. I said nothing, but simply sat down by his side.
Akhman continued to sit still, absorbing from the far desert its heartbeat, its voice, its music, its desolation and consolation, its history, its ever-presence; he absorbed it

all, and was absorbed, like a crystal gathering itself to itself out of what we call 'nothing'. (You see that I have learned something from his lesson of the desert lily!)

We remained like this until the full moon rose over the rim of the world a century later, or so it seemed. It appeared twice or thrice its normal size and was a weird terra-cotta colour, which lightened to ochre, and then lemon as it climbed. Within half an hour of its rising it was as pale as elderflowers, and in another while it shone brilliantly silver. Only then did Akhman stir, as if awakening from a trance.

"Mauhin will come. He has been gathering his strength. Soon, very soon, Kip Blacksmith, you must leave. It is time. Take the road north, into the mountains. Watch for the cliff with eyes." He gave me further directions. "Your journey will require courage and perseverance, but remember what we have spoken of. And remember the wise words of one of your island's poets: 'That which purifies us is trial.' Yes, yes." He almost whispered his assent.

"Why do you give me directions? Will you not come?"

"You have forgotten what we said. I will not come. We will not come. This is your journey, though it is also everyone's. We have simply been your guides and fellow travellers for a while. You don't believe in yourself as yet, but you have hidden resources waiting to be discovered by you as you are tested."

16th HAWTHORNMOON

I feel unready to face what I have to write in my journal today.

When the vain princess in Agouti's tale realized her selfishness and stood before her father, the Sultan of Yar Khill; or when Akhman and I sat last night awaiting the moonrise: these were minutes that lasted centuries. Today, for different reasons, I have lived for a thousand years each hour a weight of misery and hopelessness.

Falseface came today, an embodiment of vindictiveness

and negativity. All the frustration of his failed attempts to deflect me from my purpose (whatever that might be!) fell with his gathered strength upon the rock-town of Kayya. There was hatred, resentment and spite abroad, to add to the physical terror that he brought. The moment has come when I must put down in words what I do not even want to think of. It was late morning; Agouti and Ussa were at the stables making arrangements for the final leg of my journey to The Inward-Looking Houses. They had said that they would obtain for me a few basic supplies, as I lack their skills in self-sufficiency. Fadouma, Akhman and I were drinking together at the tea-house. I was feeling self-conscious because I wanted to say worthwhile things during those last minutes with my friends; but, of course, I could think of nothing, so I kept on blurting out inanities, which made Fadouma laugh. Outwardly, Akhman seemed utterly calm, drank his rose-petal tea, and watched the passing world with interest and detachment. And yet there was an underlying wariness, an uneasy watchfulness, which belied his apparent nonchalance.

Suddenly, I seemed to be in the grip of an attack of dizziness. Was I ill? Then, I was on the floor: I must have fainted, or lost my balance. But strangely, Fadouma was sprawled by me; had she jumped solicitously to my side to reassure me? No; I saw tables and chairs tumbling all around me. I was disoriented and alarmed. Then a yell from Fadouma re-focussed my attention. "Earthquake!"

Immediately, with an alarm alien to his familiar reserve, Akhman cried, "Mauhin! He has come!"

He seemed instantly aware of a specific threat.

"Ussa and Agouti! We must go to them!"

Recovering our bearings, we rushed from the tea-house, and down to the stables, avoiding falls of rock more by luck than by design. We found them in one of the ground floor caverns that served as stabling. Two huge cracks had split the solid rock ceiling of the cavern, and Ussa and Agouti were helping to lead llamas, horses, mules and camels out to the comparative safety of the open ground away from the increasing cascades of dislodging rock.

As we joined in with the assistance, slabs of stone began to slide from the cave's ceiling, where seams were splintering and snapping, and they crashed to the floor as we went to and fro, leading the terrified beasts to safety.

Akhman stood in the centre of the stable, and seemed for a moment or an age to be motionless in the midst of the chaos and the shivering of the world. Then he shouted to us as we were about to gather some panicking creatures from the back of the cavern: "Leave now! I shall go to the desert spirit. Leave now!!" his voice resounded. There was a frozen pause from the rest of us, a moment of realization.

"LEAVE NOW!!!" roared Akhman, in a voice unlike his own, with a volume and tone that could not be countered, and in an instant he was gone, and there was a huge mammoth holding the weight of fracturing rock on its back like a living pillar.

Ussa decisively ushered us out, and we were barely on open ground before a primeval, thundering bellow, the source of which it was hard to fathom. Maybe it was the cliff from which the stable was hewn groaning as it gave way; maybe Mauhin hailing a supposed victory; or maybe Akhman himself in his monumental labour.

Then, with a cataclysmic quake, the whole internal structure of the cliff collapsed into the cavity of the stable, crushing the last few animals, and the great mammoth.

We stood, dazed, disbelieving. Then Fadouma let out a screaming sob and fell onto Ussa, who stood immobile. Agouti stared uncomprehendingly at where the stable had been, but it was now a mass of disjointed rock, with billowing clouds of dust swirling and settling all about it. The earth tremors ceased.

******

The town is largely undamaged. Falseface concentrated his attack where he wanted to do the most hurt, and achieved what he apparently set out to do, on this occasion at least. He was in mortal combat with Akhman. It appears to be a mortal danger to support me in my task, though I do not understand why, or to whom it so important that I be prevented from reaching my goal.

My initial thought was that I could not carry on now that Akhman was gone, but the others were emphatic that that would be a betrayal of Akhman's sacrifice. So now it seems starkly clear that it is my turn, that I must achieve what I set out to do, and to deliver the Thirteen Moons to The Fortress of the Inward-Looking Houses.

******

18th Hawthornmoon *from Kip's journal*

I am camped a day's walk north of Kayya. My progress today was relentless. I used walking, physical endurance, as a solace; something to do. Not only was I trying to cope with the death of my friend and 'guide', but also with parting from Ussa, Fadouma and Agouti. It was a solemn farewell. Ussa gave me pieces of practical advice; Fadouma fussed about me lovingly; Agouti encouraged me to be a fearless adventurer, so that he would have plenty of material for an epic ballad about my exploits! We drank together one last time in the serene, dark corners of the tea-house, and then the time to go was inescapable. I was moved because they seemed as reluctant as I was to part, but we hugged: Fadouma cried, Agouti's eyes glistened even as he smiled his ready, white smile; Ussa was calm, but the tightness of his grip on my shoulder gave away his emotion. And I, I was a tumult of feelings: grief, fearful apprehension, hopelessness, determination, elation, deep misgiving and dark melancholy; all jostled together within me.

Then all too soon I was walking away from the rock-town, along the dusty track between the crops, with a heavy pack slung from my shoulders, looking back towards the golden stone triptych which is Kayya, and at the three diminishing unmoving figures in their robes of cobalt, turquoise and black respectively, until I passed over a ridge about a mile from the town and lost sight of my Tu Darshaq friends for the last time.

20th Hawthornmoon
'...when a fight begins within himself,
A man's worth something.'   Robert Browning

'But I have that within which passeth show'   William Shakespeare

I have walked for a couple of days, always uphill. It is peaceful: the only sounds are the wind on my ears, the occasional lean mew of a bird of prey wheeling high above. My nomad friends assured me that Falseface would not make an appearance for a while.
"He is not the Great One," Ussa said. "He will need much time to recoup after such an expense of energy as was his earthquake."
So I have made as much progress as I can in the undisturbed calm of the mountains.

******

Today I came along the ridge known as 'The Spine'. It is terrifying. I have heard and read of 'dizzy heights' in conversations or books, but until today I had not had any experience of them. The ridge is about a mile long, and the ridge-path itself varies in width from barely a yard most of the time to about eighteen inches in several short stretches. This sounds a reasonable platform on which to walk, but seems grossly inadequate because of the fact that the rock-face falls away on either side for a thousand feet in such a precipitous drop that I continually had to force myself to look ahead. However, despite my efforts, the sheer precipices attracted my gaze again and again, and many times I had to stop and crouch and screw my eyes shut, because I felt my head beginning to spin, and feared that I would be drawn to plummet down the vertiginous depths. At the narrower sections, I actually went like a baby, on all fours, and all this meant that my progress was hampered, but at last, and with what thankful relief, I reached a point where the causeway widened.

23rd Hawthornmoon

I am resting after some days uneventful journeying. I have lost count of exactly how many, but estimate from the size of the waxing moon that it is about four or five. Ahead of me is the 'mountain-with-eyes'. Akhman assured me that I would know it when I saw it, and he was right. However, the striking feature had been indiscernible as my twisting path gradually looped around the skirts of the high peak. Now, from where I sit, they are plain and obvious, and also very curious. Someone, many ages past, has carved two great eyes over an area of flat surface. It is a strange decoration, quite disconcerting, and I cannot imagine what the artist or artists were thinking or feeling when they decorated the rock in this way.

Now, according to Akhman's directions, I must find a fork in the path close to a triangular rock.

******

I have made camp for the night. I found where the paths diverge, but I nearly missed my way, for this track is so little used that I wasn't sure for a while whether I was imagining a way where none existed. I was even about to turn back, but I seemed to hear the voices of my four companions encouraging me closer and closer to the mountain. So I kept going and, almost immediately, I encountered definite signs that this was a track that had been used by others: an old campfire of cold ashes, a shred of torn fabric on a thorn.

The next cryptic direction which Akhman had given me was to seek the Veil of the Vale. When I asked what to look for, he only said: "Some call it the Silver Door."

I shall eat and sleep and then, in the morning, I shall explore and consider my next move.

25th Hawthornmoon

It is lunchtime, and a day and a half since my last entry. Yesterday I searched fruitlessly. I have found what I am sure is the Veil of the Vale, or the Silver Door. The path was running along the foot of an extended wall of rock which rose vertically from the skirt of foothills and did not slope to any peak, but ended in a rough crenellation at about two hundred feet high, as if the top part of the edifice had been snapped off roughly. The cliff-face appeared to be impassable, other than by a long detour, but in one place I discovered a deep indentation, which I investigated, and it was in this hidden gap that I found what I was looking for: the Veil of the Vale is a waterfall!

I have decided to eat some of my black rye bread and dried figs before investigating the cataract. If this is the Silver Door, then it must open into somewhere!

******

Evening. I have just returned to my encampment after exploring. This is it!

Acting on the reasonable supposition that its name describes aspects of its character, I assumed that the waterfall hid something (Veil) and led somewhere (Door). So I climbed up close to it and discovered that the upper rock-face slopes out to form, as it were, a nose, and consequently directs the force (as we call a waterfall where I come from) out from the lower rock-face, creating a curtain of water behind which the lower rock remains relatively dry. Here, there was a cave entrance, above which was carved and painted an eye (though there was only the faintest residue of paint surviving). The eye was just like the ones on the 'mountain-with-eyes'.

So my next move is obvious: tomorrow I pass behind the Silver Door and find out what it is that the Veil of the Vale conceals.

26th Hawthornmoon

'this Birth was
Hard and bitter agony for us, like Death, our death.' T. S. Eliot

Well, I have come through, though after the vast, open spaces of desert, sky and ridge, today's ordeal was sorely trying. Indeed, there were times when I wondered whether I would ever be seen again! I shall attempt to set down my experiences.

After my breakfast, I lit a candle and began to explore the dark recesses of the cave behind the force. It was quite large: the roof must have domed about twenty feet above my head, and it began to taper down towards the back. However, from the flickering pattern of candlelight as I cautiously advanced, it became apparent to me by degrees that the taper extended into a recess, or even a tunnel.

I decided to explore, so I gathered my belongings and followed the tunnel which, gradually but relentlessly, narrowed and lowered until I was walking with my torso at right angles to my legs! Then I had to take to my hands and knees, in which position I proceeded with some difficulty, especially as I was simultaneously trying to keep aloft and alight my candle.

It soon became evident that my difficulties had only just begun, because the tunnel continued to contract, and I had to remove my pack from my back and laboriously push it ahead of me as I tortuously advanced. This became increasingly awkward, as I soon had to go from my hands and knees onto my stomach. I considered hooking my pack onto my foot and dragging it along behind me, but with so little room for manoeuvre I realized that I should be unable to reach it when I required any of its contents. At this stage, I had to make a critical decision: should I go on? Was this apparent tunnel just going to peter out into a dead end? Curiously, about the question of going on, I had no doubt; but I should have to proceed in darkness as I could not crawl on my stomach, push my pack, and carry a candle. In a way, this would be a relief, because I would not be able to see the various subterranean creatures that inhabited the cracks and crannies close to my face. I only had to hope that none of them would prove belligerent *and* poisonous. Shy and poisonous would be fine; belligerent but harmless would be nearly as acceptable. I blew out my candle, and wished that I could blow out my imaginings of awaiting perils as easily.

I could not gauge how much time passed as I made my restricted and sometimes painful way along the tunnel, but I guessed several hours had passed, with many rests and forebodings, before a strong impression came to me linked with the word 'candle'. I rested, pondered, and decided to light my candle in response to this impression. The lighting of it was made easy by some little fire-sticks which my Tu Darshaq friends had presented to me shortly before my departure.

As the light expanded into the narrow passage, and I became aware of my situation, I gasped. The impression that had come to me with the accompanying word 'candle' had obviously been some strange intuition, for the tunnel ceased its forward progress a couple of yards ahead of me and turned down at right angles to become a shaft. At the top of the shaft, where it met with the tunnel, the angle had been hollowed out to make a sort of rounded socket, thus allowing room to manoeuvre oneself in order to descend the shaft feet first. This also indicated to me that I was not the first person to use the tunnel; this angle was at least modified, if not created, by human hands. With great difficulty, I positioned myself at the top of the shaft, bracing myself with the soles of my footwear on the shaft-wall ahead of me and my back pressed against the one behind. My pack and lighted candle sat a couple of feet away in the tunnel, and I retrieved them gingerly, all the time struggling with the temptation to relax my muscles, which would, if I relented, instantly cause me to plunge into who knows what depths.

A voice inside was telling me to turn back, that once I started down the shaft there was no going back up because the sides were sheer and without foot- or hand-holds. I tried putting this thought of unknown depths out of my mind, because I was aware that, by attempting to climb down this well of darkness, I was putting myself in great potential peril. If the flue was a few feet deep, which my candle wasn't powerful enough to reveal, then there was little problem, beyond a small discomfort and a passing fear of the uncertainty. On the other hand, if it were so deep that I would become fatigued before I reached the bottom, then I was in serious trouble. All these considerations kept coming up in my mind, and I would keep forcing them back.

Inch by painful inch, I crept down in the pitch black, saving my candle: right foot down and secured; left foot down and secured; slide my back down the rear wall until I had regained the 'resting' posture which I held between movements. I say 'resting', but in reality the tension needed simply to maintain my position was such that I was beginning to shake with the muscular strain, and at this point my legs began to shudder violently and I felt a hopeless certainty that I was about to plunge to my death. I began to whimper, and heard my voice cry out for my mother, a sort of primeval plea for comfort and help. I took a long, slow, sobbing breath and stilled my panic, then continued my faltering progress down the shaft. Eventually, for what seemed the thousandth time, I stretched down my leading foot and could feel nothing to brace it against.

After a moment of new panic, I replaced my foot in the 'resting' position and considered the possibilities coolly. As I did so, I became aware of a change in the physical atmosphere: there was a draught of air different to the still, stale air I had become used to. It was clear to me that I needed to discover how far the shaft continued below me, so I removed a metal drinking-cup from the pack that I was awkwardly cuddling as I made my descent and, with a sigh and an invocation to the Desert Spirit, let it go into the blind abyss below me.

Almost immediately, to my utter relief, there was a clatter as the cup hit ground and rapidly bounced to rest. Next, I forced my pack down between my knees and heard it thud comfortingly in confirmation of my relative safety. I then felt around with my feet to help me form a mental touch-picture of my surroundings, and discovered that, of the shafts four sides, one (the plane ahead of me) ceased just below my feet, but so far as I could judge, the other three continued. Also, there must, I told myself, be a floor about six feet beneath me, according to the evidence of the cup and pack. I concluded, therefore, that the tunnel was taking another right-angled turn and resuming its original horizontal progress. I managed to shift and twist myself so that shaft-wall ahead of me, with its opening, was then on my left; this enabled me to continue my awkward descent until I reached the bottom of the shaft.

******

'Alas! I have nor hope nor health,
  Nor peace within nor calm around,
Nor that content surpassing wealth
  The sage in meditation found' Percy Bysshe Shelley

SECOND YEAR: BIRCHMOON TO HAWTHORNMOON

The relaxation as I sat there was blissful! I let my head drop between my knees in exhaustion and gratitude, sighing and letting out deep breaths of relief and utter thankfulness. There had been a constant voice in the back of my head lamenting, convinced I was going to die in that suffocating and seemingly interminable tunnel. Then another sigh emanated from me, this time with a different quality, indicating a sense of renewed resolution, for though I was grateful to be sitting in a dark pit deep in a heart of rock, this was only a promising position in relation to hurtling down a black shaft! I had to get on, so I lit my candle.

How can I describe the sight which met my eyes? I cannot do it credit, despite all of Mr Sloethwaite's tutoring. The visual aspects I could begin to relate, perhaps; but not the atmosphere, not the 'presence' of the place.

What I beheld was a cavern, and I was crouched in a recess below the shaft, like an inglenook fireplace at the foot of a chimney. Beholding, then stepping into, that space from my 'hearth' in that first flicker of candlelight was like being born, coming into a world through that black tunnel.

******

The ceiling of the cavern was entirely covered in paintings depicting planets orbiting, constellations processing in their courses, shooting stars: all silver and gold against a deep blue background. The walls were also completely covered in decoration, showing scenes representing the alternation of day and night, the progression of the seasons; and a frieze in thirteen sections, each showing the moon in its phases above a different tree with a few related symbols. It reminded me of the strange sphere that I carry. The painted cavern seemed to be a representation of the ever-changing nature of the world, the mutability at the core of existence; yet the cycles emphasized simultaneously and paradoxically that nothing changed! Indeed, at the very centre of the ceiling's night-sky was a single eye, and the artist had somehow skillfully lent it a look of suffering-yet acknowledgement; a compassionate gaze that seemed to me to say (and I don't know where I was getting this knowledge from or this relationship with the symbols) that although everything in the universe constantly altered so that there was grief in the heart of being, yet something existed that did not move on with Time, but watched it passing, and with its passing, ultimately, also the fading of remorse and yearning. These seemed to be very strange ideas even as I had them, but they came to me with a feeling of absolute rightness.

******

Eventually, what roused me from my awed contemplation of the tranquil, painted cave was the simple realization that I was hungry and thirsty. I sat in the recess and satisfied what is incongruously called 'the inner man'. Then I looked for, and quickly found, the exit from the cavern. I need not detail my continued progress; suffice it to say that there was a matching recess opposite the one I had entered by, and that above them were written the words 'Veil' and 'Vale' respectively. The exit-tunnel appeared to mirror the entrance-tunnel, and some hours later (though the outward journey seemed much shorter) I emerged into daylight, thankful to see the end of that particular obstacle.

Now I saw what it is that the waterfall hides: it is in the name! For I looked upon a landscape in the form of a bowl: the high, jagged ramparts, which I had just crawled through the heart of, curved round on themselves to form the rim of a gigantic bowl. The veil of cascading water at the entrance to the tunnel is an entrance to this concealed vale. Ahead of me, on the opposite side of the vale, the bowl's rim rises steeply to form a mighty rock-formation. I recall Akhman describing to me that this is where The Fortress is sited. I estimate it to be about two or three

miles across the intervening vale, which is greyer and greener here than back in the lower foothills.
Beyond and above The Fortress, towering into the distant, thin atmosphere of sky and ice-wind, are the glistening peaks, the formidable and forbidding granite horns of the sacred Mount Matluj, and the angled, white purity of the glacial fields.

27th Hawthornmoon
I have crossed the vale, but what faces me now, practically at the walls of The Fortress, is yet another great difficulty. This place I am headed for is certainly no place for the faint-hearted!
As I sit writing this journal, I am looking down on something that wasn't apparent to me when I gazed across the vale: it is a gorge which must be at least five hundred feet deep, about a hundred and fifty across, and its sides sheer. I can see, but barely hear, a torrent thrashing down its bed. The walls of The Fortress rise up directly and dizzyingly from the ravine-side, and are marked with a few dark openings, possibly windows, but it really appears at first glance to be a continuation of the rock-face.
There is a bridge across the gorge, but describe it as a bridge is an exaggeration.
Tied to some short, stout shrubs, and strung out across the sickening depths of the gorge, there are three ropes: one for the feet, and two above forming hand-rails, as it were. This minimal structure is all there is to cross this awful chasm! The Spine Ridge caused me bouts of vertigo; I am not sure how I can cope with this rope-bridge over the
yawning fracture that mesmerizes me even from my present safe distance.
(Evening) I've decided to sleep on it and then make my attempt tomorrow.

28th Hawthornmoon *About noon*
I awoke at first light full of resolve. My morning has been

spent watching my determination rise and fall, but rise a little less each time so that it has gradually dissipated. I have used every argument, every persuasion, every castigation, to get myself across the gorge, but to no avail. Each time I grab the two rope-rails and place my foot on the foot-rope, I find that I have used up all my courage getting to that point. My knees go weak, I shiver, my head swirls, and I break into a cold sweat. I really don't think I can possibly get across. This is a crisis, even without the attentions of The Shifter. I keep trying to shame myself onto the rope-bridge by telling myself of Falseface's delight at my weakness, but so far without success. I am distraught. To have come so far only to fail within sight of my destination. I feel quite without hope, and utterly exhausted.

******

DOCUMENT DISCOVERED AMONG KIP'S PAPERS AND TRANSLATED BY HIM INTO LOCAL IDIOM: A DESCRIPTION WRITTEN BY AN OCCUPANT OF THE INWARD-LOOKING HOUSES FOR KIP, TO REMIND HIM OF HIS BATTLE WITH HIMSELF AT THE ROPE-BRIDGE, WHICH HE COULD NOT RECALL AS HIS PHYSICAL AND MENTAL COLLAPSE ERASED HIS MEMORY OF IT.

*Today at usual prayer in window above Deep Ghyll Gorge_ complete sitting meditation, opened eyes_*

*Instant saw young man far side bridge_ he kept try cross bridge but returned rock where sat_ obvious he in turmoil_ desired cross bridge_ not summon courage or overcome fear_*

*I watch deep interest_ at last young man find will_ put on pack, grasp hand-ropes_ took few steps_ seemed overcome imaginings_ then he master himself and move again forward_*

SECOND YEAR: BIRCHMOON TO HAWTHORNMOON

*Not quite halfway he slightly miss footing_ bad effect_ legs began shake, seem full of terror_ bend knees, sink curl crouch, head bowed chest, eyes tight shut_*

Decide assist best I could_ I call out "Do well!"_ I encourage_ ask name, use often to help him, show he not alone:

"Kip! Stand slow, keep eyes shut. When ready, open eyes, keep fix to end bridge_ let feet feel way."

He manage start_ I just say: "Do well, Kip!" "Close now, Kip!" "That right, Kip!"

One more shake, only small_ he reach ground, collapse_ I go tell"

THE INWARD-LOOKING HOUSES

'Die, and be quiet!...
...Your old life was a frenzied escaping from silence.
A wordless full moon now rises.'   *Rumi*

1st Oakmoon *a.m.*   *from Kip's journal*
I am told that I have been in a deep sleep since I arrived
It seems like a miracle to me that I am writing this! I am gazing in wonder as my quill nib scrapes along the rough surface of the paper and leaves a trail of ink that represents language! I look at my supposedly familiar hands with a sort of first sight, or the shadows of rose-leaves quivering on the white walls of my small room; I hear a distant, echoing call and a bellow of laughter, a thrilling burst of birdsong; I feel the soft, clean, comforting nap of the bed-sheet. I experience all of these ordinary, everyday events with a sense of wonder heightened by my amazement that I am here at all to receive these impressions and record them.

Someone is knocking at the door.

Same day. Afternoon. The entry above was written when I awoke this morning. For quite a few minutes, I struggled to orientate myself. I wasn't sure where I was, or how I'd got here. I wasn't even clear who I was! As I lay still in the tranquillity of the room, I began to recall myself, my home island, my Tu Darshaq friends, and even my ordeal through the tunnel. But how I had got from the tunnel to here was a blank enigma to me. Then I saw a sheet of paper on the table by my bed. With a weak and quivering arm, I dragged it into my grasp and read it. Only on my second or third reading did I start to realize that it described something that had actually happened to me! Even the mention of my name had not at first registered. The sheet contains some notes made by the kind resident who raised the alarm at my inauspicious arrival, and they have inched back my recollection of my ordeal. How did I not fall from the rope-bridge? I was curling into submission. I was ready to release my hold and plunge into obscurity. Yet I am here!

A doubt has suddenly entered my head: did I let go after all? Is this what comes after? Then I saw a quill, some ink and writing paper, and with a surge of energy I began to write rapidly, but it quickly tired me, as if I'd done hours of hard, physical work.

5th Oakmoon

Now, I have had a few days rest, so I will attempt to bring my journal up-to-date with a description of this place, at least the little I've experienced of it from my bedroom window!

From without, it is very difficult to discern a man-made structure. The edifice is of the same rock as the surrounding mountains, and has the appearance of cliffs, crags and pinnacles, and the entrance is through a rough-hewn arched gateway, which looks from any distance like a cave. There is a curve to the pathway leading in so that you cannot see the interior as you stand under the arch; indeed, all you can see is intense darkness. The sight when you complete the pitch-black curve is breathtaking. The land that any visitor leaves outside is rocky, scrubby, with a few trees, and more hints of green than the desert and lower foothills had made me accustomed to, though still quite severe; but inside there is a garden the equal of which I have never seen.

I am aware of dappled sunlight, the sound of running water, quiet paths leading through groves of bright, shaking leaves, and- somewhere beyond the leaves, trunks and branches- I see pillars, balconies, and the blue sky. A cloistered path runs to right and left from my window, hugging the building and presumably forming a square; I haven't been able to investigate yet, having taken only aided strolls a few yards from my door.

The Fortress contains what are known as The Four

Inward-Looking Houses, presumably because the sides of the quadrangle comprise four separate buildings (the four Houses, including service offices) which look in on the gardens. It seems to be a sort of place of learning. I'm not sure.

My guide today as I walked in the gardens, which seem to me so far to fill the courtyard, was an old man called Laduni. He walked with the aid of a stick, and wore thick spectacles from the edges of which radiated deep crows' feet, for he was generally smiling, and was quick to laugh. He led me along the main paths, which quarter the gardens, all of them bordered by singing channels of water which intermittently run in and out of shaded pools.

"It is hot and dry for much of the year," he said. "Water is a mercy."

"Where does the water come from?" I asked.

"It filters down through the mountains from the snowfields," he replied, pointing to where Mount Matluj seemed to float in the blue, rarefied heights of sky and sunlight beyond the roofs of the Inward-Looking Houses.

Minor paths meander through the groves, but the main paths are straight, quartering the gardens, and intersecting at the centre, where there is a beautiful, towering cedar with great shelves of blue-pined branches which uphold the light and shade the heart of the garden. Around the base of the cedar's mighty bole is fixed a circular bench, and here, in the heat of noon, you may sit and rest.

"The tree is beautiful, Laduni," I observed.

"It has stood here for many centuries."

The quartered gardens contain a mix of shrub borders, rose-gardens, little woodlands, but each quarter has its own area of fruit-trees: one has orchards of pomegranates, the second copses of fig-trees, the third has stately date-palms, and the fourth groves of olives. And wherever we walked, the restful murmur of water accompanied us. Whether it was this sound, or the unhurried manner of my companion, or indeed the sense of having finally arrived at a long-sought destination, I quickly began to feel restored.

******

The days pass, and I do not count them (though I'm told it is the 12th Oakmoon). It is just a quiet period of recuperation. I've only seen Laduni to speak to, apart from passing pleasantries with people working in the gardens, or those who bring things to my room. I could almost swear that I have been kept apart: convalesced. This evening, though, Laduni said something that I didn't fully comprehend, but which held the suggestion that my period of rest would imminently cease.

"Kip, you have asked no questions since you came here. Apart from enquiring where the waters in the garden come from!" He rocks back and laughs. This was true. I had sunk into the recuperative sibilance of leaves and water, the shaded warmth and peace of the garden, as if this were the whole object of the journey from my home.

Laduni's observation immediately awakened something in me: I rediscovered an inner need to know about the Thirteen Moons, which, amazingly, I hadn't thought about at all! I cannot say what it is I want to know, but it feels more important than anything else in my life, now that it has re-awoken.

"No, I have asked nothing, it is true; but I see that the time has come to question."

And then I fell silent! At first, no question came, but then, without forcing, something I had wondered about came to me.

"Why are the buildings in The Fortress called The Inward-Looking Houses: is it just descriptive?"

"It doesn't only mean that they look in on the gardens, though that is part of the meaning." His usual smile suddenly disappears. "More importantly, they and the gardens represent our contemplative nature, and the water is the living spirit within."

"How long will I be here?"

"Not long!" he laughs. "It is time for you to leave the Hall of Healing. You must attend the Three Houses."

He took a sweeping view of the gardens and distant outer walls which were occasionally visible through gaps in the foliage. Again, he is suddenly serious.

"This place protects ancient secrets. Each of the Houses holds and passes on these secrets in its own way. Tomorrow, you will be introduced to the first House.

"It will be a testing time for you: remember what brought you here. But also, you may enter a time of great discoveries if you remain open and courageous."

I am filled, simultaneously, with an upwelling of dread, excitement, trepidation, anticipation. What awaits me? Something in me knows, and desires it more than anything else in the world, recognises it as the whole purpose of my journey; but something else in me also knows, and recoils from it in fear and repugnance. When I hear that voice I just want to go back to Straight and take up my blacksmith's work and forget all of this.

******

Walking softly in the warmth of early morning. The paths are spread with nets of dew which spiders spun at dawn. Following Laduni step by slow step, I feel lost in a forest of Kips; I am suddenly aware of their presence, as if someone had tilted a crystal so that light shone back from previously invisible faces.

I am a condemned king walking to his execution; I am a lost traveller being directed onto the narrow way; I am a child treading in the footsteps of his father.

We sit beneath the cedar on the circular bench. We sit, and stillness comes. Out of this stillness I hear Laduni's voice, clothed in the silence, not disturbing it:

THE INWARD-LOOKING HOUSES

"What is this journey we are on?"
"We?!"
He raises his eyebrows, then rocks back and slaps his knee in glee.
"You still think that you are on a lone quest?! You left your home, accompanied. You crossed an ocean, accompanied. Other companions were with you across the desert."
In my head: "How does he know?! Did I speak in my sleep?"
"Now, Kip, our paths cross; yours and mine. It's the same journey. We are all on it."
He laughs as if this is the most obvious, simple and joyous thing in the world.
I sigh. I feel that I'm out of my depth. "Yes, Akhman said the same thing."
This is not an ordinary conversation! It grows out of the peace of the garden, the white brilliance of the morning sun, the dancing leaves, the dappled and scented shadows, the rainbows on the webs, his inner stillness, my struggle.
"The Four Houses look inward, Kip. What do they see?"
My eyes scan the scene.
"A garden?"
"Perhaps."
There is only the song of dawn bird and the water-channel.
"And when we look inward, what do we see?"
A frown is the outward sign of my mental effort to track down an answer.
"Don't reply, Kip. Ponder. Stay with the mystery." He smiles at the garden and the praising bird. It's as if he delights in every moment. We sit. It feels like a preparation for something. The stillness deepens. Eventually (ten minutes? an hour?) he points:
"Look: the new moon! Almost invisible in the brightness of dawn."
Then another age passes. Then:
"Come, you shall be the guest of the Masters of the

Houses; each in turn will be your guide."
Through groves where figs are swelling, to a colonnade of pale-blue arches, into the cool shade of the cloister walk, to a door.
His thumb is on the latch. I am at the threshold.

SAHADA, THE HOUSE OF STARS
'If you split an atom, you will find within it a sun and planets, revolving' Rumi

"A new moon teaches gradualness..."
I am before the Mentor of Sahada, Yazir Ja. She is grey-haired, olive-skinned, and is dressed in a suit of cedar-blue cotton. I have never seen a woman dressed in trousers before. Her face is at once stern and kind; and her eyes!... it is her eyes that embrace me. How deep they are: such knowledge, such suffering, such acceptance.
"...and also it teaches us deliberation: how to give birth to oneself in due time."
Laduni is sitting nearby, in attendance. We sit for a duration. We sit; we eat occasionally, lightly; we sleep for short breaks on soft mats; we sip water from delicate bowls of translucent porcelain. How long passes? Do I dream? Do I see visions? Or do I see without the scales of 'reality' on my eyes?
She stands, becoming vertical with the least effort, as if she were weightless.
"Follow me."
We walk along passages; doors open and close; latches click, lift, and fall; we pause in vestibules; pass under finely carved lintels; keys turn in locks; we approach a door with an intricately decorated architrave: moons, oakleaves, crowns and suns. The door is old, smoothly polished with wear. In the giant lock is a key shaped like a cedar. We enter a hall through the door, its walls and ceiling painted with constellations and planets, reminding me of the cavern through the tunnel. The room seems to stretch impossibly away beyond eyesight.
Many people sit on firm cushions on the hall floor, heads slightly bowed, in robes of midnight blue: "Pupils of The House of Stars: Sahada," says Yazir Ja.
She explains that we are halfway through the Oakmoon, so it is at the full, serene and silent. I am confused: surely it

was only this morning that I saw the new moon. How long did she and I sit together? How far did we walk through passages, thresholds, ante-rooms? She smiles at my confused look. "Time is simply one of many dimensions."

Then she announces in a tone of anticipation, "But we have reached the turning of the year!" as if this is far more important than my unspoken question about the passing of time. "To triumph, we need endurance. It is time for the execution of the Royal Tree!"

I recall my feeling like a condemned king, this morning long ago.

A procession forms. We pass through door after door, till we emerge into muted cloister-light, then out to the garden until we come to the great, central cedar. Many pupils disrobe to reveal loose shirts and trousers gathered at the wrist or ankle. Suddenly, it seems, they have ropes and saws slung over their shoulders, and they swarm over the towering tree like ants over a bean-plant. Such speed, such agility! They are like the sailors on the rigging of The Tariqa. Hours pass, lopping and gathering a pyre of twigs and branches, then the mighty trunk in sections. Yazir Ja speaks to us of self-sacrifice.

The tree is down. The cedar-king is dead. I cannot deny a strong sense of sorrow and regret. It was a noble heart to the garden.

******

Back in Sahada's main hall, we sit in huge, concentric semi-circles, facing Yazir Ja and Laduni. At midnight, the Summer's eye, the solstice point, we all stand and leave the hall through a great pair of double-doors of oak set with star-shaped studs, and swung on enormous semi-circular hinges in the likenesses of a half-moon and a sun half out of cloud.

Over the brink of Midsummer, we begin to run, faster and faster, until it seems effortless. We are running on air; we climb and climb in utter silence till we are high in the sky to the north of The Fortress, way above Mount Matluj. We form a circle round Yazir Ja, who holds aloft a crown of cedar-wood, and says: "To that which must die, again and again, so that there may be birth."

She throws the crown high over her head, and we watch in quiet wonder, like children at a firework party, as it explodes; but as it cascades, instead of falling earthwards, it freezes into place as a constellation: the Northern Crown.

We then follow her back to Sahada, the House of Stars, where, from a verandah, we look up at the night sky and see Corona Borealis, the Cedar King, dipping behind the northern peaks. "He has gone to serve the Queen of the Circling Universe."

The pupils settle to an hour of stargazing through 'farsights' such as Fadouma had invented, though these are much larger and many times more powerful than hers, and bring the planets and stars to closer view. Yazir Ja instructs and assists everyone in the forms of constellations, and speaks of things which I do not understand, such as how to interpret the influence of celestial movements in our own psychologies.

"As above, so below," she quotes.

******

Oakmoon 16

The following morning, after a few hours sleep, we walk with Yazir Ja in the Garden. I gasp. At the garden's heart where the main paths intersect, there is a tall, wide-spreading holly, where yesterday there remained only a cedar stump and piles of sawdust.

"The king is dead! Long live the king!"

******

Oakmoon 24

Every day now there is study: geometry, algebra, secrets of hidden calculus, charts of constellations, precession of the equinoxes, facts and mythologies concerning planets and the night sky. And all the time, Yazir Ja's commentary, which seems to give another, deeper level to all our studies, a link to ourselves and the infinities of our own inner universe. For, every evening, we observe the skies, monitor the passage of moon and stars, ponder the movements and stillnesses not only above and around us, but also within us: for Yazir Ja constantly draws parallels, speaks of microcosm and macrocosm, reveals eclipses, dawns, orbits in our own minds; moons, suns and galaxies within our hearts.

Well, it's all very strange and not a little confusing. I'm used to a world where you know where you are, a world of facts. Since meeting up with Brag all sorts of odd things seem to have happened; and then the Tu Darshaq and the people here seem to make the world shimmer and shift. And I still haven't worked out how they create the illusion of flying and all the other stuff. I asked Akhman about it time and time again, and he just gave replies that seemed like evasions. I'll try with Yazir Ja tomorrow. Something inside me is struggling, and I feel very uncertain suddenly.

******

1st Hollymoon

This morning, we were walking in The Garden, Yazir Ja and I. There is a new moon, so slender and so sharp it had the fineness of a paper-cut on the finger.

"Look!" said Yazir Ja, pointing at the shrubbery. "The holly is in bloom."

She indicated a bench and we sat. Her movements seem never automatic, but always deliberate and natural. Intentional. I remember seeing sailors in Fiskemouth with almond-shaped eyes like hers. Brag said that they were from Oriri, far away in the East. Maybe she's from there, where the sun rises.

I take the opportunity to ask about the things which are bothering me: what she has been saying in her talks, the flying tricks, and so on. When I have finished listing what is bothering me, I add: "It suddenly seems a bit airy, a bit untouchable. What about some facts? Something solid."

"What about numbers?" she replies.

"Well...," I hesitate, unsure whether or not I'm being lured into a trap.

"What is 1 add 7?"

I look at her quizzically, and she laughs.

"There's no catch, Kip."

"Then the answer is eight."

"And the holly is the eighth moon of the year. Eight is the number of increase in old lore. Nature seems aware of this; certainly the holly is aware: it is flowering.

"Or lay 8 on its side and ∞ is the sign used by mathematicians for infinity. It is a very interesting number."

"But the thing about numbers," I interjected, feeling that she was wandering from the point, "is that they are reliable. They always do what's expected of them. Numbers don't lie or confuse or evade. They are hard, like facts. You know where you are with them."

A faint smile shimmered at the edges of her mouth. "How would you define a fact?"

I considered this seemingly innocent question. "Well, it's something that everyone recognises, and agrees is real and true. Something that can't be denied. Something that... that just _is_!"

As I was saying this, I had a sinking feeling. The comfortable, solid world that we call 'real' has a way of dissolving like a desert mirage as soon as we try to define it.

"And what is it," asked this woman whose height only reaches to my chest, yet who carries such a presence that something in me is intimidated by her, even while I am touched by her care and concern for me, "what is it that everyone 'recognises and agrees is real and true'?"

"Well... there must be some undeniable things," I hedged, to gain a few moments in which to think.

"Do numbers fit your definition?" she asked, helpfully.

I trampled on, with a growing feeling of misgiving, wondering where I would end as I hacked blindly through the jungle undergrowth of this dialogue.

"Yes!" I asserted. "Everyone knows what 4 is, for example... Everyone recognises that 2+2=4, or that 4÷2=2."

"Or that, if 4÷2=2, then 2×2=4," she added.

"Precisely," I confirmed with relief. She seemed, at last, to be persuaded by the strength of my argument.

"What about square roots?"

I was immediately wary. "What do you mean?"

"Well... what is the square root of 4?"

I assumed there were still no catches in her questions, but approached my answer carefully. "Well, a square root is a number which, when multiplied by itself, makes the original number. So, as 2 multiplied by itself makes 4, the answer must be 2."

She laughed fondly at my extreme cautiousness. "That is correct."

"You see!" I exclaimed, sensing a sort of victory.

"So what is the square root of minus 4?" she rejoined without a pause.

"Well, it must be minus 2," I answered unhesitatingly.

"Dear, oh dear! What was Mr Sloethwaite teaching you in your mathematics lessons!" she chuckled with gentle, chiding irony.

At the mention of my old mentor's name, I suddenly recalled his voice explaining to me how "two minuses make a plus". The look of confusion on my face amused Yazir Ja: "Yes, -2×-2 = 4, the same as 2×2=4. We can't find the square root of a negative number. So there are

limits to what our mathematics can do for us. We crave answers; we want everything explained. We ask for mystery to be explained away. But mystery lies at the heart of everything." Then she added with unaffected solicitude and kindness:
"Let's walk in silence under the fact of the holly blossom; let's feel the fact of the earth under our feet!"

******

Moons have waxed and waned, and I have lost track. The time seems brief, yet, paradoxically, as if I have been here for a lifetime. However, a lifetime is brief. We are all mayflies, I think: over and over again, from the surface of the river, we rise into the sunlit blueness where martins and swallows are shying and skimming.

I'm not sure why (or how!) I wrote that last paragraph, or even what it means! The influence of this place and of my Tu Darshaq friends has started to give me unusual thoughts and feelings. I'm not so sure that I even know who I really am anymore.

MILFA, THE HOUSE OF MASKS

*"When a man makes up a story,
he becomes a father and child
together, listening."   Rumi*

I am approaching the House of Milfa, which lies on the next side of the courtyard. I call it a courtyard, though you will have gathered that there are such shrubberies, glades, groves, fountains that there is quite an acreage within the square of buildings which comprises the architectural portion of The Fortress, as distinct from its gardens and grounds.

However, despite the fact that you can only see glimpses of any House from its opposite side due to the intervening trees and vegetation, there is still an intimacy about the space within its walls. It retains an air of protection and secrecy.

Whilst referring to the architecture, I should mention the beauty of the buildings. There could hardly be a greater contrast between the severity and plainness of the outer rockwalls of The Fortress and the delicate intricacy of the carved interior. Each inside face is a grace of arches and slender pillars, the ground floor set back and half-hidden behind the arches of the cloister-walk, the first floor overhanging, and forming a verandah with traceried balustrades between the supporting columns. As far as I can gather, everything is made of stone, cedar or adobe, but always marvellously carved. Despite certain generic similarities, each of the four facades has its own character, being distinctive in its detail, such as the shape of its arches. One obvious difference is in the colours: Sahada is golden ochre, Milfa a rose-madder, Safin pale blue like a morning sky, and the offices and House of Hospitality where I recovered are white as the tip of Mount Matluj.

So, here I am, approaching Milfa, which rises from its olive groves in a dream of blushed ogee curves.

I knock on the door. I wait.

THE INWARD-LOOKING HOUSES

No answer.

I knock and wait twice more with the same result.

Tentatively, I try the handle and push the aged cedar door slightly open. Immediately, I inhale stillness: it almost has a scent, a taste. This stillness is barely ruffled, like a deep pool. I enter the softly echoing calm of the interior. I am in a high hall with ornate, tiled walls reminding me of the baths at Kayya, and a floor of cool marble. A dark, wooden staircase ascends the wall to my right and leads to a gallery which goes round all four walls; in the wall opposite are two paneless, filigreed windows and an open doorway framing green leaves and red flowers, unblemished sky, sunlight. There is no furniture, save a low, circular table and a cushion on a beautifully woven rug in the middle of the floor.

As I approach these, I notice a sheet of textured, handmade paper on the table, and with a shock, I see my name at the top:

'KIP

Sit and watch for what comes'

'H'm. Well, I am here, so I might as well play the game!' I reason, though even as I have that thought, the word 'game' seems to jar with some inner part of me. I don't know why.

I take up my position on the cushion, cross-legged and facing the open doorway. I recall how Yazir Ja led me into sitting peacefully, aware of the sensation of my body and releasing tension. I sit like this for half an hour, perhaps a whole hour. Suddenly, I become aware of the sound of running water where before I was only conscious of quietness. This is what has come, so I go in search of the source of this sound. I walk through the open doorway into a rear garden, rocky, ferny and with many trees and a brisk stream tumbling between boulders into a curtain of branches. I follow it, clambering down the mossy precipice. It is easy to ascertain where it is headed, for there is the distant sound of cascading water muffled by the dell's vegetation. I make for this sound, and eventually come to an edge, over which the torrent leaps in a hail of diamonds, which seethes in a froth where it lands in a clear, dark pool, which is surrounded by dry, mossy ground and overhung by a nut-tree. On the carpet of moss, which is starred with tiny, white flowers, sit about twenty people, one of them being an old man with a permanent smile in his eyes.

"Good morning!" he calls genially. "We're having a breakfast picnic. Do join us," he adds in a quaintly old-fashioned idiom.

So I climb down to the little sunlit glade and join the breakfast party. No-one, to my own surprise, seems the least bit surprised at my arrival. There are brief introductions.

The old man is called Qisasi, which I recognise as the name of the mentor of Milfa, and he invites me to help myself to the breakfast food. I take a roll of coarse, brown bread, some goat's cheese, olives, a beaker of water. It is frugal, but sustaining. The olives are succulent, the size of pigeon's eggs, like pieces of edible, concentrated sunlight.

"I thought we might linger here, since the weather is so kind and clement," says Qisasi.

I am fascinated by him, because he is so unassuming, but he is the Master of this House. And yet, yes, there is a quality about him... What is it? And then it comes to me: it is his presence. He is <u>here</u>.

"We can tell stories," he suggests. "Who would like to begin? I well remember," he continues before anyone can draw breath to volunteer, "how my teacher, Dr Vikol, used to encourage us to have campfires and tell stories. He knew who liked to slide back into the shadows, and would turn to them suddenly and unexpectedly: "How about you, Qisasi?" Of course, one need not panic in the face of a blank mind. One learns that there are stories all around; that our own lives are full of wonder and adventure. Once upon a time-." He stops abruptly.

THE INWARD-LOOKING HOUSES

"Now that is an interesting phrase. We need go no further for the time being. 'Once upon a time.' Once... the stuff of this tale happened only once. Never before had those particular characters met in those particular circumstances; and never again in the ageless remotenesses of passing time will they ever meet again in those particular circumstances. That is a wondrous and fruitful thing to ponder." Qisasi pauses as if to allow a space for this to sink in, and cracks a few hazelnuts, crushing them before casting the kernel's morsels into the pool, where a large, silver fish rises from the invisible, dark depths and consumes the bits in bubbling mouthfuls.

"On the other hand, having occurred once, those particular circumstances then inhabit vertical time."

I am puzzled by this phrase: "Excuse me, I'm not sure what you mean by that."

"It means, Kip, that the story goes on. A story has no ending and no beginning. Whenever we tell a story, we choose a point and enter. But the tale must already have been in progress, or we should have had nothing to enter. And when we leave, the characters will carry on with their lives. 'Once upon a time' is a recognition of the uniqueness of each moment, its 'once-ness', and also of the arbitrary nature of our entrances and departures."

Qisasi smiles all the time he is speaking, but when he stops the smile fades slightly, and he looks from mild, watery eyes at all of us in turn, his gaze alighting for a moment before moving on, like a bee gathering nectar and spreading pollen.

******

And so, through the Hazelmoon and into the Vinemoon, I have stayed in Milfa, the House of Masks, sometimes listening to Qisasi's tales, during the telling of which he seems to wear masks, becoming the characters he portrays, at other times sitting with him and his group of pupils in silences or sessions of question and comment. And through his questions he reveals to me that I have more than one face; more faces, indeed, than I can count.

Vinemoon *Final day*
Tonight, Qisasi has announced, there is to be a special evening picnic and storytelling. What will be special about it he does not say.

******

The trees are hung with little lamps. Mountain crickets are chirping. The evening holds on to its warmth in a way that evenings at home rarely do.
The picnic so far has been all casual talk, jest and anecdote, eating simple, delicious food, and sipping an earthy, fruity, purple wine that Qisasi calls his 'Eastern Ruby'. Qisasi is telling one of his stories: "The boar must be tracked down," said the young hunter. "Otherwise he will wreak havoc."
So the party went out into the forest and searched high and low. The morning passed without success, so they rested and refreshed themselves. Then all afternoon they tracked the beast. But at every turn it seemed just ahead of them, never in sight.
Eventually, the sun was touching the hills, and all the birds were chorusing their praises of its splendour and beauty; the first shadows of evening were emerging. The hunters' thoughts were turning to hot baths and supper. Suddenly, in a glade ahead of them, there it was! An enormous boar, with tusks like scimitars. It just stood and stared at them defiantly, playing the air with its bristled snout. The young huntsman yelled and led the charge: "Release the boarhounds!" Then the boar was gone.
As I listen to Qisasi, it is almost as if I am riding in the hunt. His descriptions are so vivid that I feel the steed moving beneath me, the smack of twigs against my face,

THE INWARD-LOOKING HOUSES

the shouts and halloos of the hunters, the smell of exhilaration, sweat and fear...

******

'The wound is the place where the Light enters you.' Rumi

Suddenly, as I listen to Qisasi and picture the tired, questioning young huntsmen, there is a blood-chilling roar, and into the edge of our glade crashes a huge boar. I am stupefied. Is this a trick? A practical joke? Magic!? The others seem as dumbfounded as I am, all except for Qisasi. He sits calmly, unperturbed.
"Where does a story begin and end, Kip? When do we make our entrances and exits? What is the real world, Kip, and what is make-believe?"
Suddenly he shouts: " To the horses! We must catch the boar!"
For the first time, I notice a group of horses, tethered and ready, on the outskirts of the glade. In a moment the boar has crashed out through the undergrowth into the surrounding woodland, and we are in pursuit. This time I am really, physically, in the story!
We have given chase for a few minutes when I find myself parted from the others. I hear some distant shouts, but I cannot seem to locate them. I dismount and sit on a rock to recover my breath and give my mount a rest.
At a faint rustling sound, I look up and see the boar a few yards away down the path, staring at me malevolently, and immediately I know, with a sickening lurch in my stomach, where I have seen those malicious eyes before.
I shout, as much to try and give myself courage as anything: "You? Here?"
I rush to grab a weapon as, in response to my voice, he roars and charges. A slash of glinting, curved bone. A scream. My voice?! The boar turns. I am on my horse, and I have a spear. The horse leaps forward at my urging. We

are bearing down on the boar, my own blood glistening on his right tusk. He is cornered. But in a flicker of shadow, the boar is gone, and a monkey is darting up a tree. I find myself running up the tree as easily as he.

The chase is on! He seems genuinely surprised to see me on his tail, and he becomes a bird of the wood: a jay, a woodpecker, I don't know. I see a whirr of wings, hear a flap and a squawk. I realize that the flap is my own wings; I am a forest hawk pursuing its prey. Again, as I close in, he changes. The desert merchant, Eqbir, awaits my arrival, his falconing wrist held aloft, the hood prepared.

Who is chasing whom? I am human once more and draw my hunting dagger. The desert merchant has a look of Bob Nixon about him, shifting like cloud-shadows into the terrifying figure who chased me from his lamplit home near the Kingfisher Inn, and I recognise his claw of a hand as the one that was at the window of our attic room at the inn, the claw which Maddy claimed she had kept from us with her breath-symbol on the dormer-window.

Next, he assumes the form of someone I do not recognise. This stranger draws his own weapon, and we circle one another.

"Who are you, Falseface? What do you want?"

"You know what I want, Kip, and the time has come for you."

"The time has come," I reply with bravado, "but it's for you that it's come!"

I become still, outwardly and inwardly. I am focussed. I feel no tension. I watch this strange man whose face is like melting wax. I could be disconcerted and distracted by the horror of his altering features, each face presenting a new emotion, an altered relationship.

"Let's be friends!" "Go back home while you can." "You are pathetic and weak!"

I remember my lessons in stillness through the last several moons: I am patient. I wait. I watch.

"I warned you of these navel-gazers at The Fortress. They are leading you down a dead-end. Worse! They are planning your death."

There must be the slightest flicker of concern on my face, for he responds:

"Oh, yes, Kip! Your death. All that you have come to know and love will be taken from you."

All the time he stares at me, through all his facial shifts. Then, as I blink, he is gone!

I am tempted to look around, but I keep my head still, allowing myself only to flick glances out of the corners of my eyes.

A woman emerges from the trees ahead. She is the most beautiful woman I have ever seen, all I have ever tried to picture but failed; she is breathtakingly sensuous in her movements, her eyes full of welcome and desire.

"Hello!" she says in surprise. Then, because I stand dumbfounded she continues.

"Are you lost? Can I help?"

I don't know what to say. My thoughts are reeling: did The Shifter vanish because he heard this woman coming, or is this another of his guises? If I offend her, I might never see her again.

"Perhaps you were with the boar-hunt?"

"Yes," I nod.

"Ah! I don't like hunts. They are cruel. Poor creatures. But I saw your friends heading back towards The Fortress. Shall I show you the way?"

She gazes directly at me with concern. I continue to fix my eyes on her, as I did on The Shifter, and I remain still. She notices my leg, and gasps.

"But you are hurt! You must be in shock. Come, you must go to The Fortress."

She indicates a path and with a kind smile and an inclination of her head offers for me to go first. I hesitate. Her eyes say she is sincere.

"Trust me." I turn, take a step, feel an arm crooked

brutally around my throat from behind.

"You must learn not only to trust," says Falseface's merchant-voice, "but when to trust."

Then the voice alters. It is familiar, yet strange. I cannot place it. It speaks, and I know it, yet I don't.

"For so long, Kip, you have fought me. You have tried so hard to escape."

I have heard this voice so often before, yet I have never heard it.

"But no more, Kip. No more."

Who is it? Who? Where have I heard it before?

"Prepare yourself, Kip. Your long struggle is over."

The voice echoes, reverberates around the walls of my skull.

"Now, Kip. I am not going to kill you. You have learned too much from Brag, Sloethwaite, Tu Darshaq, The Houses, even Maddy. So I am going to take you into my service. It's no good fighting," he sneers, painfully tightening his grip on my neck and throat as I attempt to struggle. A finger and thumb hold a long, vicious-looking thorn before my eyes.

"One sharp jab from this thorn will bring you an endless waking sleep, helpless in my service. Sweet dreams, Kip!"

That voice! I know it now! The shock of the realization brings a surge of strength which catches The Shifter off his guard. I heave him over my shoulder and drop on him.

It is confirmed: the face fits the voice that I knew and didn't know, which was so commonplace yet so elusive. It is uncanny, but I am face to face with myself!

I recall what always came with Falseface: the air of lies, spite, negativity, fear, insincerity. Now it is me who is off-guard.

"So now you know, Kip. But let it be the last thing that you ever know."

He stabs the thorn into my thigh. Then- astoundingly, unbelievably- he explodes like a giant puffball, and all that remains of him are drifting motes like dust or pollen that scatter into the woods as the breeze eddies.

USBA, THE HOUSE OF HEALING

'No medical man should consider his education complete without a knowledge of botany.' Nicholas Culpeper

'But lo, thou requirest truth in the inward parts:
and shalt make me to understand wisdom secretly.
Thou shalt purge me with hyssop, and I shall be clean.'
1662 Prayer Book

Then into this dream, for so it seems to be, a sharp stab of pain in my leg. I look down and see the tusk's gash, which I had forgotten. My leg throbs. I feel suddenly weary. Sleep; let me sleep. Spiralling into the darkness of sleep.
But instantly I emerge into a painful blaze of white light. I shrug off drowsiness reluctantly and limp to the edge of the forest. Beyond the trees is a featureless plain. Unheeding, I step out and begin walking. It is all glare and heat. I am reminded of a desert I once knew. I can hear voices, but I can see no-one. This accursed brilliance blinds me. I must make for the voices. My leg feels like a huge weight, a great sack to drag along with me, and its contents pierce my skin with sharp points and blades.
"Easy. Lift him slowly..."
Where are the speakers? To the left. I must turn to the left. Yes, over in that direction. I see them. They are trying to carry someone. Maybe I can assist. Oh, no! How stupid of me. How can I with this leg?
I limp on. I search through the hurtful shining for some feature, a landmark. The heat grows, intensifies. I must get back to the trees. Shade. Coolness. Coolth, the opposite of warmth. My skin exudes sweat. My skin is jewelled with sweat. Beautiful jewels. Iridescent. I lick my parched lips, aware of a sudden, raging thirst, and taste only salt. I must have strayed into a salt-desert. The merciless heat and glare is everywhere: all around, above, even burning from within my body, my limbs, my head. I turn about to search back for the forest, walking for hours, and am on the point of

giving up when I catch a few words from a directionless voice somewhere in the shimmering air:
"...a decoction of borage to reduce it..."
My tongue is on fire, dry as sand. There is a throb of pure pain growing in my head. Must return to the woods. Must—. Suddenly, from the incandescent haze, a figure is emerging. At last! I falter forwards with a cry that seems not my own.
I recognise the figure. It is Maddy!
She runs to me, then stops just out of reach.
"Guess what?" she says excitedly. "I've always wanted a kitten, and now I can have one! Have you seen my star-jumps?"
She demonstrates several.
"There's crumpets for tea. Oops, sorry," she giggles. "There *are* crumpets for tea. Watch your grammar, Maddy. You're in the presence of an educated man!"
She gabbles on, flitting from one subject to another.
"Maddy!" I shout desperately. "Help me!" It is a scream, a heart-cry.
"You look silly," she laughs. "You're all limp and wet-looking. Like an old lettuce!"
She laughs in my face, her mouth like a great, black cavern. "Ha-ha-ha-ha-ha-ha!" In her quick intakes of breath the syllables shift, veer, modify, warp. "Ha-ha-na, ha-na, nana, najaha, najanna, janna, janna..." Her laughter becomes more staccato, evolves into a rhythmic chant:
"Janna janna,
Junna junna,
Janna junna,
Junna janna..."
I see that she is quite mad, utterly mad. I fall on my knees in despair. A great sob, like a huge pearl, wells up and bursts from me. I cannot go on any longer. It is too much. Brag is dead. Akhman is dead. Maddy and Prunella are lost to me. All is death and delusion.
"...saffron to strengthen the heart..."

I see it is impossible to escape The Shifter's sleep. On my knees before Maddy as she capers and chants, I imagine it must look like some sort of worship, an obeisance before this poor, dancing fool of a girl. I curl into a ball, a foetus, and let sleep take me.

******

Sounds. Human voices. No sight. My eyes don't wish to open to the pain of light. Just voices. Two of them.
"Wash the wound on his leg and apply the lotion of Honey of Roses."
A man's voice. I don't know it. Also, the familiar but unplaceable voice of a woman, replying: "... a decoction of lady's mantle?"
"Yes! Good! Wash the wound in that, and give a sip or two. Then the lotion..."
I feel moisture at my lips. Then I leave the scene in an echoing distance.

******

All of a sudden, from nowhere-somewhere, in an instant, I am aware of being 'here'. From an unconsciousness, or deep sleep, or mental wandering, suddenly I am back. I am lying down, eyes shut, aware of my senses, of being alive. Touch, smell, taste, hearing, sight: bridges to the outer world. And memory: I am aware of memory. For I recall, with a paradoxical feeling of starting from scratch, that I have a collection of previous experience; I am not newborn. And yet, in a curious way, I am.
I am lying in a sweet, clean bed. There is an air of serenity, an atmosphere of service, if that makes sense. The room is old, simply but comfortably furnished. Through an arched and latticed window there falls a limpid sunlight. A restful fragrance of herbs and roses permeates the air. It seems that this is the best– the only– place I could be in my need.

THE INWARD-LOOKING HOUSES

The only sound I can detect is the buzzing of bees and the murmur of insect-wings in the sunlight outside. I am reminded of my first experience of The Fortress when I woke to a similar scene.

I sink back into a sleep which is not forgetful, fevered and nightmarish, but recuperative. A blessing.

******

Voices are approaching. A man's voice and a woman's voice. A knock at the door. (I recall from somewhere: 'A knock at the door announces a stranger: by definition, one to be feared. A man enters. He has dark hair flecked with silver, like the last remaining patches of snow on the Spring pastures below Mount Matluj might look. He has heavy brows like stormclouds, and his eyes of coal burn with a dark fire, passionate yet compassionate, saying 'I, too, have suffered' in acknowledgement of something in my own heart that I was barely aware of myself till this moment. It is immediately obvious that knocks on the door can be of differing natures. He is accompanied by Prunella, the 'familiar but unplaceable voice'!

"Prunella!" I gasp, trying to sit up.

"Stay calm. Lie down," she replies, comfortingly but firmly. Her face betrays an obvious pleasure at seeing me.

I stammer: "But how... Maddy! Where's... How did you...?" Incoherent bits of sentences.

"Don't go exhausting yourself with questions. All will become clearer in good time."

"But what happened? Where am I? This is like the place I was in before, but not the same."

The man speaks. "This is Usba, The House of Healing, but a different part. What happened? You were wounded and weakened by the boar's tusk. Then, you were afflicted by a sickness of sleep. Your mind and your heart were undermined."

"But luck was with you, Kip," Prunella interjects. "When

you were struck, you were within a quarter-mile of this place. No-one could have helped you more than Iqaz. He is the Master of this House of Healing."
"But you, Prunella. How...?"
"I learned my art here, Kip. I am a pupil of Master Iqaz."

14th Ivymoon

At home, the leaves must be turning by now, the full of the Ivymoon. Here it remains warm, and the scents of the flowers are still borne into my room on the resinous air. Two quarter moons now I have been in my sick-bed, still much of it in sleep, but a little less and less each day as the ministrations of Iqaz and Prunella gradually counter the effects of the Shifter's Thorn.

I learn a little more from them each day. As yet I am ignorant of their story, but– amazingly, beyond belief– Maddy is here too! She is not 'ready to be seen', by which I can only guess that she has been ill or wounded: they will not say, only telling me not to worry.

21st Ivymoon

Every time I enquire about anything, they cleverly block me. They have more energy than I have, so I have given up asking questions, and just indulge myself now in recuperation. Over the last two weeks Iqaz has gradually allowed me to stroll a bit further day by day.

Outside my room is his physic garden where the herbs, roses and other plants grow from which he makes all his essences, ointments, balms, lotions and other remedies. It feels like a cure just to wander gently and weakly along its paths, between the beds of pungent botanics.

I spent a whole morning one day watching Master Iqaz tending his bees, which he considers integral to the well-being of his garden. He tends the bees without any veil or glove, and yet the bees never sting him. He is so serene, and moves, as it were, without suddenness. The bees, far from being alarmed, seem calmed by his visits.

THE INWARD-LOOKING HOUSES

******

Broths every day! Very strengthening. They are oddly fragrant, as Prunella adds rosewater and petals to them. She says they are 'cooling and cordial' and help to quicken my spirit. Oh well, who am I to argue? I certainly feel stronger and better day by day, and have the heartening impression of rising gradually in a steady spiral from a mist of somnolence.

******

I remember that El Ilam-Coram is known back home as one of The Aromatic Isles, and here in the House of Healing I cannot doubt the appropriateness of the name. Master Iqaz's garden fills the warm air with redolence, and Usba's rooms are filled with the scents of herb and flower, particularly in the chamber where he prepares his powders, juices and so on.

He also produces perfumes, essential oils and mixtures of dried leaves, petals and spices, which are used variously for scenting rooms and personages. He loves particularly to experiment in perfecting an attar, by distilling and blending different essences of petals from his rose garden.

Late Ivymoon

I have spent most of the last week following Iqaz. Just being with him I have found restorative because he has a tranquil presence and moves with such easy grace.

Having watched him tending the bees, deadheading roses, trimming shrubs, crushing seeds, leaves and petals, I finally commented on this quality in his movement, and how it seems so effortless.

"It might appear effortless, but I assure you that effort is required to do anything attentively."

******

Today I helped Master Iqaz, storing dried seedheads in beautiful jars, fixing the labels he had written, and arranging them on shelves in a dark, fragrant storeroom, whilst he worked at a pestle and mortar.

At one point he sat down.

"Let's rest for a while, Kip."

When I was settled and we had sat quietly for some minutes in the bee-murmuring serenity, he suddenly looked at me.

"Your time at Usba is coming to an end. Tomorrow, I shall take you to Safin, the House of Mercy. It is the last of the Three Inward-Looking Houses."

I nod my head. "I shall miss you, Master Iqaz. It has been a blessing to be here with you. And you saved my life."

"What you speak of, Kip, is not your life, only your carcass. I have not saved your life, but I have tried in my way to assist you to save it, for our own salvation is in our own hands only."

"Who is Master of Safin?" I ask.

"Safin is not organised like the other Houses. There is no Master there, but stewards who look after its running."

He notices my disappointment.

"Do not imagine that the stewards are simply housekeepers. They are masters in their own right; but the House of Mercy is different to the others Houses. You will see."

SAFIN, THE HOUSE OF MERCY

'Suffering is a gift. Within it is hidden mercy.' Rumi

*'Always there is music: a solemn, bright music.
If it fades, we shall fade.'* Rumi

Safin. An arched diffusion opens inside the shaded cloister beyond the garden: a doorway of light. Through the threshold, a tall room with an atrium of alternating panels of glass and pale aquamarine plaster. Perpendicularly below the dome's apex, in the centre of the tiled floor, a fountain leaps; as quick or slow as the eye that follows them, the drops fall. Everywhere, water and light play tricks, dancing on the walls and floor, flashing on the eye, making a rippled, submarine deep of the domed space. Channels in the floor chatter and giggle like young children.

Opposite the entrance is another archway, this time leading outside to the back of the house. I go through it and look down a long slope of pasture to a small river meandering through a reedbed. Some people are cutting reeds, while others gather them and tie them in bundles. Nearby is a grove of weeping-willows, and from its curtains of shimmering, silver-green leaves an invisible flute-player is breathing invisible music that makes the heart mourn. I walk down and sit at the edge of the willow-curtain, listening to the notes of longing. Within me, the music draws up from a well of emotion a sudden overflowing of homesickness, though not for my island, or The Forge. In fact, I couldn't say which place I am homesick for, just somewhere recognised by something inside me as 'home'; and my eyes respond by filling with tears.

Someone approaches and sits by me, as if in sympathy. Their figure through my tears appears as if through translucent glass: I cannot see the detail of their face.

"Ah, you hear the music of Khamush the Flute-player."

"Khamush?"

"One of the Masters of Safin. His music arises from the Silence."

"Why does it tear my heart?"

"The reed-flute always sings of separation, and so reminds us of home."

The music changes, and I feel a rush of exuberance, a joy at being alive in the moment.

"It's strange," I sigh, "it's heartrending, yet at the same time it is joyful."

"All is as it should be: even this discontent."

I brush my tears with the back of my hand to see who speaks these conundrums. It is startling to see that the supposed figure is simply a tied bundle of reeds. Then who spoke?

I return to Safin, the House of Mercy. Just outside the rear archway, Laduni sits on a bench against the wall.

"Laduni!" I call, surprising myself with my spontaneous delight. "It seems so long since I saw you."

"Longer than you think, young Kip! And yet..." he wobbles his head slightly, as if reasoning with himself. That playful smile, those creases of genuine happiness which radiate from the corners of his eyes, the familiar twinkle in his eye, the shining smoothness of his hairless head.

"Come," he says, rising to his feet. "If the reed-flute's music has caught your heart, you may be interested in the Music Room."

"How could you hear what was said way off by the river?!"

"Kip, I didn't need to."

I look at him quizzically.

"No magic trick," he laughs. "Your eyes. Your posture. We are a flowing script."

I follow him, still puzzling over his words, into a room about half the size of the entrance hall and, like the hall, domed. The notes of a flute are rippling round the curved upper space in seemingly endless echoes which weave and intertwine. Again, the flute-player is out of sight.

"The dome's perfection carries the music." Laduni smiles, drinking in its equilibrium.

Each note seems to multiply like reflections in a chandelier, or water-drops over a precipice.

Still smiling, he speaks: "Everything that exists produces a vibration. All the time we are called home. At every moment there is music: in the air, in the stalk, in the stars, in the heart of the stone. Music is life and death; music is curse and cure; music is the kiss of awakening and the spell of sleep; and it is the anger of war and the soothing 'goodnight' of a loving parent." I frown.

"I'm not sure that I fully understand these metaphors." Laduni looks surprised.

"This is not poetry, it is fact! Or say that poetry is fact. We are all orphans, Kip. We are all reeds moved by the water, flutes filled with the player's breath. Our hearts overflow with remorse but, since we sleep, all these things appear to us as dreams."

"Yes, but all that about music being life and death, war and peace, curse and cure..." I wear a look of scepticism.

"Watch!" says Laduni. "Listen!"

The unseen flute-player changes the notes of the flute and the bougainvillea on the lower walls begins to shrivel and droop. Another change of notes and they unfurl afresh. Yet again the notes alter and I am terrified by a huge splintering noise of cracking masonry as a shower of dust falls on us: the dome of the music-room has a large rent across it, but before I can yell out a warning, the music has transformed again and the gaping crack is healed.

Laduni smiles serenely. "So much that is beyond our grasp; all we can do is watch and listen."

******

Days pass. The fountains leap. Everywhere in this House of Mercy, water flows. I have sat beneath a great cedar and, at times, I have wept. More often than not, I have not known what it was I wept for. Lost friends? Lost places? Lost times? Perhaps it all comes down to 'Home' in the end. Though what 'Home' might mean I am not altogether sure.

******

Today, Laduni came to me. I sat in the warm morning against the high wall of the garden. Above my head, hyssop sprouted from cracks and holes in the mortar. Laduni sat by me silently and we remained together, motionless and peaceful, as the sun climbed above the domes and towers of The Fortress.

Eventually, Laduni broke the silence.

"The sun is moving towards the Winter Solstice. Your journey, like the sun's, is approaching its completion... for this year."

As always with the Masters of this place, I was puzzled and disconcerted by his words. What did he mean by 'completion', especially his coda 'for this year'?

"It is time for you to meet the Waluja."

"Who is that? Why is it time?"

"It is time to meet the Waluja because you have something to deliver."

"But I thought you were..." I struggled to find an appropriate description. "In charge."

Laduni rocked back and waggled his legs in the air, roaring with laughter. Wiping the tears from his eyes, he continued: "One person alone could not receive your gift, just as one alone could not tend all The Houses, or look after the whole Fortress and the needs of its inmates."

"Who or what is the Waluja? Why is his name singled out from the rest of the Court of Mentors?"

THE INWARD-LOOKING HOUSES

"I oversee the day-to-day running of The Fortress and the reception of visitors, so your perception of me is understandable. However, the Masters of the Inward-Looking Houses need support in their own work. They assist one another, of course, but they all refer to the Waluja, the Wise Woman, who is called Junnajanna, for *she* [he wags a playful admonitory finger at me for my earlier presumption] is acknowledged to be wise in the matters held in high esteem here. The late Master, close to death, recommended her to take on his mantle, and all concurred.

Questions were bursting from me!

"What shall I say to her?"

Laduni detected some concern, some agitation in me. I had travelled far and long without any clear idea of a destination or a purpose. I knew that what I carried was of great value, but did not know why. I assumed that the 'something to deliver' that Laduni had mentioned earlier referred to the 13 Moons, and, yes, I suddenly felt very protective towards it. I wasn't just going to give it up to complete strangers without some convincing.

"Who is this person that I do not know, that I have never met, and who expects some delivery from me?" I asked with a sudden and quite unexpected assertiveness.

Laduni smiled a smile of great caring and rested his hand on my shoulder: "It's alright, Kip. The Mentors are not unknown to you: there are Yazir Ja, Qisasi, Iqaz, and myself. We shall be there. Also, for an occasion as important as this one, our 'Masters-out-in-the-World' will return."

"Such strange things, Laduni. I hear a reed-flute and my heart aches for home. The song of the water in the gardens and halls eases it. But where is this home that I long for? I cannot link the feeling in my heart with the thought of my village or my birth-house."

"That is a good question, Kip. Keep it open in your heart."

"One more question. I seem to have been here for so long, and yet so briefly. How long have I been here?"

"This is curiously linked with your previous question. How long would you say?"

"I guess a year, since we are approaching the Winter Solstice."

'In a way that is so, Kip. But you have worked hard and travelled far since arriving at The Fortress. The calendar has turned its pages, and the moon has changed its phases, and yet, and yet... there is not only the time of the calendar moon. In the time of the moon, you have been our guest for a Great Year."

He pulls a hand-glass from the folds of his robe and passes it to me. I have not looked in a mirror, not seen a mirror, in this place. When I look in it I see myself, but I am oddly changed.

"Eight ordinary years of the moon calendar make a Great Year," observes Laduni.

"I look so old!" I exclaim. His eyes crease, he rocks back and slaps his thigh.

"Well, Venerable Sage," he mocks kindly, "you had better fulfil your mission before your flame peters out!"

"My mission?"

"Obtuse to the last! You knew all along that this journey of yours was to do with the strange gift you were given to look after. You knew when you left your parents that you had to bring the 13 Moons with you."

"How do you know so much?!"

"We are all on the journey, Kip. We are all struggling with The Shifter, Falseface, Mauhin, the Strangers-at-the-door." He smiles, but there is fellow-feeling and a tinge of sadness in the smile. "But,' he adds, raising his eyebrows, "there are friends, also. The power is not all with Denial and Greed and Ignorance and Fear. It is time to fetch the 13 Moons, Kip. I will wait for you beneath the Royal Tree this evening; we will go to meet the Waluja and the Mentors."

THE INWARD-LOOKING HOUSES

******

*'The moment of the rose and the moment of the yew-tree
Are of equal duration.'* T.S. Eliot

'Are these words, or tears? Is weeping speech?' Rumi

In the evening shadows of my room, I kneel before the treasured bundle of rags, drawing it from its long-held hiding place in my shoulder-bag. A sigh escapes my heart. I unfold the rags to look once more upon the Moons whilst in my care. Then I bear the rag-bundle outside, reverently. A white rose glows in the twilight. A full moon is rising over The Fortress and its Inward-Looking Houses, dashing its light into a thousand pieces in the leap of the fountain, like moonlit tears, like a blizzard of white rose-petals, like shattered words. A nightingale is singing, and something in me recognises that simultaneous ecstasy-and-longing that pours from its heart and throat. I understand, belatedly, Laduni's words: 'There is not only the time of the moon calendar.' I pause in the rose-garden for a thousand years.

******

Laduni waits in the black shadow of the great Cedar-Holly. We make our way in silence to Safin, the House of Mercy: this is to be the resting place of the 13 Moons, within the Hall of Grace.
The Waluja and the Mentors does not sit behind a bench like magistrates, or behind the masking light of torches like inquisitors. Their seats are in a crescent on the floor of a perfectly white circular room, the colour of moonlight and candlelight. It is like the interior of some gigantic seashell, so intricately and finely carved that its surface appears to be infinite. There is a fountain at the centre of the semi-circle of seats in the middle of the floor, and circles of

seats like ripples expand behind.

Standing in the small ante-room and watching, entranced, this beautiful scene, I ask Laduni a question which has kept occurring to me ever since the early days after my arrival, but which, until now, has never quite prompted my tongue.

"Why is there such an emphasis on water here? Fountains, pools, channels, not only in the gardens, but also the buildings; especially, it seems, here in Safin, the House of Mercy."

"For us, it is a living and ever-present symbol; a reminder of what we are and why we are here. The Inward-Looking Houses with the enclosed gardens of roses and cedars represent the contemplative aspect in human nature; the groves of olive, pomegranate, fig and date represent our true natures, our essential selves if you like."

I was abashed to recall my lack of sympathy when my Tu Darshaq friends showed me the preparation of these fruits for their Day of Rubies when I asked what their treasure was.

"Water represents Mercy, and the running water is the living spirit within our symbolic setting."

I nod, recalling with further humility, Ussa pouring the silver cord of water from his goatskin to the sand to show me what their treasure was, and Akhman's words when I asked him about his exploits in dowsing for the water-supply: "To find water in the desert, you must lose yourself." With remorse, I begin to see how unaware I was of the depth of what they were telling me. I remember how their cryptic replies to my questions had always caused me either to smile to myself, loftily indulgent of their rustic obliqueness, or to seeth with inward frustration at their obstinate refusal to give straight answers to my questions. Now I begin to see that my teaching had begun before I ever reached The Fortress. I feel a sudden pang, as if something in me has only just realized the loss of Brag. My tears flow, and I feel a profound homesickness.

Laduni puts his hand on my shoulder: "I know," he whispers, "I know..."
The white room is full of residents, sitting in the concentric semi-circles of seats that form the rows fanning out behind the Mentors front row. Laduni leads me to the semi-circle of fourteen seats within and indicates one of the seats to me. I take my place and he sits beside me. Soon, Yazir Ja and Iqaz enter, walking sedately, Qisasi quietly relating to them what appears to be an amusing story. As they reach their seats, they stop and bow, and Laduni returns their greeting, so I do too.
"Now," announces Laduni, "some friends of yours have come for this special occasion, Kip. First: Ussa, Fadouma and Agouti."
I smile broadly and spontaneously, but I am in a whirl of confusion.
The next three who enter transform my confusion to perplexity: Samuel Sloethwaite, Bill Pipkin, and Prunella the herbalist. 'Yes, of course,' says an inner voice, 'these people have all helped you to be here. Your preparation began long ago.'
"The next two Mentors, I believe you have met before," says Laduni, with a broad, unabashed, child-like smile. "Akhman and Brag Drufus."
In my astonishment, I begin to scramble to my feet, but Laduni lays a gentle hand on my arm. I must wait before discovering how on earth my old friends can be here. I cannot help but stare at Brag, and he winks at me, then bows his head.
"Now, it only remains for the Waluja, Junnajanna to enter. Everyone stands in order to receive the Waluja with due respect." Laduni raises his hand towards the entrance, and in comes the wise woman. But now I am utterly confounded. I have tumbled into a dream, and these wonderful reunions are turning to mist before my eyes. My head is swirling as if I were drunk. All this because the Waluja is Maddy! Junnajanna is Maddy! At least, she looks

like Maddy, but she has an ageless look. It is Maddy, yet it isn't her. Her eyes have flashes of youthful freshness and mature serenity. She walks right up to me and looks me directly in the eye; she seems to see into all the passages and rooms of my being. For a moment her eyes seem to search. Then, suddenly, like sun in April from behind a cloud, she smiles.

"Hello, Kip. You have done well, very well."

She holds out cupped hands, and I place this profound treasure, whose profundity I do not understand, into those hands.

"These inner spheres, fashioned from each of the moon-trees, represent the thirteen moons of the year, from the Birch to the Elder." Laduni is stood by her, holding another small globe, slightly larger than the complete 13 Moons, but differing from them by being hinged. "The outermost into which I now place them is made of ivory, one hemisphere plain, the other gilded, to represent the moon and the sun. It was carved by someone with the Deep Understanding in time-out-of-memory from a tusk of the Great Mammoth, which was discovered frozen in the ice-fields of Mount Matluj. We shall never know who the maker was."

She places the 13 Moons inside the ivory globe and Laduni closes it and locks the clasp, before handing it back to her. She bows her head to the 13 Moons and hands them back to me. "Place the Moons on the fountain, Kip."

I take them, noticing my hands shaking, and walk to the central fountain, then extend my arms so that my hands are in the plume of water where it spreads, the 13 Moons resting in my upturned palms. Then, I slowly and gently slide my hands apart, and the 13 Moons are held by the merciful fountain in its out-curving palms of ever-flowing water.

******

THE INWARD-LOOKING HOUSES

'And hear upon the sodden floor
Below, the boarhound and the boar
Pursue their pattern as before
But reconciled among the stars.'
T.S. Eliot

Afterwards, in the garden, I sit with Akhman, Laduni, Brag and Junnajanna/Maddy. (I cannot get used to calling her anything else but Maddy yet, even though she now looks changed somehow, and certainly is not simple or mad! Laduni told me whilst walking through the garden from Safin that the name Junnajanna in the local dialect means 'to become crazy (Junna); to veil, cover or conceal (Janna), so the sense of Junnajanna is 'to <u>appear</u> crazy <u>in order</u> to remain hidden'.)

From somewhere, I summon the courage to ask a direct question. "So am I to know what happened to my two dear friends, who I thought were dead?"

Junnajanna says, "You have witnessed strange things since setting out from your village: shapeshifting, apparent magic, and things which changed your perspective on the world and people." She looks at Akhman and he gives a slight nod of assent before he speaks.

"When the cavern roof collapsed on me in the earthquake, I was able to escape by changing my form. But that's not important. I needed to disguise my presence from Mauhin, to remain out of sight for a while. I am sorry for the upset it caused you, but it was necessary. We were having to deal with powerful and astute forces."

"Aye, Kip, lad," adds Brag. "I am also sorry for your distress, but it was judged that the time had come for you to travel without me, in a way which would draw out your own qualities, and allow me to elude Falseface. I was never very far away, though."

"Well, at least Falseface is gone for ever," I reply.

"Oh no, Kip! It would be a great mistake to think that!" Maddy/Janna warns me. "Falseface is with us always, all of

us. The more we learn to trick him, the more cunning he gets. You must learn to be more and more on your guard."
I am taken by a sudden conviction: "Throughout my journey, I have thought and acted foolishly. I assumed myself superior to many of those I met, despite repeated lessons to the contrary. The world is not as I thought, probably not even as now I think it is."
"Assuredly, it is not," comments Laduni.
I sigh, recalling when I was at a loss as to my next step, Maddy telling me to seek the Inward-Looking Houses; my first hearing of them. "I thought I was looking after Maddy, a simple girl, and it turns out that she was looking after me, protecting me, guiding me!"
"But," she replies, "it was through your act of care that you were cared for." I look at her, and it is like in a dream, when there is someone you are familiar with in daily life but they look somehow different. Maddy is Maddy, and yet... She is not a girl, not a young woman, not an old woman. I cannot actually put an age on her, because, though her complexion is smooth, her eyes have a depth and serenity which belie her apparently few decades. This is Maddy, but it isn't, but it is!
"And now, Kip, it's your turn," she says. "You have endeavoured and endured. Though you suffer the same vanities as we all do, you have been contrite when recognising them and have acquired a little knowledge some understanding.
"Now, there is a task for you. There will be help available; there always is. But it is your own task, and only you can do it. You have been preparing for it ever since the day when I gave you the 13 Moons, that midwinter night of the mummers' play in your village. From then on-"
"Wait, wait, wait...!" I exclaim. In fact, I haven't known what an exclamation really is until now! "You gave...- but...!" I am speechless. I sigh in frustration and disbelief.
Laduni rocks and hoots with laughter and claps his hand in

undisguised mirth.

"As you said yourself, Kip, the world is not as you thought!"

He smiles, and his face is a picture of compassion for my confusion and helplessness.

"Janna, the Hidden One, is one of our Great-Mentors-in-the-World. When you were chosen for the task of carrying the 13 Moons to Safin, she came in disguise as the Old Dame in the travelling play, to sow a seed, as it were. But before that, when your preparation needed to begin, Samuel Sloethwaite saw to it that you were taken in hand." I just shake my head, wordlessly. "Then, when the time was approaching for your journey to begin, Janna came again; this time as a simple country orphan. For, she is a genius of disguise: as her name tells us."

"Well," I breath, with a rueful smile, feeling utterly bemused. "I don't think I'll ever be sure of anything, ever again!"

"Good! That is a good start," replies Janna with a twinkle in her eye. "Now then, this task of yours which awaits you..."

ABOUT THE AUTHOR

Anthony Handy was born in Yorkshire in September (the Vinemoon!) of 1951. As a child, his family moved to Warwickshire, and here he learned to love the countryside and its wildlife, as well as poetry, music, and (well into his teens!) proper ale. He began to write poetry at 16.

After teacher training, he settled in Herefordshire, appreciating its wildness and sense of being on the edge of things. He quickly took up The Morris, and still performs the local Welsh Border Morris dances with The Leominster Morris.

By the early 1980s he had a son and daughter and had become headteacher of a village primary school near Ludlow, Shropshire, where he spent eight happy years before the deadly National Curriculum drove him away from a full-time career.

He has self-published two books of poetry.

ACKNOWLEDGMENTS

*Any wisdom represented at 'The Inward-Looking Houses' is not mine, but comes from my contact, over many years, with the ideas and practice of the Gurdjieff 'Work'. I acknowledge my debt to this exceptional man, Gyorgi Ivanovitch Gurdjieff, and to all those in 'The Work', past and present, who selflessly share their own experience of his teaching.

*'The White Goddess' by Robert Graves has long been a source of inspiration to me since I first read it, longer ago than I care to remember, and most of the information about the Tree Calendar and the symbolism of the trees came from my reading of Graves' book.

*My 'Tu Darshaq' desert characters are loosely based on the Tuareg people of the Sahara, whose traditional dress, way of life and music I have used as a model. Special mention should be made of the ensemble, Tartit, whose particular playing of the immemorial Saharan music is my favourite version. I had pictures of them from their record sleeves in my mind as I wrote many of the 'Tu Darshaq' passages.

*Marcus Locock has been, and continues to be, an invaluable technological help in getting the book published on Kindle and CreateSpace, and maintaining and updating the text. He doesn't just *help* me...he does it for me with endless patience and equanimity!

*I am very grateful to my daughter and son, Rose and Nathaniel, and to Marcus and Ed Locock and Mary Roberts, who all read the text and made helpful comments and observations to iron out inconsistencies and errors, and even applied themselves to the tedious work of combing the text for 'typos' and other technical mistakes.

*My thanks are due to Sarah Jane Muskett, graphic artist & designer, who designed the cover for the book.

*I am very grateful to my friend, Duncan Fox, for first suggesting the idea of e-publishing, without which I should probably still be dreaming about publishing this book in the traditional manner.

*This book has gone through several different incarnations over 30 or 40 years to arrive at its present state! Along the way, it has gathered influences from many sources. As T.S. Eliot points out in 'Four Quartets', nothing is entirely original. What we do as we write is 'a wholly new start' as we only 'get the better of words/ For the thing one no longer wants to say.' And anyway, everything has 'already been discovered… by men whom one cannot hope/ To emulate –but there is no competition-/ There is only the fight to recover what has been lost/ And found and lost again and again…/ …But perhaps neither gain nor loss./ For us, there is only the trying. The rest is not our business.' Amen.

Made in the USA
Charleston, SC
01 December 2013